I0703927

SUSAN M. THODE

# Undercurrents

A
*Do I Matter?* Book Two

By
## Susan M. Thode

Reader's Group Guide Included

ISBN: 978-1-965352-43-4

# DEDICATION


This book is for my husband, Willie, with love and gratitude. After 47 years, he generously continues to overcome my pessimism with his optimism.

.

undercurrent   *noun*
*un · der · cur · rent*


1) A current of water below the surface and moving in a
different direction from any surface current

2) An underlying feeling or influence, especially one that is
contrary to the prevailing atmosphere and is not expressed openly


*Scars have the strange power to remind us that our past is real.*
*Cormac McCarthy*

# Chapter 1



*Sometimes I have to look back where I've been so I can see where*
*not to go next.*
Sara's Diary

Star shied violently to the side. Completely relaxed and lost in my thoughts on his bare back, I made an awkward grab at his neck when something spooked him. In slo-mo, I slipped down his side and landed on my feet like a drunken ballerina. Eyes white-rimmed, nostrils flaring, Star backed away from me, pulling hard on the single rein I managed to hang onto.

"What in the world? What's wrong…Star? Shooting Star. Come on, boy. Calm down. It's okay. Everything's okay," I crooned while I walked toward him hand over hand on the taut rein. When I could reach his head, I slowly raised a hand to his nose and stroked the velvety black softness of his muzzle.

"Come on, boy. You're okay…everything's fine."

I've always felt safe on our family's small northern California farm. Santa Rosa is the nearest big town so we're not close to big city problems. Our beach and coastline aren't marred by crowds of people like San Francisco which is a couple hours away. I searched the sparse woods behind us for a clue of what spooked my horse.

Nothing. My head swiveled to take in the path we were on to get to the beach. Zilch. Overhead? A seagull or something? Blue sky. I lifted my head to take in the panorama before me and saw only the familiar stretch of sand that led to the ocean. Tide coming in, I noted. Waves creeping up the shore in front of us.

My gaze returned to my sixteen-hand tall, trembling Appaloosa who, until this moment, I considered fearless. I moved my hand from stroking his nose up to rub behind his ears. Gradually, the white rim disappeared and his eyes returned to their normal molasses brown. His breathing evened out. When he stamped a foot and lazily switched his tail a few times, I knew he was over it. Whatever 'it' was.

I tried leading him forward toward the beach. He would not move. He stretched his neck forward in response to my pull on the reins, but he stayed put.

Huh. I didn't have a clue. But Mom and Dad were waiting with dinner and I was supposed to fetch my brother, Ben, which is why we were heading to the beach to begin with, so I cupped my hands and yelled on a high-low extended note.

"Beee-eeennn!"

"Yeah?" came faintly back on the breeze.

"Diinnn-nneerr!"

"Okay. Coming."

I didn't wait and turned back towards home. Star willingly followed. I led him to a convenient rock and boosted myself onto his back. I stayed alert, but he walked toward home with his usual swinging step, ears forward. Whatever happened, it was over.

We gathered at the kitchen table for dinner. It felt cozy and I was glad we converted the dining room into a family room. We all preferred the kitchen for meals. During dinner Mom and Dad asked Ben about his marine biology project. He didn't require any feedback from me, so I let my mind wander to the upcoming school year. I wondered if it would be strange to have Ben as an incoming freshman while I was a senior. I'm glad I'm older since he's a brainiac and I wouldn't appreciate the comparison.

The clean slate of senior year loomed before me. But was it? Would it be murky from last year's chaos? Does anyone truly get to start over? Would Robyn? My fork froze halfway to my mouth. Where did that thought come from? I had deliberately deleted all thoughts about Robyn, the new girl from school last year who I had hostile history with, from my mind. At least until now. Ugh. Memories flooded my mind and my appetite was swept away.

Suddenly feeling restless, I asked, "May I be excused?" I pushed my chair back in anticipation of permission from Dad.

In my room, I drifted from my desk to the closet and back again to my desk. Memories of my toxic relationship with Robyn and Travis drifted in and out of my mind. I eased down onto the chair and sorted through the paperwork for the beginning of the school year. My heel beat a brisk tattoo against the floor until I put a hand on my knee to keep it still. Star's behavior on the way to the beach slid into my mind. What was up with that? We hadn't been back to the beach for a few months since my 'deep dive', as Ben called it. Being too close to the water triggered anxious feelings in me. Could that be Star's problem?

The opening notes to Taylor Swift's, *Shake It Off*, sounded from my phone. I pulled it from my pocket and thumbed the little green phone logo.

"Hey, Tawny. What's up?"

For the next hour my best friend and I chatted about boyfriends. Hers, Ryan; mine, Kevin. Then we segued into what classes we were taking.

"Can you believe it's already time for school? I mean, it literally seemed like the summer went by at warp speed. I wish Mom would just let me quit school and work at the salon. It's what I'm going to do anyway. I'm not going to change my mind, like, ever. Why should I wait?"

Tawny's familiar complaint prompted my usual reply. "She wants you to have opportunities she didn't have. You know that."

"Yeah, well," she grumbled, "her life hasn't turned out so bad. Why do I have to suffer for what she didn't have?"

"You know the answer to that."

A deep sigh answered my logic. "Because she loves me too much to limit my choices in life."

"Yep," I agreed. "Might as well quit fighting it and go with it. Besides, what would I do without you at school? I need my Tawny power supplement to get through the day, you know?"

"True. You do need help defining your rizz. Hey, I gotta jet. See you tomorrow?"

I agreed and she was gone before I could ask what rizz was. Tawny's slang vocabulary remains miles ahead of me. I changed into the t-shirt and shorts I slept in, grabbed my Kindle and read until I was tired enough to drift off to sleep. Sort of. I had the nightmare again. It began like it always does.

Panic paralyzed my lungs and my breath came in short gasps as I fought the ocean current. Salt water stung my eyes and sand gritted against my clenched teeth. I couldn't get my arms free and I thrashed frantically to fight entrapment. My fist hit something hard and pain shot up my arm.

Discomfort jolted me awake, but it took a minute to realize I was safe in my bedroom, caught in a tangle of sheets and blankets, face buried in my pillow. Ah. The nightmare. I forced myself to breathe deeply through my nose and exhale through my mouth a couple times then rolled to my back, loosening bedding as I went.

I continued the controlled breathing my counselor taught me to help minimize PTSD triggers. While I struggled to free my mind of the nightmare that gripped like Velcro, I remembered something new in the old nightmare. When my dream-self looked up from under the waves, I saw my parents, Ben and Kevin gazing at me from the ocean's surface. That part was a repeat. But this time, Robyn joined the familiar friendly faces.

While sweat cooled and dried on my skin, I wondered why the frightening dream was back. It had been months since I'd been troubled out of sleep by memories of the terrifying suicide attempt I so stupidly thought would solve all my problems. Why was Robyn suddenly included? The nightmare had been a rerun ever since it began, not long after my botched self-destruction. Well. Not botched so much as foiled by Star. That's a whole other story.

Heartbeat back in a steady rhythm, I stared at the ceiling and reconsidered what I knew about Robyn. Maybe I could figure out why she suddenly appeared as a new character in an old nightmare. Just before school ended last spring, Robyn had vanished. Nobody, not even Tawny, who had her finger firmly on the pulse of everything and everyone at school, knew where Robyn had gone. My cheeks and neck grew warm with embarrassment and regret when I remembered my last real conversation with her.

Robyn had foolishly participated in sexting with Travis, the jock we both liked. Travis played Robyn and I off against each other and successfully created a rivalry between us for his so-called affection. So-called because Travis didn't care about anyone but himself. I may have wised up more quickly than Robyn, but we both had Travis scars. Love from Travis was like writing my name with a sparkler. Burned hot and bright for a few seconds, then nothing but ashes left.

Once Robyn sent the revealing photos of herself, Travis pretty much focused on her. Unfortunately, like the slime he is, he shared the photos with his friends and everybody ended up in legal trouble. After that, Travis dropped Robyn like she was a fiery marshmallow at a campfire.

Robyn looked as miserable at school as I felt. Robyn, because of the sexting. Me, because I didn't feel like I mattered to anybody and the cheerleaders and jocks bullied me. Tawny suggested they should take their flying monkey friends and melt, but no such luck.

You would think our similar situations would make us closer, but one day at lunch I twitted Robyn about the suggestive photos. I basically humiliated her and we haven't talked since.

"Stupid, stupid, stupid," I wailed at the ceiling. "Why did I say such a mean thing? Especially when kids were talking trash about me and I knew how it felt. I wish I could tell her I'm sorry."

Not only had Robyn disappeared, but Travis left town, too. The difference is that we all knew his dad sent him to a substance abuse rehabilitation program in San Francisco. Travis's father was quick to tell anybody who came into his car dealership that his boy just needed to get his head straight and he'd be back.

I threw a pillow into the air and caught it against my chest. "Well. That's too bad," I mused. "We get along just fine without him."

My nightmare faded like fog in the sun so I jumped out of bed and pulled on jeans and a sweatshirt. Even though barely sunrise, Star would be glad to see me. I detoured to the kitchen for an apple, then headed out the back door catching it just in time before it banged shut. Abby, our little calico and Spot, Ben's black lab, joined me on the trek to the barn while I munched on my apple. I shivered a little. Late summer mornings turn chilly in our northern California town.

The barn door protested with a rusty squeal when I heaved it open. The heavy door slid open on metal wheels. The wheels at the bottom were encased in rubber, but the ones that ran along the track at the top of the door were bare metal. I pulled it closed and winced at another off-key metal protest. Star's startled snort let me know he was up and ready for the day. A low rumbling nicker came from his throat when I started toward him.

"Good morning to you, too." I reached up and stroked his nose then scratched under his forelock. He leaned into my hand and his upper lip twitched ecstatically against my sweatshirt. I rubbed extra hard for a few seconds then asked, "Ready for breakfast? Here, you can have the rest of my apple as an appetizer."

Star was always ready for food. If we weren't so active, he'd look like a pregnant mare. I got busy pulling a section of hay out of a bale to fill his feed net, and then measured grain for his feed bucket. While he nuzzled the mixture with an eager grunt, I climbed onto his back from the edge of the manger, lay down on my tummy facing backwards and folded my arms under my head for a pillow on Star's rump. His steady munching, rhythmic deep breaths and warm hide almost had me nodding off. His hide smelled slightly of the cedar sawdust I used for bedding under a layer of straw. I listened to him breathe and remembered the deep racking cough a few months ago that shook his body with each breath. The cough turned out to be a symptom of pneumonia and bronchitis; the result of his desperate swim against the ocean riptide that had threatened to sweep us both out to sea. My suicide attempt had almost cost my horse his life right after he saved mine.

The screech of the door interrupted my somber memories. Kevin came into the barn, pulling the door closed behind him. He tucked his hands under his armpits to warm them against the morning chill.

"Ah, I hate to tell you this, but you're facing the wrong way."

"Oh, really? And when did you become such an equine expert?"

Head still resting against my arms, I turned to look at him. My heart did a little skip-beat and happy adrenaline woke up every sleepy cell in my body. He walked over and stroked Star's neck, then stretched up on his toes and kissed my cheek. "I don't have to be an expert to know you're only going to see where you've been in that position."

I sat up. "Funny. I've just been thinking about where Shooting Star and I have been. He was so sick after he saved me from the ocean."

"I still have trouble believing you were desperate enough to try to drown yourself. How could I not have known? What kind of friend was I?"

"Well, keep in mind I wasn't exactly a great friend to you either by that time. I concentrated on pushing people away, remember?"

I swung my left leg over Star's back and stretched out my arms toward Kevin. He grasped my waist and helped me slide down Star's side to stand in front of him. He brushed a lock of hair out of my face. "Today your hair reminds me a bit of that beginning sunrise outside. Sort of reddish gold."

Man, he had a killer smile. I reached up and clasped my hands around his neck. His hands circled my waist and I stood on tiptoe to meet his lips lowered toward mine. A slight quirk curved his mouth while he paused, then his eyes closed as he kissed me.

After a moment, I pulled back and touched a finger lightly to his mouth. "You know, I love that slight smile thing you do almost as much as I love your kiss."

"What? Like this?"

He smiled more broadly this time, tightened his arms and kissed me again. Our kiss strengthened until Star's tail swished against us, coiling briefly around our shoulders before it fell away.

The intensity broken, Kevin laughed. "Hey, big guy. Way to break a mood."

I giggled then briefly squeezed Kevin's shoulders before I stepped around him to grab a brush off the shelf by Star's stall. I reached up to groom his white rump that was liberally sprinkled with varied size splotches of black, talking to Kevin over my shoulder.

"You're up pretty early for a Sunday. How come?"

He leaned against the stall door. "Mom has a huge order she has to mail out tomorrow so I told her I'd help today. We decided to get an early start. I saw the light on in the barn through the trees so came over to tell you I won't be at church this morning. You're up early yourself." There was a query in his tone.

"Yeah. I had that nightmare again. Couldn't go back to sleep."

Concern wrinkled Kevin's forehead. "Same again?"

I shook my head. "Not quite. This time Robyn was with all of you looking down at me in the water." My hand paused against Star's side. "Why would she be there?"

He shrugged. "I don't know. But you've always felt bad about what you said to her, and you didn't get a chance to apologize like you did to Tawny and me. Maybe you feel guilty?"

I turned around and leaned back against Star. "Of course, I feel guilty. What if I had something to do with her leaving town? Nobody's heard from her since April."

"But her dad is still here. He must know where she is." He took the brush out of my hand and tossed it by the stall door. He took my hands in his, tugged gently and I pushed off Star's side. I came to rest in front of Kevin. He regarded me with a steady, brown-eyed gaze. "Want to go by their house and ask? Would that help?"

I considered the suggestion. Not sure if I knew my own mind, the words came out halting. "You know…maybe…I don't know. I'm sorry I never got to talk to her. But I don't know about tracking her down. Hey. Maybe I could call her? Or text? Do you think her dad would give us her phone number?"

Kevin shrugged. "I don't know why he wouldn't. Never know unless we go ask. If that would help keep the nightmare away, I'm all for it."

"Okay, thanks. Somehow you always know exactly what I need and when." I laid my head against his chest and hugged my arms around his waist. His arms closed around my back and he rested his chin on top of my head. We stood quietly for a moment then he kissed the side of my head and dropped his arms.

"I know something else you need." He smiled a teasing smile.

"Oh, yeah? What's that?"

Kevin pulled a small gift bag out of his pocket. "Scented candle."

I cradled the candle a moment before I lifted it to my nose and inhaled deeply. "Mmmm. Vanilla and cinnamon, right?"

Kevin reached forward and circled his arms loosely around me again. "Yep. But you know what they say. It starts with vanilla, leads to hydrangea, then suddenly your free-sniffing sandalwood." He leaned forward until his forehead rested against mine. "Before you know it, you're craving lavender pear candles." He kissed the tip of my nose. "It's a slippery slope."

"Sounds dangerous."

"Oh, you have no idea. Scented candles are part of my plan to keep you going out with me. I'll get you hooked." He winked and dropped his arms.

I smiled. "So far your evil plan seems to be working. I'm not planning on going anywhere."

I held the candle close to my nose and drew in another deep breath. "You know, I really respect your mom. It must've been hard to move here with you and Chase after your dad died to start her own essential oils business. Especially since there was no guarantee of success. And look how far she's come! Candles, soap — all kinds of products. Smart lady."

"Yeah," he agreed. "She's pretty cool. She worked hard and prayed hard." He glanced at his watch and his brow puckered. "Gotta get going if Mom and I going to finish that order. See you later? Let's think about when we can go find Robyn. I bet if you get a chance to apologize, that dream won't come back."

"Def see you later," I confirmed. "I'll be going over to Mr. K's later today to talk about Star's new training, but I'll be home in time for dinner. I guess we can figure out a time to go see Robyn's dad."

My reluctant tone didn't seem to get through to Kevin. He jogged out the barn door with a quick backward wave.

I stared at the opening where he'd disappeared. "Apologize, huh?" I turned toward Star. "I feel a little sick to my stomach when I think about talking to her," I admitted to my horse. "Why should I talk to her? She was mean to me, too."

Star switched his tail. I took the movement as agreement. "Really mean," I clarified. "At her party she completely humiliated me in front of a whole roomful of kids. And that's when things got really awful at school. And that's when I began to think about how I could kill myself."

Memories of that painful time flooded my mind and my emotions did an about-face. Remembered humiliation of weight gain and the gross sore on my finger that Robyn made such a public fuss about caused a slow burn in my chest. "Apologize to her? She should apologize to me."

I stared again at where Kevin had vanished just moments before. "Yeah, I'll think about apologizing. I'll think real hard."

No. Way, I mouthed to myself while I turned to grab the water bucket.

# Chapter 2

*Parts of my past feel like anchors holding me back.
How do I cut loose so I can move forward?*
Sara's Diary

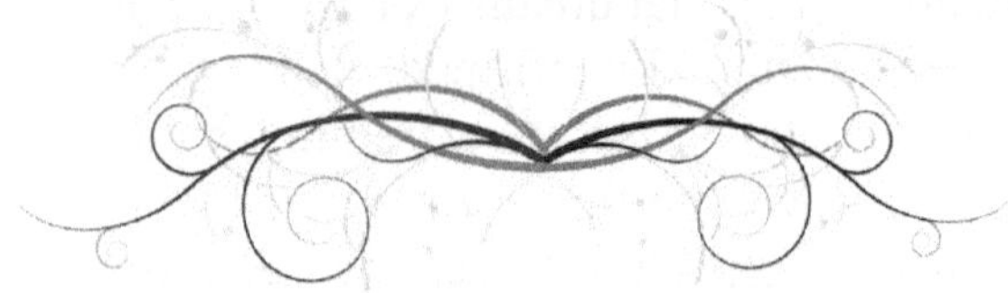

Ben and I walked out of church toward the parking lot. I tossed him the car keys. "You need to practice if you're going to take your driver's test. Try not to kill us on the way home."

"Very funny." Ben caught the keys and grinned. An old fedora hat that had been Grandpa's sat cocked back on Ben's head. It reminded me of a 50's TV detective from reruns my parents watched. It looked both ridiculous and appropriate.

"Remind me again why the hat?"

"I found it in the attic." He pulled the rim down over his forehead. "It's part of my new image."

"Why?"

He shrugged. "I don't know. Just feel like I could be more cosmic than I am."

"And the hat accomplishes cosmic?" I smoothed my frown of skepticism before he could see it.

"Well, yeah. Don't you think?"

Before I could admit ignorance, Ben effectively changed the subject by pursing his lips and letting out a shrill wolf whistle. The sound echoed around the parking lot. Old Mr. Cousins, a few rows over, turned his head. Ben pointed his finger at me. The senior citizen made an impatient brushing off gesture then shuffled toward his car. But not before I saw the smile on his face.

I punched Ben's arm. "Hey!"

Ben knocked into my shoulder with his own. "What? Oh, come on. Gave the guy a thrill. You saw that smile."

"You are such a child."

We reached our old Subaru and Ben folded his long body into the driver's side. His knees hit the steering wheel and he fumbled for the seat lever. The seat slid back to its max. I tucked into the passenger side.

"You're going to outgrow the car before you even get your license."

"Tall, dark and handsome, that's me. Or, as Tawny would say, TDH!" He started the car and backed out of the parking spot. We were on our own since Mom and Dad had a meeting after church.

"Hey, you're improving," I commented as we looked both ways before pulling onto the street. "You didn't kill the engine once."

"Ha, ha. Very funny." Ben stopped at a stop sign then turned the car to head toward home. "I haven't stalled since that first time. I think you can give me a break on my first time driving a stick shift."

"Yeah, I guess. Who was that girl you were talking to before church? She's kind of cute."

Ben immediately began humming the alphabet song under his breath. I knew he only did this to calm himself. Had done so ever since he was a toddler. "What's going on? Why are you stressing? Who IS that girl? Just take a few breaths and tell me."

He reached forward and turned the radio on. "Let me tell you when we get home. I have to concentrate on my driving."

I switched the radio off. "Okay. But go back to humming your song. I know it helps." I grabbed my phone and scrolled through messages while he hummed. Pretty soon the contagious childhood song had us singing a duet until we reached home.

Ben turned into the driveway and let the car coast to a stop. He killed the engine then turned to face me. "Her name is Zoe. Zoe Gavalas." His voice sounded like mine when I described Star to people. Totally awestruck. I faked a cough to hide my smile.

"And? What else?"

"I met her earlier this summer at that extra credit Biology class I took. The one about microorganisms and tide pools. Remember?"

I had no memory of this class whatsoever. "Ah, sure. Tide pools."

"Anyway, we got to know each other during field trips. She's incredible. She knows tons more about amoeba and bacteria than I've ever even heard of. Her name is Greek for life. So sigma."

"And she likes you, too?"

His mouth opened and a frown creased his forehead like he was going to protest, but I stared him down. Big sister superpower.

"Okay, yeah. I admit it. I like her. I don't really know if she likes me or not. She might. How am I supposed to tell?"

I was saved from trying to come up with an answer when a beat-up Ford Focus pulled up next to the Subaru and slid to a stop. My best friend, Tawny, bounced out of the car and hurried to where Ben and I sat in our car.

"Hey, sibs. S'up? What's…" She caught sight of Ben's ancient fedora and seemed stunned into silence. Not easy to do with my friend. She reached in the car window and slid the hat off his head. "What's up with the bonnet, Benster?" She placed the hat on her head, leaned down to see herself in the sideview mirror, shrugged, tousled Ben's hair then replaced the hat on his head. She walked around the car to open my door.

"Oh, hey, Tawny. We just got home from church and were talking about…"

Ben jumped out of the car and began drumming on the top like he was in a rock band.

"…about Ben's summer class," I finished smoothly.

"Boring." She opened my car door and motioned me out. "Let's you and me go chatter about what your fit for the first day of school will be."

This time I had a clue about Tawny language and knew she wanted to talk outfits for the beginning of school next week. We headed for the house and my room.

Tawny leaned over to speak low in my ear. "So, what was the heavy GDT about with the bro?"

Back to mystified by Tawny's slang, I queried, "GDT?"

"General discussion thread. C'mon, Sara, keep up. What's happening with the tall drink of water?"

"I think he has a girlfriend. Or at least he'd like to. Her name's Zoe and he met her over the summer.

Tawny giggled. "Ryan and I saw them on the beach once. Ben is for sure crushing on her. It was so cute! He looks at her like she's the science set he got in 5th grade. Like she's the microscope, even. Little bro is growing up."

I snorted and held the back door open for my friend. "Growing? He's already six feet tall. I hope he's done."

Tawny laughed. "Yep. He's a giraffe," she agreed.

We lounged on my bed catching up on news until Tawny jumped up and began to rummage through my closet.

"Let's see. How shall we make sure you're crisp on the first day?" she mumbled.

"Do I want to be crisp? Is that within my skill set?" Not to my knowledge, for sure.

"It will be when I get done with you." Tawny flashed a smile over her shoulder then turned back to the closet. "I wish you'd let me put some highlights in your hair. I have some ideas that would be trippy."

"You know my main fashion accessory is an extra scrunchy around my wrist. That's more my style. Not sure I'm up for trippy. Would you do mine like yours? Your hair reminds me of Abby." I admired my friend's black shiny hair that rippled with streaks of gold, blonde and light brown tones.

Tawny pivoted out of the closet like a sergeant major on parade. "Gee, thanks. You think I look like the family cat? Not. Even." She examined her reflection in the mirror, head tilted to the side. "Actually, I sort of do. Well," she pivoted back to the closet, "Abby is a smoking hot cat, after all."

I pushed off the bed and grabbed a shirt out of the closet. "Here, what about this? You said it's a good color for me."

Tawny took the tangerine-toned shirt from me. "Yeah. This is a start." She stood in back of me and draped the shirt around me like a bib. "Look how it makes your eyes pop."

"Popping eyes are good?" My voice sounded high-pitched with doubt.

"You're kidding, right? Your eyes are one of the most stellar features you have."

We regarded my image in the mirror. Green eyes and reddish

gold-hair were a great combo for a movie star, but freckles across my nose and cheeks, messy bun and irregular features were what my grandma called passable, but no prizewinner.

As if reading my mind, and I wouldn't put it past her, Tawny asked, "What's that your grandma says about the two of you?"

I smoothed my shirt bib and pulled it around my waist. "Passable, but no prize winner."

"Harsh." Tawny loosened my messy bun and fluffed my hair around my shoulders.

"Nope. I know I'm not beautiful. But I guess I have a nice face. And my hair and eyes are okay. I wish the meds I have to take didn't keep making me gain weight. No matter what I do, I can't seem to get rid of this extra fifteen pounds."

Tawny's face instantly lost its playful expression. "You're not that heavy, Sara. You're still really pretty. Don't let your weight bleach your rainbow."

"Really?" My eyebrows lifted. "Bleach my rainbow?"

"Yeah. You know. Like don't let it Eeyore you? You know?"

"Eeyore me?" We stared at each other in the mirror. Tawny determined, me confused. In moments we were laughing at each other. I hung my shirt back in the closet.

"So, how's it going with the lupus anyway?" Tawny leaned in and lightly gripped my shoulders. "You doing okay?"

I shrugged. "Way better than last year, that's for sure. After playing around with the dose until they got the right balance for the meds, they're stabilized so I don't have so many side effects. Remember how much weight I gained last year? Ugh. I was sooooo miserable." I sighed. "It is what it is."

Tawny wrapped me in a fierce hug then became all business when she let go and gathered my hair into her hands. "Your hair would be stunner if you'd just let me fix it for you."

She piled the hair on top of my head then combed out a few strands with her fingers. "Look. If you'd just let me cut it in a stylin' bob and maybe put in some highlights, you'd be crisp for sure. C'mon, Sara. Let's try it."

"Kevin likes my hair the way it is."

Tawny flipped my hair with an exasperated toss. "That doesn't mean you can't change it. Guys have no savvy about fashion."

I grinned. "He knows what he likes."

Tawny threw up her hands in surrender. "Okay, okay. You win for now."

I moved behind Tawny, put my hands on her shoulders and stared at our images in the mirror. "Now you, on the other hand, are completely beautiful."

Chocolate-brown eyes sparkling, Tawny struck a pose with her hand on her hip and the other behind her ear, head tilted to one side. She flicked her gold, blonde and red highlighted locks off her shoulder. "Yeah, I have to admit I'm eye candy, for sure." She held the pose briefly and then we both laughed. Tawny's self-confidence was balanced by boundless good nature and generosity. She is the least conceited person I know.

I returned to the bed and flopped on my stomach; chin propped on my hands. "What should I wear with that shirt? Please tell me jeans are okay."

"Ripped?" Her eyebrows arched almost to her hairline.

"Fine." I felt stupid in the one pair of ripped jeans she made me buy, but I could suck it up and wear them. "I'm going to get in a little trail practice and then I have to head over to Mr. K's training center. Want to get together tomorrow?"

"Yep. Remind me what trail is again?"

"It's the event I'm switching to since Star shouldn't do jumping anymore. Either trail or dressage. Trail is opening gates from horseback, walking over bridges and other things that could spook a horse. Sometimes walking through water obstacles. Just doing things in a ring you might run into on a trail ride. And it's timed so you have to keep moving."

"Oh yeah. Hope that works out." Tawny paused on her way out the door. "Hit the cell keys when you're free?"

"Text?" I hazarded a guess.

"Natch." Tawny waggled her fingers goodbye and bounced lightly down the stairs.

I changed into boots and jeans, called to Mom I was headed to Madrona Acres and set off for the barn. As always, Star's ears perked up when the barn door opened. I always imagine if he could talk, he'd be like a pleading toddler. "Is it time, huh? Can we go? Can we?"

I tacked him up and then led him into the practice ring attached to the barn. I mounted, then approached the gate to practice opening and closing it from Star's back. He's so tall I have to lean down and stretch my hand to reach the gate latch. So far he'd cooperated pretty well with gate opening and closing, but I knew the judges were looking for more than cooperation. They expect horses to assist their riders. I crossed my fingers that would come in time.

"You just don't understand why we have to go back through the gate when we've just done it, do you boy?" I reached down to stroke his shoulder. "I agree it's pretty boring compared to what we used to do." I glanced longingly at the disassembled jumps piled next to the barn. "Not like jumping at all. But at least I can ride again and you're healthy." I patted him a final time then urged him toward the driveway. "Let's get over to the Acres."

We clip-clopped down the driveway to take back roads to the training stable. Fearing training would feel monotonous for Star, I urged him into a gallop when we reached a straight section of road. Once he got rid of his initial burst of energy he slowed to a rocking-chair lope. I pulled him down to a trot when we entered the training grounds.

Mr. King must have heard hoofbeats because he came out of the barn, thumbs tucked into his back pockets and hat pushed back on his head. He smiled and motioned us toward him.

"Hey, Sara. How're things with you and Star today? Have you made up your mind if you want to go with dressage or trail? We really need to get going on training so we're ready for the spring shows."

"I guess we'll see how trail goes." I looked out beyond the training rings to the pasture where boarded horses mixed with Mr. K's. They all looked content. Wish I felt the same. My gaze returned to Mr. K. "It sounds more fun than dressage."

"I don't know about fun, but it's a different kind of activity for sure. Star could do either. He has the confirmation and class for dressage, and the smarts for trail. Just up to you to decide."

I swung down and held the reins lightly in one hand. "I know. I just can't make up my mind. I guess I'm having a hard time letting go of jumping. We both really loved the jump events. And it's all my fault we can't compete anymore. What was I thinking? Using Star in my suicide scheme. So stupid." I scuffed at the dirt with the toe of a boot.

Mr. King lifted his hat to settle it more firmly on his head. "I think the point is you weren't thinking. You were feeling. And you have to let that guilt go. You can't move forward if you're hanging on to something you can't have anymore. Pining after jumping isn't going to change the facts. Star can't safely handle the physical exertion of jumping anymore because of the pneumonia damage. Let it go so you can move on. It's not fair to him." He nodded toward Star, who watched the horses moving around the pasture, eyes bright with curiosity and interest.

"Let it go," Mr. K insisted more softly. "Star needs some new stimulation. Something to challenge that bright mind of his and give him a good safe workout. You're not being fair to him."

Mr. K's soft tone felt like a sharp blow. I winced at the truth that I wasn't being fair to Star. Mr. K was right. I blew air upward to blow my bangs off my forehead then shaded my eyes with a hand against the afternoon sun. My gaze followed Star's. I watched the horses move lazily around the pasture while my mind wrestled stubbornly with the inevitable. Remembering our successful jumping career made me so proud. And left me with such an ache of loss. I continued digging a hole in the dirt with my boot, then looked up to meet Mr. K's gaze with new determination.

"You're right. I've got to let it go. He's an amazing horse and it's not fair to keep him from learning something new. What do you think? Dressage or trail? You've known him even longer than I have."

"I think he'd find trail competitions more interesting. Dressage is beautiful and there's no denying he's got the flair to be impressive in the ring, but trail has more and varied challenges. Plus, you wouldn't have to change much of your tack and other gear."

I rolled my eyes and blew out a derisive snort. "I absolutely would appreciate not buying more tack. Do you have time to run us through a sample of what a trail competition involves? I've been practicing gates, but I know there's more."

"Sure. Let me get Blake and we'll set up a few obstacles and see how you do. Give us about a half hour then come to the back paddock."

"Okay. We'll go say hi to Justine over at Big Sky and be back in a bit."

"How's Star doing with therapy horse training?"

A full-blown laugh burst out of my mouth. I shook my head.

"Justine already eliminated him. He's fine with most of the requirements. He's good around people, doesn't startle easily, gentle with kids. He just gets bored so fast. Therapy horses have to repeat pretty monotonous tasks and Star just doesn't have the patience. He doesn't have a mean bone in his body, but he can't settle to just walking around a ring."

"Are you okay with that? Not upset with Justine? Or Star?"

"Absolutely not. It was actually kind of funny. He just couldn't understand why she wanted him to just keep walking quietly around the ring at her side. At one point he looked at me as if to say, 'Really? Is this it? Can we go now?' That's partly why I think trail will be better than dressage."

"Are you still interested in Justine's program?"

"Oh yeah! Star doesn't have to be a therapy horse for me to get the training I need to work the program. I'm filling out my application for the PATH program and hope I'm accepted for the next training session. Justine's teaching me to work with the kids who have physical disabilities which is really interesting, but I need the PATH training to work with the mental health individuals."

"What's that program again?"

"PATH. It stands for the Professional Association of Therapeutic Horsemanship. It's how Justine got started."

"Sounds like a plan to me. I know Justine will be glad of the help. She told me she has a waiting list of people who want to either get their kids enrolled or enroll themselves. She's asked me to be on the lookout for possible horses. You go on over there then bring this big fella back." Mr. K walked past Star on the way to the barn and gave my horse a friendly smack on the shoulder. "I can pretty much guarantee we'll keep him interested."

# Chapter 3

*The great thing about the past is I don't have to stay there.*
Sara's Diary

The road leading to Big Sky Hoofbeats across from Mr. K's place was well-traveled with both human and horse prints. The equine therapy facility run by Justine Myers and her brother, Jeremy, had become a destination therapy spot for veterans, as well as several mental health and disability agencies in the county. Jeremy handled the veteran's program while Justine organized all the other types of therapy.

As soon as Star saw Justine, he quickened his steps until he caught up with her. He nudged her jacket pocket insistently.

"All right, all right. Give me a sec. Here." She placed a horse treat on her palm and held it out. Star lipped it up and crunched happily. Justine stroked his nose. "He learns quickly. I haven't been carrying horse cakes in my pocket very long."

"Trust me," I laughed. "If it has to do with food, Star's a genius." I jumped down from Star's back. "I got my application in to PATH. I hope I hear back soon."

Justine continued walking to her office in the main barn. She gestured me to her side. "I want to show you something. I just got a brochure from a school in Oregon. They're offering a Master's program in Equine Mental Health Therapy."

"Master's? I'm not even done with high school."

"I know. But you should already be thinking about college and this would be a good fit for you. You should think about it."

I took the glossy folder and opened it up. "But, Oregon? What would I do with Star?"

Justine sat on the edge of her desk. "Are you going to live at home forever?" she asked in a gently teasing voice.

"Well, no, of course not. I just hadn't thought yet about what…where. I mean, I didn't think about going away. Last year got so out of control. We, my whole family, pretty much concentrated on just getting through after my diagnosis." My voice trailed off while I flipped through the pages of the brochure. "This looks really interesting. I'll think about it. But I don't know about leaving Star."

"Yes, you'd have to leave Star. Unless you go to community college here, you'll have to leave Star at some point. Are you going to put your future on hold for a horse?"

"No." My stomach tensed at the thought of not having access to Star. "I know I have to move forward. It's just…he's been…I'm not sure how…" I stared at the brochure then up at Justine. "I just can't imagine being away from him. I know I can't stay here my whole life. At least, now that I'm thinking about it, I realize that. But it will seem so weird not to have Star around. Guess I need to make some decisions."

"Welcome to adulting. You're going to manage just fine. Do you have any idea what you'd like to do? Or study?"

"Mr. K talked to me a few times about trying for the Olympic Equine team. That's sort of a vague dream, I guess."

"Star is a great horse, but he's not Olympic grade. If you're thinking about the Olympics, you might already be too late. Pretty sure you need a sponsor for one thing. You're great on a horse, Sara, and I see why Mr. K would mention it, but it's a long expensive haul and there's loads of competition." Justine reached out a hand and rested it on my shoulder. "Your whole future is ahead of you. Don't let it leave you behind."

"I won't, Justine. I'm glad you challenged me and I promise I'll start thinking about it. Actually, I had an idea I'd like to run past you." Will she think it's a stupid idea? My mouth felt dry and my stomach clenched.

"Sure. What are you thinking?"

"Last year I had some problems and ended up going to talk to a counselor. One of the things she worked on with me was developing self-confidence and not relying so much on what other people thought of me. She wanted me to understand I shouldn't be so caught up in if I matter to others that I lose sight of making sure I matter to myself." I glanced at Justine to see if she was following me. She grinned.

"I'm catching what you're pitching, as I heard your brother say the other day. Keep going."

"Okay, good. I wondered if it would be helpful for some of your younger clients to be in a group where they could talk about why they matter. Or maybe even learn that they do matter." I shrugged. "I didn't think I mattered to anybody and it made me feel depressed. I'd like to help younger kids avoid that."

Justine stuffed her hands in her back pockets while she considered my idea. Eventually, she nodded slowly. "I like it. I'll run it by Jeremy, but I think it's at least worth trying. Tell you what, you write up a proposal. Describe your purpose and what kinds of topics you would address. What age group are you thinking?"

"Maybe nine through twelve?"

"Better make it ten through twelve. Nine-year-olds are too young to be in with twelve-year-olds. The more I think about this, the more I like it. Good job, Sara."

She liked it! Warm satisfaction coursed through my insides.

Justine turned to go then paused and looked back. "And remember, think about what's next for you, too, okay? I think that program in Oregon is a perfect fit for you. Check it out."

"I will," I promised.

"Great. See you tomorrow for the Little Bit class?"

I nodded. "Yep. Four o'clock, right?"

"Yes. I'll see you then." She turned and walked toward her office with a friendly wave.

I mounted Star and we crossed back over the road to Mr. K's indoor practice ring. He explained the basic course and told me to walk through slowly so Star could get a good look at the obstacles. His phone buzzed and he pulled it out of his shirt pocket to glance at the screen. He waved his phone at me and said, "I have to go see about a feed delivery. I'll be back in a bit, but you go ahead and begin."

I sat loosely in the saddle eyeing the obstacles. A wooden bridge with rails on either side, a gate to be opened and closed, five log rails on the ground to walk over and, wait, what? I squinted to verify what I saw. Eight five-gallon plastic buckets, four on each side spaced about six feet apart to form a path. Maybe filled with concrete? Nothing to see here, folks, except each bucket had four brightly colored swimming pool noodles stuck in the concrete straight up. They looked like pails with brightly colored gelled mohawks. The noodles dipped and waved in the slight breeze blowing through the arena. Star hadn't noticed the movement, but I sat up straight in my saddle and wondered how he would handle the obstacle. It looked manic.

Then, at the far side, the last obstacle appeared to be a shallow eight-foot by ten-foot pool of water dug into the dirt. Easy-peasy.

Might as well see what happens. I nudged Star with my heels and steered him for the bridge. He stopped and looked at it, ears pricked forward, no tension in his neck, then placed one ebony hoof on the curved angle of the obstacle. The other front hoof followed and with arched neck and gusty breaths, we crossed slowly over the bridge. He rushed the last foot or so off the downside, but I was happy with his performance. We skipped the gate since we'd done that one and approached the parallel log rails. He didn't even pause. Lifting each leg high, he walked over the logs not nicking even one. Then he caught sight of the frenzied movement of the noodles. He stopped short, head raised high, nostrils gusting out air, ears flicking forward and back in a dance of their own. I paused to let him look, then encouraged him forward with a slight tightening of my heels. He took two steps then stopped again. We made it within a few feet of the bucket-based noodles, a few steps at a time, but he wasn't sure about the wild wavy things in his path. I didn't blame him.

After a couple of minutes, I tried tightening my heels once again, this time urging him forward with my hands at his neck. "C'mon, boy. Those things can't hurt you. Let's go see what they are."

Nope. Feet firmly planted; he stretched his neck forward as far as he could. His nose couldn't quite reach the closest noodle, but he wasn't moving an inch. He pulled back his neck, dropped his head to blow gustily and pawed the dirt uneasily. He jerked his head up and shook it impatiently.

I tried again. "C'mon, Star. They aren't going to hurt you. Just a couple steps closer. C'mon, boy." He flicked his ears back at the sound of my voice then took a hesitant step. Then another. Neck stretched to its limit again, he could just barely sniff the closest noodle. Then he nudged it with his nose. When the noodle bobbed up and down, he met it with his nose and pushed it again. This is good. Playful Star is good.

With my heels pressed firmly at his sides; we stepped slowly through the honor guard of noodles. Star's skin twitched when a noodle brushed his side, but otherwise it was a walk in the park. Yes. I did a mental victory fist clench and looked around for the next obstacle. I spied the pool of water and headed Star that way.

Before we got within six feet of the water, Star stopped abruptly and lifted his head high. Then he backed away. What the…what was he doing? I pressed his sides. He stopped backing, but he wouldn't move forward. There was nothing threatening. What could possibly bother him? I looked around the arena to see if I was missing something and spied Mr. K leaning against the top rail of the ring. He watched us like Spot eyes the pot roast pan containing a bone. Complete attention. My trainer gave a quick gesture I knew meant to hold up and came into the arena. He stopped by Star's side and looked up at me.

"What's up?"

I shrugged. "No idea. He just won't go forward. And it's not like the noodles where he was at least interested. He just doesn't want to move.

"Walk him in a circle and try another approach."

I pressed the left rein against Star's neck, turned him in a small circle, then tried approaching the water again. No dice. He wasn't going near that wet pit.

Mr. K lifted his hat and scratched his head.

My teeth clenched and my lips pinched. "Let me try again," I blurted. "I'm sure I can make him do it." Embarrassed by my horse's stubbornness, I wanted him to perform as he usually did. Flawlessly.

"Why would you want to make him do something he's so obviously set against? Don't you wonder why? He's not a stubborn animal. Normally he's eager to tackle whatever you suggest."

"I know. That's why this is so weird. He never balked at any jump I ever put him to."

"Stop right there," Mr. King commanded. "Just stop. Is that what this is about? You need him to be perfect at this like he was at jumping so you can feel good about riding? You listen to me. I have never seen a horse so willing to please its master than this spotted giant right here. I believe he would try to turn himself inside out if you asked him to. Are you even paying attention to which obstacle is giving him trouble? Do you know why it's giving him trouble? Just think a minute before you say something stupid."

If I had ever had any doubt that horses were Mr. K's priority, I definitely didn't need to wonder any more. I did as he directed and thought back over the last half hour.  My mind replayed our approaching the open water trench, maybe a foot or two of water, and Star shying away each time.

"It was the water." I stared off into space while I replayed the scene. "He shies away from the water. He just won't go near it." I brought my gaze back to Mr. K. "Why won't he?"

"It's about time you're asking that instead of getting frustrated. You're a smart girl. When was the last time Star was in water?"

My eyes widened. I'm such an idiot. "When he was with me in the ocean," I whispered. "When he saved me from the riptide. Oh, no." My pulse shot to about 160. A groan breathed between my lips and I choked on regret.

"How could I be so stupid? He's afraid of the water. Just like at the beach the other day. He shied when the waves started getting closer. I had no clue what was going on. I had trouble being near the ocean last spring, but I worked on my fear with my counselor. Poor Star."

The accusation in Mr. K's voice softened. "We'll work with him. He'll be fine. A horse's thoughts aren't sophisticated enough to figure out details, they just react out of instinct and emotion. But they remember." His thick callused finger pointed at me. "By golly, they remember anything that causes them pain. We can help him get through this by replacing the painful memory with positive memories. What I want to know is can we get you through your attitude?"

"What attitude?"

"You still haven't let go of jumping, have you?" Mr. K challenged. "You're still living the memory of soaring over those fences, hearing the crowd applaud. You can't let it go. You can't let

Star let it go."

I tried to face the accusation with denial, but found I couldn't. "All right. It's true. I hate the idea of not jumping anymore and I think trail competition is stupid. Dressage isn't any better. Prancing around on a braided and shined up horse. I loved jumping. *We* loved jumping. You know Star loved it, too."

"Yes, he did. And he'd do it some more if you asked him to. He's not capable of thinking it through and understanding the consequences. He just knows he'd do anything you ask him or die trying. Just like in the ocean."

Mr. K's hard tone shocked me. My shoulders hunched and my head bowed. "Yes," I agreed quietly. "He would. And he did. He's always done anything I asked." I clasped my hands, straightened my shoulders and looked straight at my trainer.

"I'll let it go. No more unreasonable expectations. What do we do to help Star?"

# Chapter 4

*There's no room for hope in a heart full of shame.*
Sara's Diary

"**Mr. K wants** you to go on an actual trail ride up in the hills so you and Star will learn what's behind the trail event?" Kevin glanced at me, then quickly returned his gaze to the road.

"I'm pretty sure he thinks I'm the only one that needs to learn anything. He believes Star is great. And he's right. I'm totally the one who messed up." Cold shame tightened my throat.

Kevin reached over and placed a hand over mine, twisted and fidgeting in my lap. "Hey. It's okay. You didn't mean any harm. Stop punishing yourself. You couldn't know how he'd react. Who knew horses could have PTSD just like people?"

"That's just it. I should have known. I should have realized what happened in the ocean affected him, too. I should have paid attention…"

"Stop it." Kevin pressed down on my hands, stilling my restless fingers. Hold on just a sec."

Kevin signaled and pulled the Jeep to the curb. "After my dad died and I went to the counselor, I used to say all the time, 'I should have listened to my dad, I should have spent more time with my dad, I should have helped my dad.' You know what my counselor told me?"

I shook my head.

"She said it wasn't helpful to should all over myself. Sara, you made a mistake. It happens. You can't change it; you can only learn from it and move on. Quit shoulding on yourself. It won't change the past. You said Mr. K knows how to help Star with this fear of the water obstacle, right?"

"Yes. He's worked with horses with trauma before. He'll help me teach Star to get over this. It was interesting to hear him talk about horses and how trauma affects them. They're different from humans because their behavior is influenced by emotion and instinct. Humans can think things through, horses not so much."

"So you trust him?"

"Absolutely."

"No wonder you like him so much. Horses are above people on your agenda, too. In a good way," he hurried to assure me. "And I think Mr. K does like you. He just wants you to be a better version of yourself."

"I guess. And I actually appreciate that he cares more about Star than he does about me."

"Ready to let go of what happened and move on?"

I stared out the window. "Seems like I'm having to do that a lot lately. But, you're right. Wallowing isn't helping. How close are we to Robyn's house?"

Kevin glanced at the GPS. "Looks like we're just a few minutes away." He pulled out on the street so we could continue on our way.

"Destination ahead on the right," the GPS droned.

Kevin slowed to a crawl. "It's house number 1729. See it?"

"We just passed 1725. Hers should be soon."

"And here we are." Kevin stopped along the curb in front of a big ranch-style house. "Ready? Changed your mind?"

I hesitated, then shook my head. "I guess not. I thought for a while I didn't need to bother, but I think I'm just being selfish. I know I need to apologize even if it gives me a stomachache to think about it. Are we sure this is a good idea? I mean, what if her dad is upset?"

"Why would he be upset? We're just asking for Robyn's phone number to check on her. It's a nice thing to do. C'mon." Kevin opened his door and walked around the Jeep to mine. He opened the door, held out his hand and waited. His eyebrows lifted in question when I didn't move.

I wiped sweaty palms against my jeans. Kevin reached in and took my elbow in a gentle grasp.

"C'mon. I'll be right behind you."

I slumped out a sigh, then stiffened my backbone and got out of the Jeep. We walked to the front door, Kevin's hand lightly on the small of my back. He pushed the doorbell and we stepped back in unison.

The door opened and a dark-haired, middle-aged man peered out. "Yes?"

My vocal cords froze so Kevin spoke up. "Uh, hi. Mr. Larsen?"

"Yes, I'm Mr. Larsen. What can I do for you?"

Fighting the impulse to run, I finally stammered, "I, I mean we, are classmates of Robyn's and wondered if we could have her phone number. We, I mean, I'd like to call or text her. Could you give me, us, her number?" Smooth, Sara. Real smooth. It felt like I needed the Heimlich maneuver to get rid of the lump in my throat.

"You know Robyn but don't have her cell number?"

"I, uh, I didn't know her that well. I only got to know her a little bit before she moved away."

"She didn't move, she's right here. Just hang on a minute." He turned and called, "Robbie? Friends for you. Come on out."

No answer.

Mr. Larsen frowned then opened the screen door. "Here. Come on in. She must have her door closed. I'll get her."

Kevin dragged me by the arm into the house. I squirmed my arm out of his hand so I could face him. I swallowed hard against the persistent lump in my chest. "What do we do now?" I hissed. "I can't see her like this."

"Like what?" He answered softly out of the side of his mouth.

"Like…like in person. I was going to call, remember?" I twisted the scrunchy around my wrist into a complicated knot.

"We'll just talk to her. I'll help you."

"I can't." Shame induced adrenaline shot through my body and I gulped in air.

"You have to. It'll be fine. It's too late now anyway." He nodded down the hallway where Mr. Larsen stepped back as Robyn appeared in the doorway. Her dad motioned toward us with his head and Robyn leaned out of her room. Her eyes widened then narrowed.

She walked toward us. Beautiful as ever. But, wait. Closer inspection showed her face had thinned, and faint purple shadows lined her eyes. Still slim, she wore a yellow off the shoulder tunic over ripped skinny jeans. She'd cut her hair into a long trendy shag with light blue highlights. Tawny would approve.

"Well, would you look here. Hey, Greenie. Saint Girl," she drawled. "What brings you by?"

I backed toward the screen door, ready to bolt, but Kevin grasped my arm and anchored me by his side. "Hi," he greeted Robyn in his usual friendly way. "We haven't seen you around since last spring. Sara wanted to get in touch with you."

Robyn switched her attention from Kevin to me. Man. Nothing like putting me directly on the spot. I fidgeted, but my tongue froze.

"You worried about me, Saint Girl?" her tone mocked.

"Please don't call me that." Irritation loosened my tongue. "Not worried so much as wondering how you've been. I was hoping for a chance to talk to you."

Kevin made a move for the door. "Why don't I wait outside and let you guys talk?" I grabbed his arm. Fat chance, buster.

Robyn noticed. "Need backup, Sara?"

I swallowed hard. "No, of course not," I lied. "There's just no reason for him to leave. He knows what I want to say. I shifted my weight toward Kevin so my shoulder touched his, took a deep breath and the words blurted out of my mouth. "I'm sorry about what I said at school and for how I acted. I was a jerk, and I'm sorry."

Robyn laughed. She waved her hand in a casual gesture. "No worries. I've heard much worse. How's your finger?" She nodded toward my hand clutched tightly around Kevin's. A slight smirk played around her lips.

"Fine." Memories of Robyn and Travis's mocking tones and brutal reveal of the ugly sore on my finger at a party several months ago caused snoozing anger to roar awake. "It was just a sore. I told you that. You know what?" I turned to Kevin and yanked him toward the door. "I'm done here. Let's go."

I stalked past Kevin and slammed out the screen door. I was almost to the Jeep when Kevin caught up with me. We got silently into the vehicle. Kevin sat and held the key in his hand, waiting.

After a couple of minutes, I sighed. "Okay, okay. I blew it. She just makes me so mad."

Kevin didn't answer. He just reached over and took my hand in his.

"You don't have to say it. I know that wasn't an apology. It wasn't an effort to fix things between us. It wasn't even close to a gesture of good will. I know." I blew my breath upward in frustration. Stared out the windshield. Eventually, I squeezed Kevin's hand and sighed. "I have to go back in, don't I?"

His brown-eyed gaze met mine. He shrugged. "No. You don't have to. You can, but you don't have to. Maybe this isn't the best time."

I grunted out a laugh. "There's never going to be a best time. She gets on my last good nerve. Just wait for me, 'kay?"

Kevin nodded and pulled out his phone. I sighed, yanked on the door handle and shoved the door with my shoulder. I jammed my hands in my back pockets and walked up the walkway like I was slogging through deep snow. I knocked on the front door and waited. I heard a muffled, "Just a minute," then the door opened. My eyes widened when I saw Robyn, head down, swiping at her cheeks with the back of her hand.

"Are you all right?" My anger evaporated. I sincerely wanted to know.

Robyn's head jerked up. "You! What are you doing back here? What is your problem?"

I ignored the infuriated tone when I saw the trace of tears still on Robyn's cheeks. "You're crying." I grabbed the screen door, opened it and walked through. "What's wrong?"

Robyn brushed irritably at her cheeks with the back of her hand. "None of your business. Listen, you got Travis, and apparently Kevin, too, can't you just leave me alone?"

"I don't have Travis." My sincere bewilderment caught Robyn's attention. "I haven't seen him since before school ended last spring. About the same time you disappeared. You know his dad sent him to rehab?"

"I didn't know that."

We stared at each other. Robyn broke eye contact first. She nodded her head toward the waiting Jeep. "But you got, Kev, right?" Her lips curved in the barest suggestion of a smile, but I caught it.

"Listen. Can we start again? I really am sorry for what I said in the cafeteria that day. And I'm sorry for the dirty trick I played on you guys at the Turnabout. I knew it would drive you crazy if Kev and I came dressed like you and Travis. I did it on purpose, but Kevin didn't know. And I'm sorry."

Robyn's gaze searched my face for ridicule. I knew there wasn't any there. I felt absolutely sincere. "You really mean it, don't you?"

"Yeah. It was a rotten thing to say. The thing is I was totally jealous of you so I did a dumb thing. I found out over the summer that when I'm angry I lash out at other people. I'm trying not to be that person anymore."

"Right." Robyn's flat tone reeked of sarcasm. "People don't change."

"Yes, they do," I insisted stubbornly. "It's a choice. And I'm choosing not to be the person I was last year."

"So who are you trying to be now?" Robyn sounded genuinely interested and it was my turn to search her face for ridicule. I saw sincerity.

"I guess I'm trying to be someone I can like. I didn't like myself much last year. I kept trying to make other people approve of me to make up for it." I held up both hands in front of me and shrugged. "Trust me. That so did not work."

An awkward silence stretched out between us. Finally, I took a deep breath and asked, "What do you think? Could we have a do-over. I don't really know you and all you know about me is how I was last year. I'm determined to change. Do-over?"

Robyn smirked. My heart sank and I doubted things would be different for us until Robyn said, "You know me better than you think. My stuff was pretty public, remember? You know what I did." Her gaze challenged mine.

I looked at her without flinching. "I know what you did. I don't know who you are. *How* you are isn't the same as *who* you are. Listen, you did stuff you're not proud of, and I did stuff I'm not proud of. Can we just let that be in the past and try moving forward?"

Robyn reached to tuck her hair behind her ear. The sleeve of her tunic rolled back and I saw thin red scars on her arm. She saw me notice and quickly lowered her arm. "You know, I think I better go. No worries about last year, okay? We're good." She reached toward the screen door to push it open. "Thanks for coming by."

I took the hint and walked out the door. "Uh, okay. See you

around?"

"Sure. Yeah. Whatever." Robyn began to close the door so I turned to go. I paused when I heard her quiet voice say, "Ever notice how sometimes the past doesn't let you go? Bye, Sara." The door closed with a snap of the latch.

I guess I'm not the only one who's plagued by shame. Maybe we have more in common than I thought.

# Chapter 5

*Sometimes life seems like a foreign language I've never learned.*
Sara's Diary

The next morning, I leaned against the top board of the corral fence watching Star. He loved playing with an oversized soccer ball and kept himself occupied and exercised whenever he got bored. Nose to the ground like a bloodhound, he stalked the ball, struck it with a front hoof then shied violently with a couple bucking hops when the ball hit the fence and bounced back toward him. He raced away, his tail a flag, then returned to his nose down stalking to repeat the game all over again.

Mom joined me at the fence and we laughed when the ball ended up in the water tank. Star nosed it around the tank, pawing the ground in frustration when he couldn't get at the elusive ball. I slipped through the boards of the fence, retrieved the ball, kicked it down the corral and returned to Mom. We watched Star chase after the ball in a high-stepping exaggerated trot, head up, nostrils flaring.

"He's a big goof." Mom laughed while she watched his antics.

"Yeah. He feels good this morning. I think the cooler mornings make a difference."

"Is it going to be too cold for you to go on this trail ride Mr. K has planned for you tomorrow?"

I shook my head. "No, I'll be fine. I haven't had any problems with Raynaud's in a long time. I promise to take gloves just in case. Stop worrying, Mom. I'm okay."

The Raynaud's disease that accompanied the lupus diagnosis I got last year had given me a lot of trouble at first. Mom struggled with the memories. She rested her chin on her crossed arms on the top tail of the fence. She watched Star for a few minutes then turned toward me. "I know. It's just hard to forget how sick you were last year. I'm glad the doctor finally has your medication figured out. Are you spending today with Kevin?"

"Just partly. I'll be over at Big Sky most of the afternoon, but Kev and I are hanging out this morning. He and Ben are stacking hayfor me."

"That's convenient. How did you manage that?"

I shrugged. "Kevin likes to hang out with me so that means a lot of time with barn chores, and Ben likes to hang out with Kevin so he ends up in the barn, too."

"Yes, I get that part. But you're out here relaxing and watching Star. And the boys are?"

I laughed. "In the barn working. I know! Isn't it great?"

"I don't know how you manage it, but I hope they never catch on." Mom smiled then startled when Star nudged her arm. "Oh. Star." She reached up to rub under his forelock. "Did you win the soccer game?" She gave him a final pat then checked her watch.

"I've got to get going. I just took the last of the cinnamon rolls out of the oven so I'll be making deliveries most of the morning. Do you need anything in town?"

"Nope. I'm good. Any extra rolls?" I asked hopefully.

"Yes. I'll leave some on a plate for you and your worker bees. Best to reward them for good behavior, you know."

"I totally agree. Thanks, Mom."

"You're welcome, honey. See you later."

My attention returned to Star who was now trying to bite the soccer ball, his efforts thwarted by the slick surface. I waved to Mom as she drove down the driveway, then shaded my eyes to better see the car coming towards our house. Narrowly swerving to miss Mom, the unfamiliar car skidded to a stop next to the corral. The door opened and I watched the tall figure straighten to his six-foot height. Travis. My mouth silently formed his name. Dread felt heavy in my stomach.

"Hey, babe! How's every little thing?" He grinned. He looked different. He'd gained some weight, but still looked fit. His hair had been clipped into a sort of mohawk fade style.

A thick mop of curls fell over his forehead and down the back of his head to his neck. He had some kind of geometric design trimmed close into the shaved portion of hair at the edge where the longer hair began. He ran his fingers through the curls over his forehead to brush them back. Then lifted his Tom Cruise sunglasses to perch on top of his head. His graphic tee announced some rock band, but I couldn't make out which one. He walked toward me; arms held out for a hug. I couldn't back away fast enough.

"Wait. You're not glad to see me?" He placed both hands over his heart and stumbled as if wounded. "Oh, man. What a total setback. You're the first person I wanted to see when I got back. And now you want to ghost me?" He stopped in front of me and reached a hand as if to caress my hair.

I stumbled in my hurry to back further away. "You're back from rehab. Why should I be glad to see you? You were a total jerk, Trav. I haven't forgotten even if you have."

"Babe," he mock-whined. "I got myself cleaned up for you. What? You think I went to the hotel California for laughs? Yeah, no. I went to get off my rocket ship just for you."

Star, tiring of his soccer ball and always interested in human drama, wandered over and lifted his head over the fence.

"Wowzer. You still got the blackhead king." Travis shoved a hand toward Star like a battering ram. I noticed a dark shape coiling up Travis's forearm and realized he'd gotten a snake tattoo while he was gone. Appropriate. Star dodged the snake-clad arm. "Dude. You need some serious zit meds." He elbowed me. "Get it? Blackhead zit? I am seriously hilaire." He reached toward Star again.

Star's ears flattened back against his head and his nostrils flared. I pushed Travis just in time to stop Star's jaws from clamping onto the boy's fingers.

"Whoa!" Travis yanked his hand back from Star. My horse's head was jerking up and down, eyes white-rimmed, ears flat against his head.

"What is up with the spotted Godzilla?" Travis' gaze burned hot when he turned to face me. "Did you see that? He tried to bite me. He could've taken my finger off." He stretched out his hands in front of him as if to count off and make sure they were all there. A pinky ring glittered in the sun.

I checked his hands to make sure there had been no contact then moved over to calm Star. I put one hand on his neck under his mane and the other across his nose. I murmured softly to him then spoke to Travis over my shoulder. "I told you last time you can't rush up to a horse if he doesn't know you. You move too fast and you're too loud. Are you okay?"

When I turned to glance at him, I watched him change, chameleonlike, from furious to friendly. "Ah, sure. I'm fabulous." He kept his gaze on me, but stepped away from the fence, running one hand nervously through thick curls of draping hair. "So, like I was saying, I came to see you, babe, as soon as I got home. I know things got pretty whack there at the end of the year and I wanted to say soz and all that."

"Soz?"

"Yeah. Scusi mi, like, you know, I'm sorry. I a-pol-o-gize Get it? It was all Robyn's fault anyway. That chica is one sleeping beastie, if you know what I mean."

"I get apologize, but don't get how what you did is Robyn's fault."

"Man, that's what I'm telling you. That dudette has some serious probs."

The squeal of the barn door interrupted our conversation. We turned to see Ben emerge from the dimly lit barn. Travis immediately started toward my brother with his fist extended and a smile on his face ready for a fist-bump hello.

"Dude. Look at you. I see your wicked gains, little bro. What are you? Six, six one? One seventy?" Travis nodded his head and developed a swagger when he approached Ben.

Ben stood with his feet apart, arms folded across his chest while he watched Travis approach. He ignored the outstretched fist.

"Hey, Travis." Ben lifted his chin in greeting, but didn't smile. "What happened to Greenie? Remember me? The science nerd? In fact, I remember you saying I better be a gerd because you couldn't decide if I was a nerd or a geek. Remember?"

Travis's stepped slowed, but he kept walking. "Hey, dude. I was only punking you. You know, kidding."

Kevin stepped through the barn door opening. Travis froze. I caught up with Travis just in time to see his smiling gaze turn steely. But just for a moment.

"Killer Kev. I might have known you'd be here. What—you and Sara hooking up? Or you got a bromance going with teen Hercules here? Just kidding." He held his hands up and backed a step or two when he saw Kevin's fists clench.

"C'mon, guys. All you guys." His gaze swept all three of us. "I get it. I laid down some serious smack before. Back when I was slinging some product. But that's not me anymore. I've turned a serious corner and I came here today to make amends. Okay? For real. Like I get it. I was a jerk and I'm sorry. Can we do a Hail Mary and f and f?"

Ben turned to me and mouthed, "F and f?"

I shrugged and looked the same question at Kevin.

"F and f?" Kevin asked Travis.

"Yeah. Like forgive and forget. You know."

Silence stretched between us until I said, "Listen, Travis. It's a little soon to talk about forgetting all the things you did and said. But, yeah, we'll let it go if you're serious about changing. Just, can you leave us alone?"

Travis grasped his hands dramatically over his heart. "Sweet, sweet Sara. I knew you'd be a saint if I could just explain."

My eyes narrowed at the abbreviation of my hated nickname, Sara the Saint. Before I could protest, Travis continued.

"So, later, dudes. I've got to book it and get on the road. Posse out." He turned toward his car but paused briefly as he passed by where Star still stood by the fence. Travis raised his hand and pointed his finger as if it were a gun toward Star. His finger jerked slightly upward as if in recoil.

"Hey!" If my eyes had been daggers, Travis would have twin blades through his heart. I rushed forward fueled by anger, but not quickly enough to catch Travis who made the sanctuary of his car, roared the engine to life and skidded backwards down the driveway. He gunned the engine when he reached pavement and burned rubber down the road.

My body language translated easily to outrage and angry tears pooled in my eyes. "Did you see that? Did you see what he did?" My voice rose an octave. "He pretended to shoot Star. What kind of person does that? What kind of person could possibly imagine doing that? I'm calling the police."

I yanked my phone out of my pocket and jabbed at the numbers. Kevin's hand caught mine just as I was pushing the first 1, in 9-1-1. I wrenched my hand away from him, but he quickly regained control and grasped my hand tightly.

"You can't, Sara." Kevin's calm voice rolled off me like water off a duck's back.

I jerked against his grasp. "Let go! He can't do something like that and get away with it. That's a threat."

"You can't call the police. Travis didn't do anything illegal. He'll say he was goofing around. Please, just take a breath and think a minute."

"He's right, Sis." Ben's joined Kevin in persuasion.

"He can't go around pretending to shoot animals. That's just not okay."

"He's a jerk. Forget about him. He's an attention freak so the best thing to do is ignore him. It'll drive him crazy." Kevin put his hands on my shoulders and turned me to look at him. His steady gaze helped calm me down. He massaged my shoulders. "Relax. Your shoulders feel like a strung bow."

I jammed my phone back in my pocket, breathed in a huge breath through my nose and glanced at Star who had lost interest and was now stalking Abby across the corral. Every time his nose touched her tail it jerked, but she ignored him until she reached the fence and escaped under the lower rail. Then she turned to face the horse and deliberately began to groom herself.

"C'mon," Kevin coaxed. "Make like Abby and ignore the irritant."

I couldn't help but laugh. "You know, she sleeps on him in the barn."

"I know. I've seen her. But she ignores him when he's trying to bug her. Ignore Travis. He's trying to bug you."

"He's good at it." A martyred sigh escaped my lips. "You're right." We walked toward the barn. "Wonder if Robyn knows he's back?"

Kevin snorted. "Wonder if she cares?"

Ben joined us. "We need you to check the feed, Sara. Come look at what we did."

"Okay. Then we can go have the cinnamon rolls Mom left for

us."

Ben did an about-face toward the house. "Hay and feed, later. Warm cinnamon rolls first."

Kevin and I looked at each other and grinned. "Words to live by," I said. We raced past Ben toward the kitchen door.

"Hey!" Ben protested, then hurried to catch up.

We all reached the door together and shoved through, laughing, intent on the promised treat.

# Chapter 6

*Choose trust over fear? Not sure I can. Will Star?*
Sara's Diary

**The next morning**, barely sunrise, I jogged Star down the road to Madrona Acres. I enjoyed the jump event for the thrill, but much preferred riding with my western saddle. If felt more natural and comfortable to me since it was what I learned riding with in the beginning. Chilly morning air caused clouds of mist whenever either of us exhaled. Once at the stables, Mr. K motioned me to load Star next to Zazz, Mr. K's favorite horse, in his trailer. Zazz was short for Lotta Pizzaz, a registered Quarter Horse. Sometimes I watched Mr. K lead clinics on roping and cutting cattle using Zazz as the instructing horse. His explosive energy always amazed me because he was quiet and relatively small at fifteen-hands. His chestnut coat glistened with health. I figured the rich red of his coat and blonde mane and tail would make even Tawny happy.

Once we had the horses loaded, Mr. K and I settled into the front seat of his pickup.

"We're headed about five miles out of town. I want to check a herd of sheep I have up in the hills. I hired a new shepherd and want to see how things are going. We'll ride through some pretty rough ground so you'll be able to see why the trail class features the skills it does. And," Mr. K looked briefly my way, "we'll be able to see if there are things that spook Star. Better to know now while we're just getting started."

Before long, we pulled off the road to a wide clearing in front of a wire fence and big metal gate. Mr. K parked the truck and trailer with plenty of room to back the horses out of the trailer. Mr. K unloaded his horse first, then motioned me to follow with Star. The horses stood, ground-tied by their reins, while we tightened cinches and checked saddle bags filled with lunch, medical kit and a satellite phone. No cell phone coverage where we were going. I mounted and waited for instruction.

Mr. K led Zazz over to the gate and opened it wide. "Head on through, Sara." Star and I walked through the opening and waited for Mr. K to close and lock the gate, then swing up on the Quarter Horse. When he walked up beside us, Mr. K glanced up at me with a smile. "I forget how tall Star is until I'm next to him. Makes me feel like a shrimp."

"Zazz is an awful pretty shrimp if you ask me," I retorted.

Mr. K ran a hand down Zazz's glossy neck. "Yes. He's a good-looking guy all right." Affection warmed his voice.

Just then a brisk breeze rolled a tumbleweed toward us like a soccer player dribbling a ball. Zazz ignored the weed under his feet, but Star snorted and sidled sideways, shaking his head and going off-trail with dancing feet and tail raised like a flag.

I soothed him with a hand on his neck. "Whoa, boy. It's just a weed." Star stilled his prancing while he watched the tumbleweed's erratic course across the field. Head high, ears forward, he snorted, shook his head then caught up with Zazz.

"Doesn't get out much, does he?" Mr. K looked up with an amused smile, but not criticism.

I could feel my cheeks burning red. "Uh, not like this," I agreed. "I'm usually training in the ring or riding on the beach. I don't think he's ever seen a tumbleweed."

Mr. K nodded. "Instinctively, horses don't like anything under their feet. Understandable, but also the kind of obstacle Star will encounter in the ring. He needs to be able to tolerate and not react to sudden surprises like this. If you were out here alone and he startled enough to throw you, that could be dangerous. Now," he lifted his chin to gesture forward, "up ahead there's a good size creek. It's got a solid bridge over it, but the water is visible and loud. I want you to be ready with Star. We'll see how he reacts to this kind of obstacle and find out how deep his fear of water is. You try going first and I'll follow to see how he reacts."

I swallowed hard. I could already hear the water and knew Star did, too. His ears flashed forward, but he walked steadily on, not breaking stride. When we reached the bridge, he slowed and his nose bent down toward the dark brown planks. He stopped abruptly before the edge of the bridge, hooves at least a foot away from the boards. He cocked his head toward the steep bank on our right that sloped down to the wildly rushing water. He blew out a nervous breath.

"Just let him look." Mr. K advised softly behind me. "Don't rush him."

Star's head lowered again and his nostrils flared with his effort to figure out this unknown danger. He took a nervous step back and peered at the water rushing under the bridge.

"Give him a minute and we'll see if he'll go on his own. If he won't, I'll take Zazz across and see if Star will follow." Mr. K sounded calm and I was glad he knew what to do. I'd never experienced refusal from Star. Embarrassment and curiosity battled in my chest.

Abruptly, Star backed several paces quickly enough that Zazz had to step aside. Star had made up his mind.

"Okay, let me go ahead with Zazz. You move Star up when I give the word."

My hands slicked with sweat on the reins. I quickly wiped each palm against my jeans and settled down into the saddle. Star's ears twitched nervously. He could read my emotions like he had an owner's manual right in front of him. Great. I'm a huge help. Not.

When Zazz reached the midpoint of the bridge, Mr. K turned in his saddle and called for me to try with Star. I took a deep breath and pressed my heels into his sides. He took a dragging step, then one more. That was it. Nothing I did could coax him to go any closer.

"Let's see what happens if I go all the way over," Mr. K called. Zazz's hooves caused a hollow thud with each step until he reached the ground on the other side. Star threw his head up and whinnied sharply when it appeared his pal was going to go ahead without him. But his hooves stayed cemented to the ground.

"Hold on," Mr. K called. "Let me come back and we'll try it

differently." Zazz walked willingly back across and circled behind Star and I.

Mr. K nodded toward the bridge. "This time, keep Star's head right at Zazz's hip. Let's see if having them closer together helps. Got it?"

I licked my lips and nodded.

Zazz walked toward the bridge and I kept Star's nose even with the shorter horses's hip. Zazz clomped onto the bridge again with Star close behind. Then Star's hoof hit the wooden plank with a hollow thud. He shied violently back, and even though I was ready, I had to grab the saddle horn. Star backed several feet away from the edge of the bridge. His head nodded nervously and a coal-black hoof pawed anxiously at the ground.

Mr. K turned Zazz and came towards us once again. "Okay. At least now we know how deep his fear goes. Let's try one more approach. This time, you get down and see if he'll let you lead him across following Zazz. Slow and easy, Sara. Don't try to push him. To him, that water is as dangerous as a crazed wolf. We're going to work with him and remind him you're more trustworthy than his fear. Okay?"

Mutely I nodded while I dismounted and gathered the reins in one hand. I took a minute to stroke Star's shoulder and talk softly to him. Guilt washed over me when I remembered Star coming after me in the riptide. It was my fault my courageous horse felt unfamiliar terror. Tears felt hot in my eyes. I took a deep breath, gathered the reins and led my horse toward his fear.

"C'mon, Star. It'll be okay, I promise," I crooned in a soft voice. "It's okay, boy, c'mon. Let's cross the bridge."

I continued my soft coaxing until Star finally took a step forward. His hoof hit the plank and his ears went flat back at the hollow thud. But he didn't move his foot off the bridge.

"That's it, boy. That's great. Another step now. You can do it. You're the best horse in the world. C'mon, boy. Come with me to the other side." My low tones continued to persuade my spotted friend to trust me. Slow step after slow step Star followed until he was in the middle of the bridge. He hesitated. His neck shone slick with sweat and I knew he felt terrified. His ears swiveled to the side to catch the sound of the rushing water beneath him then pivoted immediatcly back to lie flat against his skull. His eyes were rimmed in white, but he never took his gaze off me.

"Keep him together, Sara. Don't let him stop. You're doing just fine." Mr. K's voice encouraged softly.

I continued my low coaxing tone. Star took another step, picking his foot up high and setting it carefully down. Then another and another. Finally, we reached the other side of the bridge. When Star's hoof struck dirt, he rushed forward off the bridge, knocking me aside. I didn't care. When all four feet hit soil, he turned quickly and thrust his head toward me. I reached my hands up on either side of his ears and pulled his head onto my chest, murmuring softly. He blew with gusto into my jacket. I dropped the reins and stepped forward under his head to his chest, stretched my arms up around his shoulders and clasped them over his mane. Tears filled my eyes when I leaned into Star and kept talking until I felt his breathing return to normal. Then I backed off and stroked his sweat-coated neck. Sudden swelling of affection for my horse caused a lump in my throat. He trusted me over his fear.

Mr. K rode up beside us. He looked down at me and smiled. "Well done young lady. Let's continue on to the sheep herd. When we come back, we'll see if we can get him to cross with you mounted."

I gulped. "We have to do that again?"

Mr. K grunted. "Well, yeah. Unless you want to go down and then back up these sheer creek sides. Which I wouldn't recommend as they're tangled with tree roots. The bridge is the safer bet. It's fine. We have to teach him not all water is going to hurt him. Now, c'mon." He turned Zazz toward the trail.

I mounted then followed the Quarter Horse up the path. Pungent scents of pine and cedar swirled around us as we rode through a forest on our way to the open pasture where the sheep grazed. After a twenty-minute ride, the trees thinned and we could see the wide-open area dotted with small white forms resembling giant cotton balls.

"What the…" I pulled Star to a stop so I could verify that I had no idea what kind of contraption I spied up ahead. It looked like a big metal box with gaily colored flags flying from each of the four corners. Like some kind of medieval carnival wagon.

Mr. K motioned me forward. "It's Adam's shepherd's hut. Actually, an old Winnebago, but it works great. The flags help with visibility when it gets foggy up here. How about you find a place away from the sheep where you can eat your lunch while I talk to Adam."

I looked around and spied a fallen tree at the edge of the woods. It made a comfortable back rest when I sat in the grass and leaned back. Star's reins kept him ground-tied near me. He cropped at the grass, pausing occasionally to check out the white fluffy animals grazing not far away.

Mr. K ate his lunch while he talked business with the shepherd. It didn't take long before we were back on the trail headed home. Star heard the rushing water at the bridge before I did, and we both knew what was coming. Mr. K stopped Zazz at the edge of the bridge and turned to face us. Star planted his feet several feet away.

"What do you think? Want to try on your own?"

Suddenly hot, I unzipped my jacket and unbuttoned the top couple buttons of my shirt. "I guess. Maybe since he already did it, it'll be okay this time?" My voice squeaked a little when I talked.

"Could be. Give it a try. Let me go first with Zazz."

I nudged Star to move up toward Zazz. He obeyed, but his steps were deliberately slow. Zazz walked across the bridge. Mr. K halted him halfway across. He turned in his saddle to check our hoped-for progress.

Star stopped at the edge of the bridge. He pawed the ground restlessly then lowered his head to sniff suspiciously at the wooden planks. He tried to back up, but I stopped him and encouraged him forward. He shook his head and pawed at the ground again. Moist with sweat, his neck made the reins darken.

"Come on, Star. You did it once and it was okay. One more time. Let's go with Zazz. Come on, boy." I applied gentle pressure with my heels and hands, talking constantly. I stroked his neck and patted his shoulder in encouragement. When I was just about to give up, Star placed a tentative hoof on the bridge. One more step and both front feet were on the boards. I kept up soothing reassurance, one hand constantly stroking his neck and shoulder. My hand was soaked with his sweat.

Mr. K urged Zazz to continue then waited for us at the other side.

One hesitating step after another, Star made his way slowly across. His nose remained inches from the surface of the boards. I could hear his stressed breathing above the sound of the rushing water. His ears flicked frantically back and forth alternately listening to my voice and the blast of water below his feet. A couple feet from the edge, he gave a leap and cleared the bridge completely, rushing up to where Zazz waited patiently.

When we drew even with Mr. K, he nodded his approval. "That's a great first step. It amazes me what that horse will do for you. I hope you don't ever take that kind of trust for granted. You'll need patience to get him completely over his fear."

I nodded, swallowing past the lump in my throat. "Whatever it takes, I'll work with him. He saved my life. I'll never take that for granted. If it's patience he needs, that's what he'll get even though that's not what I'm known for. Guess I'll be learning some new behavior, too. He's worth it."

Mr. K turned Zazz toward the waiting truck and trailer. "That he is. That he is, indeed. Now let's get these two home. They've earned their dinner."

# Chapter 7

*I can choose to get off the wrong road.*
Sara's Diary

**The next morning**, I hurried downstairs to find myself joining a rare family breakfast.

"Hey! How come everybody's home?" I slid into my chair and reached for the platter of waffles and bacon.

Mom passed me a glass of orange juice and a pitcher of syrup. "It's my morning off from baking, your dad has a doctor's appointment before his summer class and Ben made time when he smelled bacon."

Ben looked up from his plate and grinned around a mouthful of waffle.

"So, Ben." Dad pushed away his empty plate and pulled his coffee mug close. He glanced at Ben while keeping an eye on pouring cream into his coffee. "I understand you've become friends with Zoe Gavalas."

Mouth still full, but chewing suspended, Ben's gaze darted toward me. His eyes narrowed. Glass of juice halfway to my mouth, my eyes rounded in surprise and I pivoted my head slightly from side to side. "Not me," I mouthed.

Dad carefully took a sip of coffee while he watched our silent exchange. "Slow down, Turbo," he nodded toward Ben. "Remember we talking about you jumping to conclusions? Your sister hasn't said anything. I ran into Zoe's mom at the college. She's guest teaching an intensive botany class for two weeks before fall term begins. She said they're enjoying getting to know you." He set his coffee cup down and looked at his watch. "I can't imagine why," he added dryly. "How'd you meet Zoe?"

Ben swallowed his bite of waffle and wiped his mouth with his napkin. He cleared his throat and looked up at the ceiling. Hoping for written instructions up there? He shot a glance at me again. I smiled broadly at him while I poured syrup on my waffles. This was going to be as good as a TikTok routine.

"Ah, yeah. I kind of know Zoe. We took a class on tide pools and microorganisms this summer so she was there and I was there and, ah, we were there together and stuff. So, we, ah, learned about stuff, ah, she's a girl. I mean, of course she's a girl. It's just she's a smart girl and so we kind of know each other from the class. And I met her mom when she dropped Zoe off and picked her up and stuff."

My gaze met Mom's and we both unsuccessfully swallowed a laugh. Mine came out a squeak, while Mom turned hers into a cough. Ben's face was as red as the strawberry-themed tablecloth.

Dad took a last gulp of his coffee and pushed up from the table. His gaze remained neutral but a smile tugged at the corners of his mouth. He stacked his dirty dishes and placed them in the sink, kissed Mom's cheek then grabbed the folded newspaper by his plate. "And stuff," he quoted his son. He thumped Ben lightly on the head with the folded newspaper. "No one would ever guess you scored a thousand on your vocabulary SAT. Thanks for breakfast, honey, I'll see you all later." He gripped his briefcase and headed out the door.

Mom stood up and nudged her chair back, gathered up her plate and teacup and put her dishes on top of Dad's. She bent to open the dishwasher but looked over her shoulder at my brother. "Do you want to invite Zoe over for dinner sometime, Bennie?"

I took a bite of bacon and grinned at Ben. "Yeah, Bennie. Why don't you ask Zoe over for dinner?"

Ben made a quick grab for a piece of my bacon and stuffed it into his mouth before I could react. He was already out of his seat and handing Mom his plate by the time my indignant, "Hey," burst out of my mouth accompanied by a soggy piece of waffle.

"Snooze you lose, Sis," he taunted over his shoulder. "No thanks, Mom. I'm good." The back door slammed behind him as he made his escape.

The door had barely stopped vibrating before there was a light knock. Kevin's voice called, "Anybody home?" The question floated in the air while he closed the door behind him and entered the kitchen.

"Hi, Mrs. Mitchell. Hey, Sara." He sat down in Dad's empty chair. "What's up with Junior? He sure rushed by me in a hurry."

Mom and I laughed and took turns explaining Ben's embarrassment. While we talked, I finished breakfast and loaded my dishes into the dishwasher.

"I've gotta go feed Star, Mom. Anything you want me to do today?"

"If you could go to the store for me that would be a big help. I have the list right here."

"Sure. I'll go when I finish with Star. Thanks for breakfast. See you later." I reached for Kevin's hand. "Have time to help me?"

"Yep. Bye, Mrs. M."

We clomped down the back steps; hands clasped loosely and headed for the barn.

"Did the trail ride yesterday help you figure out what you want to do for competition?"

"Yeah. I get what it's all about now. And we found out for sure Star is afraid of water. You know, I haven't wanted to go right down by the surf since my dunking in the ocean, I should've realized Star could have a problem, too."

"I don't know." Kevin looked thoughtful while he considered my self-accusation. "He's never been afraid of anything. He just seems so invincible. I don't think beating yourself up about it is helpful. At the very least, forgive yourself and let it go. You didn't know and now you do. And you're getting him the help he needs, right?"

"Yeah. Mr. K is going to help him."

Kevin shrugged and pulled me in for a sideways hug. "Then you're doing all you can."

We reached the barn door and both winced at the metal screech when Kevin pulled it open.

"I'm going to oil that while you take care of Star. That sound will wake the dead if it gets any worse."

I thumbed on a favorite playlist, set my phone on a stall rail, then got busy gathering feed and fresh water. Star seemed fine after his hard ride the day before. Relief seeing him feeling good after the exercise relaxed the stress I felt about horse PTSD. Star would be okay. Mr. K would make sure of that. Kevin joined me in cleaning the stall until an oldies song we both liked boomed out of the phone speaker and a brief spell of dance fever broke out. The east coast swing we'd been forced to learn in seventh grade PE was still strong in our muscle memory. Laughing and shuffling through the straw and cedar shavings on the floor felt like a good break. Once the last notes of the song died away, we quickly finished the stall job. Pitchforks stashed in the tack room, Kevin took my hand to guide me toward the stacked hay bales. He sat on one of the bales and tugged me down next to him. He shifted slightly so he faced me on our hay couch.

"We need to talk about our relationship. Know what I'm talking about?"

I nodded. "Think so. You mean what Tawny would call sucking face?"

Kevin laughed. "That and other things I'm sure, but yes, sucking face. We need to figure out what's okay and what's not. I don't want to hurt you, number one, and I don't want to go against what the Bible says is okay for unmarried people."

"What does the Bible say is okay for unmarried people? I haven't read any of those parts yet."

"Would it be better if we went and talked to Pastor Jake? I'm sure he'd be glad to talk to us together."

Immediately my neck and ears felt like a thousand sunburns. Talk about sex with our youth pastor? Yucko. I grabbed my ponytail, pulled off the scrunchy and got busy retying my hair, then pulled down the sleeves of my hoodie and fiddled with the tie strings from the hood. But I could feel Kevin's steady gaze on me. I darted a quick look at him. "Uh, pretty sure that's a hard no. It's uncomfortable talking to you about sex, let alone an adult guy I hardly know. We'll figure it out. Just tell me what the Bible guidelines are as you understand them." I glanced at him and realized he apparently had the same sunburn problem I did. A-ha. I'm not the only one who's embarrassed. This made everything so much better.

"Ah. Well. I guess…I guess this is harder to talk about than I thought," he admitted. He combed a hand through his hair and rubbed the back of his neck.

We fidgeted on the hay until the tension made me uncomfortable. "Listen. We can figure this out. How about we just agree actual sex, hooking up as Tawny would say, is off the table? We both just watch our comfort zones and stop whenever either one of us feels uncomfortable?"

Kevin used his feet to move the loose hay in front of him into a little pile while he considered my suggestion. "I guess we could try that except…"

"Except for what?"

Kevin blew out an explosive breath and raked both hands through his hair. He leaned forward, elbows propped on his knees and cradled his head in his palms. Finally, still leaning forward, he turned his gaze toward me. "Except…it's really hard to stop. I mean…really…hard to stop. And I don't want to treat you like Travis did." His words rushed out tumbling over each other just like the tumbleweeds on the trail ride. "I mean, you were so scared that night, and he hurt you, Sara. He bruised your arm. What if I hurt you because I don't want to stop? What if I scare you…?" His voice raised as he expressed his fear. "What if I hadn't been there, what if…"

I reached over and placed two fingers over his lips. "Shhh. But you *were* there. And you protected me. You'd never hurt me. You're so not Travis. Not. Even. Close. Travis demanded what he wanted no matter what I wanted or needed. You," I removed my fingers from his lips and held his face gently between my hands so I could look in his eyes. "You never demand. You ask. I trust you. I think I trust you more than I trust myself. You'll stop when we shouldn't keep going. We definitely won't have sex and we'll watch ourselves from going too far. Okay?"

Kevin reached up and placed his hands over mine. "Okay. I'd feel better if we had more definite guidelines, but this is a lot harder to talk about than I thought. I really want to do our relationship the right way. For me that means thinking about what's best for you, and me, but also what God wants for us."

I turned my hands to grasp his and squeezed. "Me, too. We'll both be careful. Mostly because I never want to have this kind of talk again." I laughed, stood and pulled him up beside me. He released my hands and grasped his around my waist. My arms reached up around his neck. "You know," I smiled up at him. "This wouldn't be so hard if you weren't such a bodacious babe magnet. As Tawny would say," I teased.

He blushed so I placed a smacking kiss on his lips. "Listen, I've gotta go to the store for Mom. Want to come?"

"No. I promised Mom I'd help her for an hour or two today. I think I'll do that while you go to the store. Catch you later?" He quirked an eyebrow at me.

"Yep," I agreed. "I'll text you when I'm back."

I wrapped my arms around his waist and leaned in against his chest. His arms gathered me close and he rested his chin on top of my head. We stood quietly. I'm pretty sure nobody has felt like this around another person. Safe. Loved. Appreciated. Wanted. At least I've never felt like this around another person before. It's so different than I felt about Travis. This is a whole different level than my family or even Tawny. Not more, necessarily. Just really, really different. A sigh of contentment breathed quietly between my lips. His arms tightened momentarily then slowly dropped away from our hug. Bummer, but also, yeah, it was time to go.

We slid the barn door closed with zero accompanying screech. Nice. Kevin turned and waved. I blew a kiss.

# Chapter 8

*I can't tell Robyn what to do. But I can tell her what I wish I'd done.*
Sara's Diary

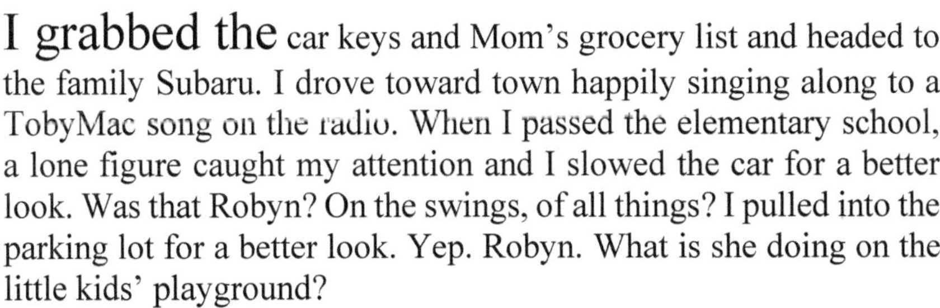

I grabbed the car keys and Mom's grocery list and headed to the family Subaru. I drove toward town happily singing along to a TobyMac song on the radio. When I passed the elementary school, a lone figure caught my attention and I slowed the car for a better look. Was that Robyn? On the swings, of all things? I pulled into the parking lot for a better look. Yep. Robyn. What is she doing on the little kids' playground?

Intrigued, I shifted into park and switched the engine off. A swift grab for the small leather clutch that held my phone and doubled as a wallet, and I was out of the car headed over to the playground. Robyn looked up at my approach and scowled.

"What are you doing here?"

My answering shrug didn't change her scowl. "I was driving by and saw you here so thought I'd stop." Robyn's puffy eyes and tear-stained cheeks made me pause, but remembering my regret of how I'd treated her pushed me forward. I squirmed into the U-shaped rubber seat of the swing next to Robyn. "Are you okay?"

Robyn tried to rub all trace of emotion from her face. She failed. "Actually, no, I'm not okay." She tossed her head, reminding me of

Star when he was in a snit. "But I'd be better if you'd just leave."

"Come on. Give me a chance here. Any way I can help?"

Robyn sighed. "Fan. Tastic. Just what I need. A completely useless offer of help. Please just leave me alone. I know you don't like me."

"I don't even know you," I protested. "Look. We got off to a really bad start last year. Mostly my fault…" Robyn's mocking snort interrupted me. Old memories and lingering shame caused heat to creep up my neck.

"Okay, all my fault. I was a jerk. You're still pretty new in town and I just think…" I shrugged my shoulders. "I don't know. Maybe we might even like each other if we give it a chance. But I get it if you're not interested. I won't bother you anymore."

I wobbled and swayed as I tried to untangle from the rubber seat. Finally getting my feet under me, I stood and flung the chain swing away. I brushed dirt from the dusty swing off my hands and walked toward the parking lot.

"Wait."

I paused without turning around. I heard a loud sigh.

"Come back. I'm sorry."

I turned, walked back to the swings and wrestled myself back onto the rubber.

"Truce?" I held my hand toward Robyn.

She stared at my hand then her gaze searched my face. Slowly she lifted her hand to grasp mine. "Truce. I'm not sure what good you think this will do, but you, you like seem pretty stubborn."

"So true. You have no idea."

I let go of Robyn's hand and an awkward silence developed between us. I squirmed around on my swing and began to pump my legs to gain height. A quick glance at Robyn revealed her mouth dropped open.

"Bet I can get higher than you," I challenged with a grin.

"Really? You're challenging me to a swing contest? You're on Saint Girl," Robyn answered, her smile taking the sting out of my hated nickname.

We strained forward and back as our legs pumped for height. Pretty soon we were laughing while our hair alternately covered our faces and streamed out in back of us. Robyn's cheeks were pink with exertion. Gradually we coasted forward and back and let our swings reduce to a gentle sway. Robyn grasped the chains on her swing and leaned back until her hair lightly brushed the ground, legs extended in front of her.

"Oh, God. I haven't swung since forever." She glanced over at me. "Oops. Sorry. You probably don't like swearing and stuff, do you?"

I shrugged. "People can talk how they want."

"But don't you, like, go to church and stuff?"

"Stuff." I laughed and shook my head. "My brother's favorite word."

"That's Ben, right? The baby hunk?"

"Ewwww. He's so not a hunk. He's my little brother." My nose wrinkled at the description of Ben. Yuck.

"Oh, trust me. He's hunk material. And definitely not little."

"Well, he is to me. Yuck. A hunk."

"Think he's interested in older women?" Mischief lurked in Robyn's laughing gaze.

"I repeat. Ewwww. That would be beyond weird."

A friendly silence floated between us, finally broken by a loud sigh from Robyn.

"What?" I looked at her with curiosity.

"It's just that nobody's going to want to hang out with me once school begins. Even a baby hunk won't. I am so not looking forward to going back. But my parents insisted." Robyn stared down at her toes digging into the loose soil under the swings.

"You're kidding, right? You're so popular."

Robyn looked up and over at me. "No way. Pretty sure I've burned my bridges at this school."

"Pretty sure you're beautiful and popular and last year isn't going to matter. Duh." My snort wasn't exactly ladylike.

Robyn dug her feet into the ground and halted her swing. "You don't think what I did last year will matter? You know. The photos and stuff." Robyn's cheeks were red. She stared at her hands clasped in front of her and began picking at her nail polish.

Last year's events and Robyn's actions played tag in my mind. I hesitated. Because Travis shared the revealing photos that Robyn sent him, everybody at school pretty much knew what happened. Would it matter?

I cocked my head toward Robyn. "You know, honestly, I'm not

sure if anyone will give you a hard time or not. My guess is maybe a few people like Alyssa and her crowd, but if you ignore them, I bet they'll stop. Travis leaving right after you did was a huge deal, too, and Travis will be back just like you so maybe that will take some of the heat off. Everybody knows he went to drug rehab."

Robyn stared straight ahead and now her face paled. "Yeah. Travis will be back." She breathed in a huge breath of air and blew it out. "Got to admit I'm not looking forward to that either." She peered over at me from behind a curtain of blue-streaked hair. "You know?"

"Ha. Do I know? Absolutely. Trust me, I know about not looking forward to seeing Travis. I am so with you there. But he can't hurt you—can't you just ignore him?"

"You're kidding, right? Are we talking about the same guy? Self-centered, conceited, it's all about me, Travis?"

"Well, yeah. He hasn't changed, that's for sure. So?"

"So, Travis doesn't walk away from anything or anyone he believes messed him up in some way. I'm sure he blames me for anything that happened after I…well, you know…after the pictures." Robyn stared at the ground.

"Yeah, but what can he do? It was his own fault for sharing your text to the entire football team. That's on him," I insisted.

Robyn shook her head. "He won't see it that way and one thing I know for sure about Travis." She turned toward me and regarded me solemnly. "Travis gets even. If he thinks somebody got the better of him in some way, embarrassed or hurt him? You can be sure he'll get even. I lay awake at night wondering what he's going to do to me."

"Well, we won't let him. We'll help you; we'll make sure he knows you're not alone."

Robyn studied my face until I squirmed. "What? I have dirt on my face?" I laughed uneasily.

Robyn shook her head. "No. I just…I was as awful to you as Travis was. Maybe more, and yet you're here talking to me. I don't get it. So are you apologizing to him, too?" We were back to sarcastic.

"Sort of. He came by the house and asked me to forgive him." I included air quotes around my words. "I don't think he meant it. But I did tell him I forgave him. I also made it clear I wasn't interested in spending any time with him. As for you, I told you at your house the other day that I'm really sorry about what I said to you in the cafeteria that day. About the…I mean, what you did with your phone."

"You can say it. Sexting. I was convicted of sexting which is against the law." Robyn's bitter tone turned her face sour. "I was literally willing to do anything to hold onto his attention. I had to beat you. That's how despo I was. A lot of good it did me."

"Listen, Travis is only interested in one thing and that's whatever Travis wants. You know that, right? You're so much better off without him. Really. You are. Me, too."

I glanced sideways at the other girl and noticed her eyes were bright with unshed tears. "Robyn?"

Robyn rubbed impatiently at her eyes. "Stupid allergies. Listen, thanks for stopping to talk. I appreciate it, really. But you don't owe me anything. See you around." Robyn hurried away before I could react. My uncertain, "Okay," was lost in the lengthening distance between us. I wondered if the distance will always be there. I hoped not. She reminds me of a stretch of beach north of our home. The water always appears calm on the surface, but if you try to swim you discover a fierce undercurrent. Calm on the surface. Turbulence below.

This time I escaped the clutches of the swing with better grace and walked toward the parking lot. I thought about what Robyn said and knew she was right. Travis did like to get even. What did that mean for me? And for Robyn? Nothing good, that's for sure. I wish I could convince her I'd like to help. I knew what finding out about God's love had done for me. Unconditional love is something I'm just beginning to understand, but even I know it's what Robyn needs. Especially since she experienced so much of Travis's conditional, and destructive kind, of love. She needs to hear about the kind of love Lauren Daigle sings about in her song *Rescue*. I began to plot how I could get the song to speak for me. This had to work.

# Chapter 9

*My counselor said staying angry with someone is like drinking poison expecting the other person to die. Sometimes I'm still drinking the poison.*
Sara's Diary

**Early the next** morning, before dawn, I stirred uneasily in bed. I rolled over and yanked on the sheet tangled between my legs. I had to stop dreaming about riding Star. Sometimes it seems I actually heard hoofbeats in my dreams. I punched my pillow and settled back down to sleep then groaned. Great. Now I was hearing car noises in my sleep. What had I eaten before bed?

When I woke again with the sun on my face, I lay disoriented for a few minutes trying to thrust sleep away so I could think clearly. What was the dream and what was real? I pushed up out of bed, stretched then reached for jeans and a shirt. A quick trip to the bathroom for face, teeth and brushed hair. I regarded the two prescription bottles of meds and sighed. I knew they helped me feel better, but I sure hated that I had to take them. I shook out the required doses, swallowed them dry and hurried down the stairs for breakfast. Sometimes life can feel pretty lame, but there's always hope of Mom's cinnamon rolls for breakfast. There were only a few days left before school started and I juggled practice with Star, sessions at Big Sky, time with Kevin and my friends, and, oh yeah, figuring out what to do about Robyn.

Mom and I chatted briefly while she kneaded elbow-deep bread dough, then I dashed out the door letting it slam behind me. Abby, from her calico cat loaf of bread position, jumped down from the railing to follow me to the barn. When I reached the barn, I slowed. Something was off. The door. The big sliding door wasn't closed and latched as usual. "That's weird," I noted to Abby. "I know I closed it last night."

Abby slipped in through the slight opening, but I pulled the door wide open, relieved there was no squawk, stepped through and pulled it closed behind me.

"Hey, Star. Time to get ready…wait. What the…" I rushed over to the wide-open stall door. I peered in, no Star. I raced around the outside corner of the stall and stared at the dark corner of the barn where hay bales were stacked to the ceiling. Still no Star. Half-remembered dream sounds came back to me. Hoof beats. A car in the drive. I sprinted to the door, wrenched it open and examined the ground. There. Hoof prints in the gravel. Undisturbed U-shaped impressions at first, then deeper depressions with widely spread gravel sprayed backward and scattered.

"Like from a spooked horse," I muttered. I glanced up and frantically searched the horizon. No spotted horse in view. Nothing. I studied the direction of the sprayed gravel on the driveway. Fear clutched at my throat. I wheeled and sprinted toward the house.

"Mom! Ben! Help! Star's gone." Panic made my voice a screech. Mom stood in the doorway brushing flour off her arms with a towel.

"Sara? What's the yelling about? What's wrong? Are you hurt?" Alarm sharpened her tone as well, until Ben's loud whistle topped even our raised voices.

"What's going on?" Ben stood at the door in pajamas, voice scratchy from sleep. "Why are you two yelling?"

I skipped the steps and leapt to the porch. "Star's gone. He's on the road maybe, or even the highway, I don't know. I don't know where he is, but the stall and barn are empty and there are hoof prints on the driveway. Ben? Come with me? Please come? Help me look?" I turned a pleading look in his direction.

Sleepiness vanished; Ben spoke decisively. "Right. Get the car, I'll get dressed." He turned and raced up the stairs.

Mom chimed in and motioned me to follow her inside. "I'll call the police then take my bike and search the back roads. You and Ben head for the highway. Got your phone?"

I patted my pocket and nodded. Tears streamed unchecked down my cheeks. "Mom, he could be hit, he could slip and break a leg. I couldn't stand it…" My voice muffled into silence when Mom pulled me against her in a fierce hug.

"We'll find him. It will be all right." Mom grabbed me by the shoulders and stared into my eyes. "We'll pray. Star's smart. He won't have gone far."

"He's spooked, Mom. I can tell from his tracks. Something…" My voice trailed off. Something Robyn said drifted into my memory.

"Travis gets even," Robyn had said.

"…or someone," I continued. Rage curled my fingers into claws. "That jerk! That scum! When I get hold of him…" My words hissed out through clenched teeth and jaw.

"What are you talking about?" Mom broke in sharply.

"Travis, that's who. We didn't hear the door because Kevin oiled it so it was perfect timing for that creep. He hates Star and he hates me. He did this. I know he did."

Ben jumped the last five stairs and landed almost at our feet in the kitchen. "Why aren't you in the car? Let's get going." The air, vibrant with unseen tension, stopped him like a wall.

"What's going on?"

I turned a dark, fierce gaze on my brother. "Travis is what. He did this. I'll bet you any amount of money. He came early this morning, let Star out then spooked him. I'll kill him. If Star's hurt, I'll kill him," I vowed. Fist-clenched hands rested on my hips.

"Yeah, okay, tough girl." Ben grabbed my shoulders and turned me toward the door. "You can kill him later. Let's go find Star. I'll drive, you look. Give me the keys."

Still fuming, I raced after Ben toward the car.

"Where should we look first?" Ben called as he dodged around the car to the driver's seat.

I slid into the passenger seat and jerked the seat belt around to the buckle. "Let's head toward the highway. He wouldn't be able to cross because of the cars so he might be wandering alongside the road. Or…" my voice choked and I couldn't continue.

"Don't go there," Ben advised. He patted my knee awkwardly. "Concentrate on finding him safe. There're no sirens and that's a good sign."

Ben pushed the speed limit by a few miles per hour. We reached the highway. He pulled off to the shoulder before we reached the traffic light that controlled entry to the double lane road.

I hopped out of the car and ran forward to scan the traffic. I searched both directions, but saw no sign of my horse so returned to the car.

"No Star, but no flashing lights either," I informed Ben as I got back in the car. "You're right. That's a good sign. But I have no idea which way to go. What do you think?"

Ben considered the choices. "I think if he came this way he'd go right. He could go that way, avoid the highway and cars and stay on grass. If he went left, he'd be in the line of traffic. Let's go right on the highway for a mile or two."

Biting my lip in frustration, I glanced right then left. "I guess. He could be anywhere," I wailed in despair.

"We'll find him." Ben's voice was emphatic and desperate at the same time. "Let's go. Eyes sharp."

He turned the car carefully into merging traffic and stayed in the slow lane to give me a good view of the side of the road. After a couple of miles, he glanced at me. "Turn around?"

I nodded miserably.

Ben exited the highway, turned left under an overpass to go back the way we'd come.

"What was that you were saying to Mom? About Travis?"

My gaze scanned desperately forward, side and back as we drove as slowly as allowed down the road. "Remember when Travis came over last week? What he did when he left? The gun gesture?"

Ben nodded, his gaze also searching right and left.

"I think he did this. I heard hoof beats this morning and a car in the driveway, but thought I was dreaming. It was Travis, I know it was. Getting even with me and hurting Star because Star doesn't like him. Travis can't stand not being liked or admired. He's such an arrogant stuck-up JERK!" My hand slapped the dashboard. "I can't stand him. Him and his, oh, please forgive me, oh, please, I'm so sorry. Bull-oney, he's sorry. Robyn told me the one thing he always does is get even, and she's right."

Ben's gaze returned briefly to me. He looked startled. "Robyn? When were you talking to Robyn?"

"The other day. It's kinda weird, but we're getting to know each other. Sort of. Not really. Oh, I don't know. But I know what she told me is right. Travis gets even. And this is his way of getting even with me and with Star." This time my fist pounded my knee. "I'll kill him. If Star's hurt, I'll kill him," I vowed.

"Okay, even if that's true, you can't kill him. Calm down, will you? You're talking crazy. If he did it, we'll figure it out, but you have to calm down. Concentrate on finding Star, then we'll figure out what to do next. Now, where shall we go? We've been driving around an hour and I'm out of ideas. Toward town or back past our house?"

"I don't know," I wailed. "If he was spooked, and I'm sure he was, he'd just run."

"You said you could see hoofprints in the gravel. How about we go home and see if we can tell which direction he went?"

"Okay, that makes sense. Mom's last text said she's heading back home, too. Let's go check in."

Ben U-turned the car toward home. When we drove in the driveway and coasted to a stop, I saw a familiar figure walking toward the house. I opened the door and hurled myself out of the car before it came to a stop. I raced toward Kevin, collided with him and threw my arms around his neck. He rocked back a few steps to keep his balance, his arms instinctively closing around me.

"Kev, Star's gone. We've been out looking but haven't found him." Kevin pulled me in close, tucking my head onto his chest. I relaxed. The hard strength of his grasp calmed my panic. I nestled against him and felt enclosed in a safety net. A sigh breathed out that felt like it came from the soles of my feet. I sniffed appreciatively at his jacket. Honeysuckle.

"You've been working with your mom, haven't you?" I murmured into his chest.

He bent his head toward me. "What?"

I lifted my face off his chest. "You've been working with your mom. I smell the honeysuckle." He nodded and I burrowed back into his embrace. Ben joined us.

"Hey, Ben. What's this about Star?"

"I guess when Sara went out to the barn this morning, the door was open and Star was gone. We've been out driving around trying to spot him, but no luck. I'm going to check with Mom and get some breakfast. Want some?"

"I don't need breakfast, but I'd like to hear the whole story." He leaned toward my ear. "Ready to go to the house? You could probably use something to eat, too. Okay?"

I nodded but kept one arm tightly around Kevin's waist while we walked to the house.

Ben looked up from a giant bowl of cereal when we walked into the kitchen. Mom turned from the stove where a pan of freshly backed rolls rested, waiting to be frosted. Kevin and I grabbed chairs. I put my elbows on the table and propped my head on my hands.

Mom came and sat down by me, her hand on my shoulder. "I didn't have any luck either, honey. I'm so sorry. Dad says wait for the police. They'll send someone out to talk to us. Shall we go out looking again? We'll do whatever you want. We could go different routes this time and stop to ask at people's homes to ask if they saw anything. That might be worth a try."

"Ben thinks we should check the driveway for hoofprints to see if we can tell what direction he went. That's probably a good idea." I looked toward Kevin. "Will you help me?"

He nodded. "Fill me in on what's happened so far." I began talking as we left the kitchen to see what story the driveway could tell.

"Looks like right here is where he took off." Kevin pointed to half-moon shapes dug into the dirt beneath the loose gravel. The gravel fanned out from each dug-in mark. We followed the tracks down the driveway almost to the road. There they veered sharply to the left. The gravel fanned out in an even wider pattern to the right.

I shaded my eyes and peered in the direction the tracks pointed. "I guess we could start walking that way. Maybe he stopped as soon as he calmed down and is grazing down that way."

Kevin stuffed his hands in his jacket pockets and looked back the way we'd come, then swiveled to the direction the prints pointed. "I always come the opposite way." He nodded toward the path in front of us. "What's down there?"

"Most of our five acres is that way and it's all fenced. Then after that there's a house or two, then the state park. But it's closed right now because of the damage from that last earthquake we had. The beach access caved in and is dangerous, I guess. I used to ride there, but not since they closed the park. He could've gone there."

Just then, a patrol car turned into the driveway. We moved to the side. The officer rolled down the passenger window and leaned toward us. "Is this the Mitchell residence?"

"Yes. I'm Sara Mitchell." I walked toward the patrol car.

"You're reporting a lost horse?"

"Yes. He's my horse."

"Can I meet you at the house?"

"Sure. Of course. We'll be right there."

Kevin and I followed as the patrol car made its way slowly toward the house. We reached the car just as the officer stepped out of the vehicle.

The officer held his hand out toward me. While I shook his hand he said, "I'm Officer Talbot. Someone called in the report of a lost horse. Said he could be out on the road?"

"He could be anywhere. I'm not sure what time he was let out and spooked from the barn. Would you like to come inside?" I gestured toward the house.

"Why don't you show me where the horse is kept. Do you have a picture of him?"

Kevin put his hand on my arm. "I'll run in and get one from your mom."

Kevin held his hand out toward the policeman. "I'm Kevin Richards. I'm a friend and neighbor. Be right back." He hurried toward the house while I walked toward the barn with the officer.

Kevin returned to the barn to find the officer and me seated on hay bales. He walked up in time to hear the police officer say, "Miss Mitchell, there's no proof this young man actually let your horse go and deliberately spooked him. You can't accuse him with no proof."

Kevin handed a recent newspaper clipping of Star and me to the policeman.

"Thanks. Hey. I've seen this horse." The policeman looked up at me. "Are you in 4-H?"

"Yeah. Since I was twelve. Why?"

"My daughter's in your club. She has this photo in her room. I recognize his markings. She's too young for you to know, but you and this Star are all she talks about."

He stood up, carefully ripped off the top copy of the report he'd filled out and handed it to me. "Here's your copy of the report. If you think of anything else, or if Star comes home, please let us know. I'll circulate his description to the rest of the patrol and we'll keep an eye out for him. And no," he insisted when he saw me open my mouth to argue, "I won't go talk to Travis Baker. There's nothing concrete to indicate he could be responsible."

He touched the rim of his hat, nodded to Kevin and me, and walked out of the barn. We heard his car crunch slowly down the driveway toward the road. Kevin joined me on my hay bale seat. He put an arm around my shoulder and I leaned into him.

"Want to go out and look some more?" Kevin reached over and gently hooked a loose lock of hair behind my ear. He hugged me close to his side. "We'll find him. He's too big to miss."

"He could be injured and down, he could be caught in wire. Maybe a car hit him." I looked up at Kevin. He caught the tear that brimmed over my eyelid and put both arms around me.

"He could also be happily grazing in someone's yard or raiding someone's haystack. He could just as easily be fine somewhere out of sight. C'mon. Let's go look." He stood up and reached out his hands toward me. I grasped them and he pulled me up just as his phone rang. He pulled his phone out of his back pocket, checked the screen then answered. "Hi, Mom." He listened intently then nodded as if she could see him. "Okay, I'll be right there. No, it's okay. I'll be right there," he repeated.

"Mom just got a huge shipment and she's got heavy boxes she can't move. I've got to go help her get them put inside." He grabbed my hands and squeezed lightly. "I'll come back as soon as I can, okay?" He brought one of my hands to his lips and kissed it.

I nodded. "Just call when you're done. I'm going to take the car and keep looking on my own."

A few hours later, I pulled our dusty Subaru to a stop in front of the barn. I rested my head against the steering wheel. No one I talked to had seen Star. The back door slammed and I looked up to see Mom walking toward the car. She opened the door and got in the passenger seat.

"Nothing?"

I shook my head. "Nope. I drove down to the state park then crisscrossed the roads between here and there. That's the direction it looks like he ran, but I didn't see him. I stopped at the houses where it looked like somebody was home and asked them to watch for him." I rested against the steering wheel again. "He's vanished. He doesn't even have a halter on so even if somebody sees him, it will be hard to catch him."

Mom reached over and combed her fingers through my hair. "He's smart and healthy. Once he calms down, he could just wander home by himself. Let's not give up yet. I've been praying all day God will keep him safe. Let's trust that, shall we?"

I nodded, but didn't lift my head off the steering wheel.

"I've got to get dinner started. Come in and help me?" Mom pulled back the drape of hair so she could see my face.

This time I looked up. I wiped my eyes with the backs of my hands. "Yeah, I will. But can I get a bucket of oats and set it out by our gate first? Maybe if he gets close enough, he'll smell the oats and come the rest of the way down the drive."

"Sure, honey. Go ahead. Good idea." Mom got out of the car and headed toward the back door.

The barn door slid open easily. What I wouldn't give for that deafening sound to have woken me last night. I got a bucket for oats, added some of the molasses mixture I kept for treats, closed the feed bin and turned toward the door. My eyes swept past the small mirror I'd hung in the tack room after I started dating Kevin. I took a step back and stared at my image. All my flaws seemed magnified in the mirror. I knew there were more inside, unseen. I scowled. But the scowl relaxed when I thought about Kevin. He didn't see many of my flaws, visible or not. And he loved me in spite of the ones he saw. But, Star? Star knew me inside and out and his love and loyalty never faltered. He just stayed solid in support and devotion. Kind of like God.

"Whoa," I whispered uneasily. I glanced up and around the tack room. "Ah, sorry, God. Didn't mean to compare you to a horse. It's just; he is kind of like you. I know you love me no matter what, and if I could see myself the way you do, I wouldn't see my mistakes and flaws because you don't. And I know he's just a horse, but that's kind of how he is, too. Please, please, God keep him safe. And please, help me find him. Amen."

I placed the bucket of oats by the gate at the head of the driveway, then went in to help Mom with dinner.

Star was the main topic of conversation that night while we ate. Ben helped me clean up after dinner, then I sought the sanctuary of my room. Conversations with both Kevin and Tawny helped the evening pass, but by 11:00, I was in bed, reading. I knew I wouldn't be able to sleep and prepared for a long night. My phone vibrated on the nightstand. I picked it up and saw Mr. K's name on the screen. I hit the answer button quickly.

"Hi, Mr. K."

"Hi, Sara. I know it's late, but I was sure you'd want to know Star is outside my corral trying to steal hay from my horses."

"He is?" My voice squeaked and I thumbed the speaker button and placed my phone on the table. I jumped out of bed, pulled sweats on over my pajamas, slipped on shoes, hopping around my room in my hurry, while I continued talking. "Is he all right? How long has he been there? Is he hurt?" My next question was muffled by the sweatshirt I pulled over my head, but that gave Mr. K a chance to break into the conversation.

"Hold on, hold on. I don't know how long he's been here. He wasn't there when I came in for dinner, but just now I went out for my final nightly check. He seems sound, but he won't let me near him. I could throw a rope around his neck, but thought I'd check with you first."

"I'm coming, Mr. K. I'll be right there. I'm leaving now." I thumbed off my phone and raced out the door to be met by the three members of my family.

"What?" Ben asked, uncharacteristically to the point.

"Star's at Mr. K's. But he won't let Mr. K near him. I've gotta go. Dad?"

"We'll all go," he answered. "You go get the car, Sara. We'll be right there."

I detoured briefly to the barn to grab a halter, but still beat my family to the car. Mom and Dad made no comment while I drove almost within the speed limit to Madrona Acres. I pulled up next to Mr. K and we poured out of the car.

Mr. K pointed. "He's just on the other side of this corral. You might need to get up on the fence so you can see over the other horses." Mr. K thumped the top rail of the fence.

I climbed each rail until I could see over the dim shapes of several horses. "It's so dark out there. The light doesn't quite reach."

With a frustrated exclamation I jumped off the fence. "I'm going over there."

"Is that a good idea?" Dad appealed to Mr. K who shrugged.

"He's her horse."

"It's okay, Dad. I just need to get him safe," I called over my shoulder. I started around the curved fence line calling Star's name. A soft nicker answered me, then he loomed up in front of me. I dropped the halter and reached both hands, palms up, toward him. He stepped straight toward me until he was close enough to lower his head to my chest. He leaned slightly into me while I reached up and gently stroked from the base of his ears as far down his neck as I could reach. I murmured soft nonsense.

"Got him?" Mr. K called softly.

"Just a sec." I reached down for the halter, slowly drew it up over his nose and fastened it. Stroking his neck, I moved my hand toward his chest to scratch him. My hand froze when I felt sticky wetness. My eyes strained, but I couldn't see in the darkness. I held up hand toward the bright yard light outside the barn and forgot to breathe. Gleaming red moisture told its own story. Blood.

# Chapter 10

*I wish I could stop listening when fear talks.*
Sara's Diary

**"Mr. K! I** think he's hurt."

"See if he'll come into the light with you," Mr. K suggested, his voice calm and low.

I gripped the lead rope and gently urged Star into step beside me. I kept a hand on his neck. He came willingly, ears nervously swiveling forward and back. When he saw my family gathered by the corral, he stopped, shook his head and took a step back. Mr. K shook a bucket of oats. Smart man. Food is Star's love language. His ears perked up and he moved forward, his nose stretched toward the enticing bucket.

While he snuffled up every last morsel of grain, my family quietly gathered around him, stroking and patting. I waited impatiently while Star finished his treat. I wanted to get him in the barn where we could look more closely at his chest.

As if reading my thoughts and feeling my impatience, Mr. K lowered the bucket and nodded toward me. "Let's get him in the barn and take a look. I think he's settled now."

When I tightened the rope and encouraged Star beside me, he started out willingly enough, then his energy deflated like a balloon with a slow leak. He walked more slowly, barely lifting his feet, and his head bobbed down toward the ground.

"He's exhausted, Sara." Mr. K commented from behind Star. "He must have run quite a spell today. He's got a bit of a limp to his left fore." The older horseman moved in front of us to open the barn door. He gestured toward two sturdy poles about five feet apart. Each pole had a large solid metal ring embedded toward the top of the pole. "Let's crosstie him here."

Once we had Star secured between the two poles, I stood at his head speaking softly, while Mr. K examined Star. He placed a hand on top of Star's back at the base of his mane. He stroked the normally silky black shoulder, now gray with dust, and murmured softly while he moved toward Star's chest. Star shifted uneasily when the man's hand came close to the smear of blood.

"Whoa, there, big fella. Not going to hurt you. Shhhh, settle now." Mr. K's low monotonous tone soothed my exhausted horse. He stood still.

"Ben," Mr. K's voice did not change in tempo or volume. "Fill that pail by the feed bin with warm water and grab a clean towel out of the tack room, will you? Bring them over here."

Once Mr. K had the bucket and towel, he hunkered down by Star's chest to carefully clean away the blood and dirt. He looked up at me, his forehead creased with concern. "He's got quite a gash here. Looks like a wire cut." He glanced over my shoulder at Dad. "You folks have barb wire on your property?"

Dad shook his head. "No. My father replaced all the wire with split rail when he bought the place years ago."

Mr. K's attention returned to the wound on Star's chest. "Well, he's a jumper so he probably jumped those. He must've run into a neighbor's wire fence somewhere. Probably didn't even see it if he was spooked." He shook his head. "That wire is cheap, but deadly."

He stood and wiped his hands on the towel. "I don't know if this will need stitches or not, but I think he'll be fine if we keep him quiet until morning. Let's put him in a stall here. The vet is coming to worm my yearlings in the morning and he can take a look then." He glanced at me. "Want me to call when the vet gets here?"

My throat tightened at the thought of leaving Star when I just found him. My anxious gaze darted toward Mom and Dad, then flicked back to Mr. K. "Can I…" my voice quivered so I cleared my throat to speak clearly. "I want to stay here with him." My gaze returned to my parents and I continued with a plea. "You know I've slept in our barn and been fine. I'll be all right. Mr. K has a bathroom in here and everything. And I have my jacket." I flapped the front of my coat as if to prove its existence. "Please?"

Mr. K added his assurance. "She'll be fine. I have a sleeping bag I can bring her. Spent a night or two myself out here. It's a secure building."

My parents spoke together, then Mom answered for both. "That will be fine. I'll put some things together when we get home. Ben and Dad can run them back for you so you can put yourself together in the morning before the vet comes." She took a few steps forward to gather me in for a hug. "Star will be fine, honey. He's safe now, and the doctor will fix him up." She stood back and took my hands. "You okay?"

"Yeah, Mom. Thanks. I'll call you in the morning and let you know what's going on."

Dad added a bear hug of his own, Ben gave an awkward half wave and my family left.

Mr. K glanced at me; his wiry eyebrows more tangled than ever. "Nice family."

I nodded. "Yeah. We've been through a lot together."

Star walked willingly into the corner stall I chose so I could make myself a hay bale bed in the aisle out of his way. I filled the water bucket and gave him a section of hay. He munched half-heartedly, then turned away to stand head down, a back hoof cocked on point. I grabbed a brush and began to clear away the dust and grime from his day on the loose. I worked carefully around the ugly gash in his chest. The angry red of the ragged edge of the wound showed up harshly against his black hide. Fury as red and black as Star's chest began a slow burn in my heart. Travis making a mock gun and aiming at Star filled my memory. I remembered his sarcastic comments last year about my weight and the cruelty on his face when he exposed my infected finger to his friends. I remembered the countless careless slights and lies. Memories fueled my anger to inferno and my thoughts turned toward revenge.

"Here you go, Sara. This should help you get some sleep tonight." The stable owner's cheerful tone clashed with my dark thoughts. I accepted the rolled up bag and tried to smile.

"Thanks, Mr. K. I'm sure I'll be fine. Thanks for taking care of us."

"Cowgirl belongs with her horse. You're right where you should be in my book. See you in the morning." He tipped the brim of his hat toward me. He left the barn just as Dad drove up and stopped by the door. Ben got out.

"Here you go, Sis. Mom packed your toothbrush and some other stuff. Girls." He shook his head. "Sure are high maintenance."

I grabbed the bag out of his hands. "I'm not any more high maintenance than you. Mom's just being Mom."

"Whoa. Chill." Ben rocked back on his heels and spread his hands out in protest. "Star's back and he'll be okay. What's up with you?"

"It's Travis. I know he did this. He's such a slime. All that stuff he pulled last year and now he's back and worse than ever. I know he let Star out this morning and spooked him. He's just…he's so…he's a scum-sucking pig is what he is."

Ben's raised eyebrows shrieked astonishment. "A scum-sucking pig. Really? That's all you've got?"

I glared. "I can't think of a bad enough word. He's a black hole of awful."

"You can't prove he let Star out."

"Who else would do something like that?" I demanded. "Everybody loves Star, you know that. Travis is the only one who's ever been negative. And all because Star has the good sense not to like the jerk. Horses are so smart." I scowled. "I'll get even." I looked at Ben and promised. "I'm so going to get him back."

"How? You can't even prove he did it. There's nothing you can do. And considering Travis, and who he is, I think you better let this go. School starts Monday and there will be enough going on. It's your senior year. Don't try to take on the biggest jock in school. It won't turn out well for you, trust me."

"It's not right that he can just treat people like they're nothing. Like nobody matters but him and what he wants. Somebody needs to show him what it feels like."

"And that somebody is going to be you? For reals? Travis has about as much depth as a mud puddle. He's not worth it." Ben shook his head and jingled the car keys. "Think about it. Star's back and he'll be okay. I've gotta go. I promised Mom I'd come right back.

See you tomorrow." Ben waved and was out the door.

Still seething, I watched him go, fists clenched at my sides. I turned to watch Star doze in the stall and a small smile curved my lips. Fatigue hit like a brick wall and I yawned. I wrestled some hay bales into a cot-size space and spread out the sleeping bag. My jacket made an adequate pillow and soon I joined Star snoozing away.

A deep hacking cough woke me from a sound sleep. I bleared sleepily around the still dark barn. I heard the deep ragged sound again and sleep vanished. Fumbling impatiently with the sleeping bag zipper, I lost patience and slid the bag past my hips so I could wriggle out. I stumbled to Star's stall, still in my stocking feet, tugged the sliding lock bar back and heaved the door open. Star stood in the far corner; his front feet braced as if for balance. Another cough racked his lungs.

I hurried to flip on the light switch, pulled my shoes on and returned to the stall. When Star had been fighting for his life battling pneumonia, the veterinarian told me a horse's normal respiratory rate was twelve to sixteen breaths per minute. I stood next to Star and simultaneously stared at the second hand on my watch and counted each exhaled breath for a full minute. Twenty-five.

"Too high," I muttered. "What happened, boy? Too much excitement and running around?"

I refilled his water bucket with fresh water and offered it to him. He drank until another cough shuddered through his body then he turned away. I set the bucket down and placed my hand under his chest between his front legs, carefully avoiding the bloody gash. No sweat. I checked his groin area on the inside of each back leg. No moisture. Good. He wasn't sweating. I ran my hand down his back, then stroked his neck and smoothed his mane. Several minutes passed, and while his breathing remained rapid, there were no more coughs. Maybe he just needed fresh water.

I retrieved my jacket then sat against the stall wall, brought my knees up to my chest and folded my arms over my knees for a headrest. My eyes fluttered then gradually closed. Star's coughing woke me twice more during the night, but he didn't break a sweat. When a stray sunbeam glowed warmly against my eyelids, I stirred with the sunrise. A memory floated through my sleepy mind. I saw myself sitting on a hay bale in Star's stall. He was in the body sling the doctor used for support during the worst of the pneumonia last year. My dream self ran a finger down my open Bible and read a verse out loud.

Sunlight poured through the window opposite the stall and I yawned, stretched and tried to stand. My legs had stiffened during my uneasy night and I grunted when I pushed up off the floor. I stretched up on my toes, arms reaching overhead, then settled back on my heels. I stared unseeing at Star while I tried to remember what I'd been reading in my Bible. Oh. Yeah. It was the verse about as much as possible being at peace with everyone. My blurry vision sharpened. I stared at Star's spots while I pushed the dream out of my thoughts.

"How can you sleep with just straw for a bed, S?" I scuffed my boots through the thickly piled straw at my feet. "This stuff is brutal."

Star took a few steps toward me and butted his nose against my stomach before raising his head and letting his chin rest against my shoulder. I reached up to scratch under his chin, then stroked his cheeks. "You okay? The vet will be here pretty soon and we'll get you fixed up. Want some breakfast?"

He drank deeply from the water bucket, setting my mind somewhat to rest, then turned his attention to the hay in the manger. My fingers combed through the black strands of his mane, loosening bits of straw. "You don't suppose that verse is talking about people like Travis, do you? I just can't believe God means for me to try to be at peace with him when he's such a jerk."

Star's ears swiveled back at the sound of my voice, but his only answer was to blow hay dust enthusiastically out of his nostrils. "I mean, I get being at peace with those who want to be at peace with me. But, Travis? That would mean letting go of what he did to you. Like forgiving him when he hasn't even asked for it or apologized for what he's done."

The rattle of the barn door interrupted my conversation with Star. Mr. K stepped inside.

"How's he doing?"

"He coughed early this morning. Does that mean the pneumonia is back?"

"Not likely. It's probably just the scar tissue the vet told you about. I imagine Star overdid yesterday and his lungs are inflamed. The vet should be here any time. Let me take a look at that gash."

Mr. K stepped into the stall and ran his hand down Star's shoulder. Star ignored him and continued to much his hay.

"Good," the ranch owner grunted. "He's not touchy about his wound." He bent forward for a closer look then straightened at the squeal of truck brakes outside the barn.

"Darn Doc," he muttered. "Still hasn't fixed his brakes." He raised his voice. "Morning, Doc. Got something in here you need to look at before we start with the yearlings. C'mon in."

"Morning, Pete. What's going on?"

The doctor stepped inside the barn and stopped in surprise when he saw me.

"Sara. What are you doing here so early?"

I gestured toward the stall where Star continued to crunch hay.

"Shooting Star. What's wrong, Sara?"

"Somebody let him out of his stall early yesterday morning. Whoever it was spooked him and he was on the run most of yesterday. He showed up here late last night. He has a bad cut across his chest."

The doctor quickly stepped around me, but quietly approached Star. "Hey, big fella." Dr. Heins reached out a hand to Star's side and stroked his way forward. "What have you been up to, huh?" His low tone barely rated a twitched ear from Star. "Let's take a look here."

Only when the doctor's gentle hand neared the wound did Star's feet shift uneasily. "Sara, let's get a halter on him and bring him out into the light. I need to be able to see."

I haltered Star, led him out and cross-tied him between the posts. I stood at his head while the doctor took his time examining the wound.

"Well, you surely did come up against something, didn't you? You've got quite a gash. Here, calm down, calm down." The doctor's voice soothed, but when he began to clean the gash, Star's head tossed and his feet shifted fretfully.

"Hold him, Sara. He's got to stay still. Pete, move to his other side, will you? See if the two of you can keep him still. I'm going to have to stitch this and I'd rather use a local and not sedate him. It's just deep enough I think it will heal better and leave less of a scar if I stitch it."

Held by me at Star's head so he couldn't move forward or back, and blocked on either side by the two men, Dr. Heins was able to clean and stitch the injury. I bit lip while I watched the doctor administer a local anesthetic, then suture the gash.

He cleaned his instruments and returned everything to his bag. "Let's give him a tetanus booster since it's been a while. He's all stitched up so you can trailer him home. Keep him quiet. You can walk him, but nothing strenuous. I'll come by and remove the stitches in ten days or so."

A deep cough from Star interrupted the doctor's treatment. His keen glance sharpened.

"How long has he been coughing?" The vet reached for the stethoscope in his bag.

"He started early this morning. After midnight anyway. Do you think he'll be okay?"

Dr. Heins settled the earpieces and placed the diaphragm against Star's side, listened intently then moved the stethoscope under Star's belly and motioned for quiet. My body felt as stiff as a store mannequin while I waited for the doctor's answer. I had longer to wait.

The doctor straightened and rummaged in his bag for an equine thermometer and lubricant. He smoothed his hand down Star's back toward his tail. He lifted the silky black waterfall of tail and inserted the thermometer. After the right amount of time, he slid it out and peered at the numbers.

"Temperature is normal and there's no congestion in his lungs. He's got a ragged cough, but it's dry so I think we're okay. I think whatever strain occurred yesterday probably irritated his lungs and throat. Try mixing four teaspoons of sage in his oats and see if that helps. Sage is a natural remedy for coughs. Can you find a supply?"

Picturing Kevin's mother's storehouse of herbs, I smiled. "Yeah. I'm pretty sure Mrs. Richards will have some."

"Ah, yes. The oils and fragrances lady." Dr. Heins nodded. "She'll have good quality." He gave me final instructions, patted Star on the hip then left the barn with Mr. K. I called Dad and asked him to come with the trailer. A half hour later he pulled up by the barn. He and a surprise passenger, Kevin, jumped out of the truck and hurried toward me. Kevin reached me first and pulled me in for a hug.

"How is he? Everything okay?"

While we loaded Star into the trailer, I described the vet's diagnosis and suggestions.

"I'm going to ride in back with Star, Dad," I called once we were all set.

"Me, too," Kevin added.

"I'm so shocked," Dad answered, a smile neutralizing the sarcasm. "It's not far. I'll take it easy. Bang on the window if you need me to stop."

I nodded and Kevin and I took up positions up by Star's head. We braced as the truck slowly moved forward and picked up momentum.

"Remember that verse I read about being at peace with people?"

"Of course, I remember. That's what made you finally come and talk to me. Why?"

"Think it includes Travis?"

"I know this isn't what you want to hear, but 'fraid so." Kevin shrugged. "It doesn't say be at peace with only the people you like. In fact, other places in the Bible it says we need to forgive those who jerk us around. I know you want to get even with Travis, and I agree with you it's most likely him who let Star out and spooked him, but going for revenge isn't what God wants you to do."

Sometimes it is a real drag to have a godly boyfriend. I don't get a break from reminders of right relationship in God's eyes. Like, ever.

I moaned. "I knew you were going to say that. Isn't that impossible? To forgive somebody who does things like this? Especially when they're not even sorry."

"Yeah. It's rough. But we're supposed to do what Jesus would do. And guess what?"

"Jesus would forgive him. Rats. This is so hard," I complained.

"Yeah, but just think. Travis being who he is, I bet he's waiting for you to accuse him and try to get back at him. It's what he would do. What he won't expect is for you to just let it go. I bet that'll drive him nuts. I mean, don't you think it'll freak him out if you kill him with kindness? He'll never in a million years expect that."

"Probably," I said, quietly thinking it over. Forgiveness is totally not what Travis would expect. "Still, I'd rather get even somehow. But I think you're right. I won't get payback. I promise

I'll think about this and try to do the right thing. Maybe by Monday when school starts, I won't be so mad. But don't count on it. When I think about what he did and how hurt Star is, I just see red."

The truck slowed for a turn. I looked out the window. "Almost home. Once I get Star settled, can we go over to your house? I want to ask your mom is she has some sage I can give Star for his cough."

"Sure. Anything for the other male in your life. You're lucky I'm not the jealous type."

I slipped my arms around Kevin's waist. "You have nothing to worry about. You're my favorite human male."

"Is that so?"

Kevin's superpower is that just his smile can make me feel loved. But the kiss we enjoyed didn't hurt either.

# Chapter 11

*Fitting in isn't the same as belonging.*
Sara's Diary

I knew Tawny would arrive bright and early Monday morning to braid my hair so I was up and dressed in the outfit she chose when her car pulled up by the house. I gasped when I saw my friend.

"Tawn! Your hair!"

"Yeah. So. What about it?" Tawny plunked her backpack down on my desk and grabbed the chair. She positioned it in front of the mirror on the closet door then motioned for me to take a seat. I got up from the bed and walked toward the chair but couldn't take my eyes off Tawny's gloriously untidy hair.

"You let it go curly. I haven't seen it this way since fifth grade when you discovered your mom's flat iron and figured out how to use it. Your hair looks like the curly ribbon on a gift package."

Tawny shrugged. "I'm doing me. No biggie. Now, let's do you. Sit."

Obediently, I sat but turned to look at my friend. "Does Ryan like it?"

Tawny turned my head to face the mirror. She expertly gathered my hair, smoothed it completely with a brush then parted it down the middle. She began a French braid on the right side at my forehead, then continued to gather and braid while she talked. "Don't know. He hasn't seen it yet, but do you think I'm worried about what Ry thinks about my hair? Seriously? Have I taught you nothing?" She paused and turned my head to the right then left while she considered her handiwork. She finger-combed the braided hair loose and began again with another handful of hair at my right temple. Her clever fingers angled the braid up and over the crown of my head.

"How's the cut on the celestial Star doing?"

Transfixed, as usual, by my transformation under Tawny's skillful fingers, it took me a moment to answer. "He's doing great. His cough is gone and the stitches haven't gotten infected. Worst part is trying to keep him quiet because he feels better now. He wants to go and do."

"I can so relate," Tawny murmured. "I don't do sitting around either. There." She stepped back and considered her work, head tilted to one side. "What do you think?"

I turned my head from side to side admiring the thick braid that began on the right side of my head, curved over the top so it ended up behind my left ear with some loose strands curling gently to my shoulder. "It's beautiful."

"Yep. It's crisp, all right," Tawny agreed.

I sure hope that's a good thing.

We gathered up our stuff and clattered down the stairs to the kitchen.

"Hey, Mrs. M." Tawny dodged the kitchen table and closed in on Mom for a hug. "You have the best mom smell ever," Tawny said into Mom's shoulder. "All vanilla and cinnamon." She leaned back, but kept her arms clasped around Mom's waist. "When shall we give you some highlights? I could fix you up with some sweet blonde highlights. It would be totally lit."

"Is that good?" Mom frowned. Her head tilted to the side and her eyebrows arched high in confusion.

"Absolutely, Mrs. M. It's what you maybe called the bomb."

Mom's frown twitched into a smile. "I'm pretty sure I never called anything a bomb. Unless it really was a bomb, of course."

Tawny rolled her eyes. "C'mon, Mrs. M. Like cool? Or rad? Is that one you know?"

"Thank you, Tawny, cool is one I know. But I think I'll pass on the blonde streaks. I'm not sure I can pull off lit or rad," Mom laughed. She gave Tawny another quick hug, then returned to her baking. "You girls have a good first day of school."

"Right-e-o, Mrs. M. We're off to slay the dragons of ignorance and stupidity." Tawny's arm slashed through the air as if her arm was a sword.

"Bye, Mom. I'll see you later if I survive following the warrior princess around."

We drove separately to school because of different afterschool activities, but found parking place in spite of the busy first-day traffic. We clambered out of the Subaru and headed for the gym entrance. Tawny spotted Ryan, right away.

"There's my boo." She waved and hurried forward to meet Ryan with a giant hug. He returned her hug then grasped her by the shoulders and held her at arm's length, eyeing her hair. He took one springy curl between his fingers and pulled it gently straight to its full length. Then he let go and the lock immediately recoiled into a springy spiral. "That is crazy sweet," he drawled. He did it again and again until Tawny impatiently swatted his hand away.

"Get over yourself," she commanded. "It's just hair."

"I like it," he protested, laughing. He turned toward me and lifted his chin in a friendly greeting. "Hey, Sara."

"Hey, Ry. Didn't see much of you this summer." Our trio headed for the gym. Ryan looped his arm around Tawny's shoulders, but glanced down at me.

"Yeah. I visited some schools. Checking out possibilities. How about you? What're your plans? I know gorgeous here is headed for beauty school."

Tawny batted his hand off her shoulder. "Beauty school? So lame. I'll have you know I'm headed to the Cosmetology and Salon Academy in San Francisco."

I stopped dead in my tracks. I grabbed Ryan's arm and tugged him to a stop, which stopped Tawny as well.

"Wait. What? San Francisco? Since when? You said you were going to stay here and have your mom train you."

"I know, right? Is that not the best idea, ever? But, nooooo. Mom says she's not having anybody working in her salon who isn't certified and licensed. I did not know she is such a sorry toe-the-liner. So, I have to go to school." She shrugged her shoulders and lifted her hands. "What are you going to do when the parentals take a stand? And since Ry's eventually going to the University of San Francisco law school," she shrugged again. That's where I'll be." She reached out a hand and rubbed my shoulder. "I'm sorry. I know I should have told you sooner, but I just couldn't. Telling you would make it too real and I don't know how I'm going to handle not having my bestie around."

I stood like a rock in a river while students streamed around me. Am I the only one who had no firm plans what I'd be doing next year? How will I manage without Tawny? And Ryan? What WAS I going to do with my life?"

"SJ?"

Tawny's hesitant tone caught my attention. "Uh, that sounds awesome you guys. I'm happy for you both, really. Just surprised is all." I tried to inject enthusiasm into my voice, but even I could tell it was forced. "And law school? Ryan? I thought you were headed for a huge track star career. What happened to your track scholarship?"

"Oh, I still have the scholarship. And I'll run track. But track is just a way to get me where I really want to go. I want to be a lawyer. And I want to work in family law. You know my mom's a social worker, right?"

"Yeah."

"She talks about her work a lot. One of the things that upsets her is the court system. I think I could be good at helping parents and kids through rough situations. At least I want to give it a try."

Great. Everybody has a plan for their lives, and I'm not even sure what I'm doing tomorrow.

Just then a familiar fragrance and grip around my waist told me Kevin had arrived. He pulled me in and aimed a kiss at my cheek. It missed and hit my ear, but I turned and did him one better by giving him a quick kiss on the lips.

"What's up? Why is everybody looking so serious?" Kevin rested his arm around my shoulders. Some of my anxiety melted away when I leaned into his comforting presence.

"Tawny and Ryan were just telling me about their plans for next year. They're both going to schools in San Francisco." I tried with a lot of difficulty to keep my voice calm and light.

"No kidding. That's awesome." Kevin sounded genuinely

excited for our friends. "Hey, we better get headed in or we'll all be late. Three people were late for my zero-hour AP class on marine biology and the teacher gave them a hard time. See you guys at lunch? I've gotta dash." He gave me a quick kiss, then rushed into the school building.

"He's right. We better jet. I'm glad we all have the same lunch this year. Catch you two later." Tawny blew Ryan a kiss. He waved at us both, and we all scattered.

Knowing running into Travis was inevitable, I had thought long and hard about how I should react. Kevin suggested I ignore Travis. Since I couldn't think of a better idea, I decided to go with that as much as possible. Only, he's so unpredictable, it makes me nervous. I'd just have to do the best I could. I followed the crowd into the building.

At lunch, I looked around the chaotic room searching for my friends. I noticed Courtney, Alyssa and the other cheerleaders at a table in the middle of the room with most of the football team. Courtney was still part of the in crowd, but she remained neutral toward me. A relief from last year. There was a lot of loud laughter, nudging and checking out each other and others in the cafeteria. No sigh of Travis which gave me a weird feeling of mixed relief and dread.

"Living large," I said to myself when my gaze settled on the group for a moment. "Not."

I spied Tawny's curly hair tilted toward Ryan's close-cut sandy brown hair and hurried over to join them. I settled onto the bench just as Kevin walked up. We chatted about our morning classes until one-by-one, we noticed a change in atmosphere in the lunchroom. A sort of stillness when people's voices gradually died away. We looked around until Kevin nudged my arm and nodded toward the far side of the room. Travis and a couple of his friends sauntered into the room. Though Travis appeared aimless in his direction, I'm pretty sure he made deliberate moves toward his former posse. He meandered, talking and joking with students, then paused when he reached the cheerleader's table. He reached out and tugged at a lock of Alyssa's hair while he leaned down and whispered in her ear. She must've liked the attention because she smiled and a hot pink flush began at her collar and flooded toward her hairline. She glanced at Courtney, then stood and pushed away from the table. Her arms snaked around Travis's waist. He put his arms around her and lifted her off the ground in a full-body hug. And just like that, he was once again part of the group.

"And that's how it's done, folks. Seamlessly back in the fold." Kevin muttered.

Travis kept an arm around Alyssa, but reached over and traced a finger along Courtney's cheek. Then he fist-bumped and clasped hands with a couple of the football players. His periscope gaze took in the entire cafeteria in a slow revolution. When his gaze narrowed and his body tensed, I knew he'd spotted my friends and me. After a few minutes he spoke into Alyssa's ear then walked deceptively aimlessly toward our table. A couple of his friends followed him. When he drew near, he nodded toward Tawny.

"What's with the Orphan Annie look? You know, my grandma had a mop that looked kinda like your do. Is this the latest Cuban chica craze?" He elbow-bumped one of his friends. They all laughed with a mocking tone.

Before Ryan could react, Tawny, eyes narrowed into cat-like slits, hopped to her feet, put her finger right in front of Travis's nose and let fly with a string of pure fluent Spanish. There was no doubt from her tone how serious she was, but Travis clearly had no clue of what she actually said. Suddenly, as abruptly as she stood, Tawny sat with a little hmph sound under her breath, picked up her sandwich and took a dainty bite. Travis's face turned dangerously red, but he saw Ryan's equally enraged expression and turned toward me instead.

"What's up, oh saintly one?"

His friends laughed. One of them muttered, "Saintly one. Good one, Trav."

Encouraged, Travis turned to his friends and confided, "Sara here supposedly has one claim to fame. She's got this monster horse she rides in shows and stuff. She thinks he's some big deal, but he's not so much. I've seen him. Kind of a nag, if you ask me."

My body stiffened. My mouth opened to snap an answer, but then I felt Kevin's hand under the table on my knee. He applied gentle pressure. I took a drink of vitamin water, picked up my apple and took a bite before I answered neutrally, "Well, maybe. A lot of people think he's a better ride than that gas guzzler of yours though. Prettier, too."

Obviously not used to my standing up to him, Travis leaned down and placed both hands on the table next to me. His gaze locked onto mine. "Yeah? How is the that vicious spotted demon of yours anyway? I heard he's not reliable about staying home."

Anger that began a slow simmer when Travis insulted Tawny with a racial slur began to boil over. More gentle pressure from Kevin's hand centered me. My resolve to ignore and not let him get to me returned. I may not exactly forgive him yet, but I'm not going to give him the satisfaction of rattling me.

I glanced at him as calmly as I could manage. "Oh, he's home eating hay as usual. He's pretty smart about finding a safe place when he needs to." I hoped the look in my eyes conveyed as clearly as possible that I knew exactly what he had done but wasn't going to stoop to his level of warfare.

Travis watched me like a wolf eyeing its prey. He straightened up. "Later, Saint Sara. Or not. All the same to me." He turned and ambled away with his friends.

I glanced at Tawny and Ryan, then finally, Kevin. I let out a breath I didn't realize I was holding. "What did you say to him?" I asked Tawny.

Tawny shrugged and inspected her nails. "I recited the words to the Pledge of Allegiance to him. I knew he wouldn't know the difference." She peeked at me from underneath her curly bangs and grinned. I felt the tension drain from my body. I grinned back.

"That's beautiful, Tawn. Perfect."

"That's my girl," Ryan announced. "Smart and beautiful."

We picked up our interrupted conversation until I noticed Tawny's eyes widen and heard a quiet, "Oh, no," from my friend.

"What?" I asked.

"Don't look, but Travis just stopped by a table where Robyn's sitting reading a book. She's by herself." Tawny's fingers touched her lips in dismay. Her eyebrows drew together in a frown of concern.

"Should we do something?" I glanced at Kevin and Ryan.

"Wait," Tawny cautioned. "He's just slowing down and checking her out." Tawny's gaze hardened. "That creep. He paused then walked by and made the loser sign behind her back. He's ditching her. Poor girl."

I made up my mind in an instant. I got up, grabbed the rest of my lunch and motioned my friends to follow me. We walked over to where Robyn sat alone.

"Cafeteria food's bad enough. You shouldn't have to eat it alone." I took a seat next to Robyn and Tawny sat on her other side. The boys slid into seats across the table from us.

Robyn looked at me. Her eyes were bright with unshed tears.

"What are you doing?" Robyn asked, her voice sharp. "I'm not a project you know. I'm fine on my own."

"Don't think so," I retorted. "Nobody is. I learned that last year."

Robyn pushed her untouched tray away. "But you. Of all people. Why you? Or you?" Robyn turned and looked at Tawny. "None of you bothered with me last year. Why now? I'll tell you why." Her gaze took in each of us in turn. "You feel sorry for me. Well, forget that. I don't need anybody's pity." She grabbed her tray and pushed up from the table.

I put my hand on her arm. "Please stay a minute. Just a minute, okay?"

Robyn hesitated, then sat down. Her knuckles turned white from her grip on the tray. "What?"

"I told you how sorry I am for how I acted last year. And I am. I was a jerk, and I'm really hoping you'll give me another chance. But even if you don't, these three never did anything to you and they make great friends. Believe, me, I know. Can you give them a chance even if you don't want anything to do with me?"

Robyn stared down at her tray. "None of you were friendly last year. Why should this year be different?"

Kevin spoke up. "I don't know about Ryan and Tawny, but I didn't think you were interested. I'm what everybody calls a greenie, and you're a cool girl. Usually, girls who are interested in Travis aren't interested in guys like me. I'm sorry, I just assumed you wouldn't like me, and, if you'll let me, I'd like to try being your friend now."

Ryan finished his apple and threw the core toward a trash barrel. It dropped in the exact center of the trash can. "Yessss," Ryan crowed while he raised a fist in the air as a victory sign. He looked at Robyn and shrugged. "Sorry. I don't like any girls but Tawny, really. Nothing personal."

"Hey!" I protested.

"Oh, well, sure. You. But you're sorta like a Tawny attachment. Or a clone or something. Anyway, Robyn, you weren't on my radar last year, but nobody's much on my radar except Tawny, so no biggie. I'm good with being friends, though. He beamed a good-natured smile at her. A reluctant smile curved Robyn's lips.

Tawny sighed. "I don't know if my reason for not being your friend last year is sketchy or not. Sara's been my best friend, like, forever, and when it seemed like you and Travis were ganging up on her I guess I took her side. But when everything broke loose?" She looked at Robyn to see if the girl understood what she was talking about.

Robyn nodded. Color stained her cheeks.

Tawny continued, "I felt really sorry for you. You shouldn't have had to go through that. But by then I didn't know what to do. Should I have told you I felt bad? What would you have done?" Tawny's sincere gaze searched Robyn's.

Robyn was quiet for a moment then replied. "I know you're Sara's friend. And I know I was crummy to her." She turned and looked at me. "To you." She turned back to Tawny. "I wouldn't expect you to be friends with me after how I acted. Any of you really. You're right, Kevin. I try to hang out with whoever seems popular because then I feel popular, too. But even I know fitting in isn't the same as belonging. And I don't belong."

Robyn grabbed her tray and stood again. "You know, I can tell you all mean well. And you're right, I didn't make it easy to be nice to me last year. It isn't your faults. Well." She looked down at me. "It's a little your fault," she said with a small smile. "But, really, we're all good. Don't be fazed." She took a step away. "I'll be fine."

I took her arm, careful not to jostle the tray. "Wait. Just tell us one thing about yourself. What did you like doing before you moved here."

Robyn dropped her head back with a sigh of frustration. "God, you're stubborn." She looked at Tawny. "Is she always this stubborn?"

Tawny nodded solemnly. "You literally have no idea. Do you know how long I've been after her to let me highlight her hair? Girl, she's like no mule you've ever met."

"That's cray. I'd love for you to mess with my hair."

"That would be lit. You should come…"

"Hey." My exasperated tone interrupted them. "Remember me? Question on the table here?"

"Seriously?" Robyn demanded.

"Yeah. Come on. Tell us one thing you were really into before you moved here. How else are we going to get to know you?"

Robyn stared at me. Finally, she brought her face to within inches of mine. "Horses, Sara," she admitted softly. "I was into riding." Then she turned quickly and hurried toward the door, barely jamming her tray onto the shelf at the kiosk.

I froze. Then thawed and rushed after Robyn.

"Hey! Wait. Please? You can't take off after telling me that. C'mon, Robyn. Wait up."

I burst forward and darted in front of the fleeing girl to stop her headlong rush. I put a hand gently on her arm. "Please. Please talk to me. I know you don't trust me, but just try. We both love horses. I don't have any friends my age who like to ride or love horses like I do."

Robyn face was an open book while she struggled with conflicting emotions. Finally, she looked at me with an anguished gaze. "Listen. I know you probably mean well. I get that. But what you don't get and never will is where I am right now. I'm in a pit. There's no light at the end of the tunnel, there's no hope to hang onto. There's just a deep dark pit. You can't help me. Nobody can. Just do me a favor and leave me alone, okay? There's no way out for me. Like ever." If eyes are the windows to the soul, meeting Robyn's gaze revealed a torture chamber of pain. I had never glimpsed such misery in a person. Before I could respond, Robyn rushed past me and down the hall.

For a second, I felt Robyn's pain like it was my own and I flinched. How could she stand it? Resolve strengthened my determination to get to know my former enemy.

"God, make a way for me to talk to Robyn. Don't leave her in the dark. Help me help her. I want to help." The bell interrupted my pledge and I hurried to class.

# Chapter 12

*Sometimes I think what I really need is a relationship GPS.*
Sara's Diary

At the end of the day, I wandered out of school toward the parking lot checking my phone as I went. I noticed Robyn several feet in front of me, head down, walking slowly, and quickened my pace to slide up beside her.

"Okay, don't be mad. I know you don't want to talk to me, but I just want to tell you about one thing and then I'll leave you alone. Promise."

"I can't even believe you're stalking me." Robyn increased her stride toward her car. "I mean for real stalking."

"I know, I know. Usually I'm not this annoying," I protested, "but I think this is really important and it could help a lot of people. Please?"

Robyn face-palmed and shook her head. Then she stared at me with a laser gaze. "All right, all right. What? What is so important?"

"I was thinking about how you used to ride and I thought you should know about this place called Big Sky Hoofbeats. It's an equine therapy ranch outside of town. The owner always needs qualified volunteers to help with the classes. She'll even train some people to help with therapy sessions. Her programs have become so popular she seriously needs more help. How about if you follow me out there, I'll introduce you and then I promise I'll leave you alone.

You'd really be helping her out."

"And you'll leave me alone if I meet her?"

"Yes. Well. I'll try. I'd really like for you to meet Shooting Star, my horse, and I'd like to have a chance to be your friend, but, like, I get that it might seem weird. But I will really try not to bug you. Don't you want to be around horses again? Don't you miss it? I'd go nuts if I couldn't ride or at least be around horses."

Robyn's gaze looked out over the parking lot then down at her shoes. She blew out a slow aggravated breath between pursed lips then glanced at me. "Okay. But only because I seriously have nothing to do. And I like the idea of helping someone. C'mon. Show me this place."

I kept looking in my rear-view mirror to make sure Robyn didn't peel off and escape. But she followed me faithfully out to Big Sky and parked next to me. We got out of our cars and I motioned Robyn to follow me.

After pausing to look around, Robyn caught up with me. She put a hand on my arm to slow me down. "What's that?" She pointed across the road to Madrona Acres.

"That's Mr. K's stable. He boards and trains horses. He also gives lessons. That's where I learned to ride and met Star."

"Star's your horse? An Appaloosa?"

"Yeah. He's great. Shooting Star. I wish you'd come over and meet him," I repeated. Where did that wistful tone come from?

"Yeah, well, don't push it. I said I'd come here and here I am." Robyn's scowl returned.

I swallowed a sharp answer. "You're right. This way. We'll find Justine."

"She's the owner?"

"Yes. She and her brother, Jeremy, run this place together. It started when Jeremy came home from active service and Justine realized he was calmer when he helped with her horses. She researched horses as therapy animals, did a lot of training, got certified and started this place. Jeremy helps her. Especially with other veterans. He's a wizard kind of guy."

"I bet." Robyn answered with a nod.

We passed a corral where five students on horseback circled the ring encouraged and helped by volunteers. I motioned Robyn past corrals of loose horses and other classes until we came to a small outer pen where Justine stood with Mr. K. Both had their arms propped on the top rail of the corral with chins resting on their folded arms. Justine turned when I called her name.

"Hi, Sara. Who's your friend?" Justine pushed off the fence and turned to meet us.

"Hey, Justine. Hi, Mr. K." He tipped his hat but returned his gaze to a horse in the corral.

"Justine, this is Robyn. Robyn, this is Justine Myers, the owner of Big Sky Hoofbeats. And Mr. King, the owner of Madrona Acres."

Mr. King nodded. Justine reached out her hand and gripped Robyn's. "Hi, Robyn, it's nice to meet you. You a friend of Sara's?"

Robyn glanced at me with a small smirk on her face. "Sort of. She told me you could use some volunteers, but I'm not sure what for."

While Justine explained what Big Sky was all about and what volunteers did, I joined Mr. K at the corral fence.

"Who's this?" I nodded to the most striking tricolor pinto I'd ever seen. "She's beautiful."

We watched the pinto mare lip listlessly at the hay in a net attached to the fence. I admired the flashy coloring of black, white and shiny red bay with white and black streaked mane and tail. The mare had black legs up to her knees then bright white hide blending into red bay and continuing up to her chest. The rest of her body was interspersed with varied-sized interesting splotches of white, black and bay. Her forelock was black, but right behind her ears the hair turned white until the middle of her neck where it became black again. Her long tail was streaked white and black. She looked like Tawny could easily have had a go at her.

I turned to Mr. K. "Where'd she come from? I think Star is splashy, but he's nothing compared to this. She's awesome."

"Yep. She's a sweet looking lady. I brought her over for Justine to try out. She might work out over here, but we're just not sure." Concern filled his eyes while he watched the mare.

Justine and Robyn joined us at the fence. Justine gestured toward the horse. "I sure hope she'll work out. With her background she'll be great. So far she's pretty disengaged though. I tried her in with the other horses, but she wouldn't settle so we're going to leave on her own for a bit to see if she perks up. She's been here about ten days and I can't make up my mind about her."

"What's her name?" Robyn could not take her gaze off the pretty mare.

"Diva."

"Wow. You think?"

Justine laughed. "I know. Couldn't have named her any better myself. Her owner was a young woman who lived on a ranch over by Santa Rosa. Her dad gave her this horse as a foal and she became Diva then and there. In her twenties, Diva's owner developed symptoms of Multiple Sclerosis. Diva here became her owner's therapy horse as the disease progressed. When tremors and impaired coordination became too severe, Diva just naturally became what her owner needed. Never had any training. Just a natural. It's an incredible story. Eventually, the young woman's symptoms became so pronounced she knew she had to give Diva up. The horse is too young to be inactive. Generous young woman." Justine shook her head in sympathy.

"Anyway, she knew Mr. King here, and that's how Diva ended up at Big Sky. It's not going well." Justine nodded toward Diva. "That horse is grieving as sure as God made little green apples. I don't know when, or if, she'll come out of it. Be a shame if she doesn't."

Justine turned to Robyn. "Can I give you the paperwork to become a volunteer? I sure can use you. You can work for rides if you want," she joked.

Taking her seriously, Robyn answered eagerly, "I'll take you up on that."

"Wait here and I'll go get the paperwork." Justine walked off toward her office.

Robyn climbed up on the rails of the corral and leaned over the top. She held her hand out toward the apathetic horse. "Come on, Diva. Come on, girl. Come and meet us," she coaxed.

Mr. K slipped Robyn a horse cake and she held it out toward the horse. "Come on, girl. I've got a treat for you."

The pinto lifted her listless head and stared at the people across the corral. Her ears lay slack. Her body drooped with disinterest.

Robyn tried again, still holding the horse cake. "Come on, girl. Here's a treat." She tried a high, low-pitched whistle to try to catch the horse's attention. Diva's head snapped up and her ears swiveled forward. Robyn whistled the same sequence again. The horse dragged her feet through the dust of the corral, but she moved toward the sound of the whistle.

Diva moved slowly up to the fence and sniffed at the horse cake in Robyn's hand. She took it, not at all like Star would have. He would've snatched it up neatly in a nanosecond, but at least the mare took it. She crunched it slowly, without energy. Finished, she went a step further and sniffed at Robyn's hand. Her ears pricked slightly in interest.

Robyn leaned further over the top rail to stroke the white blaze down Diva's nose. "Hey, girl," she said softly. "You're so pretty. That's a good girl," she murmured and kept stroking. She scratched carefully underneath the mare's forelock. Diva leaned into the pressure.

Justine returned. "Here's the form…whoa. What's going on here?" She slowed her steps and talked more softly as soon as she saw Diva at the fence with Robyn.

Robyn turned to look at Justine. I couldn't believe the look of pure joy on Robyn's face. I'd never seen her with anything close to that look. The weight of the world seemed to be lifted from her shoulders.

Just then Robyn's phone chirped out the opening of Taylor Swift's, *We Are Never, Ever Getting Back Together*. Diva snorted and backed a few steps away.

Robyn grimaced and silenced her phone with a scowl on her face and suddenly I understood the song choice. Travis strikes again. Trying to get back in touch.

Robyn's phone vibrated and she backed down the fence reluctantly. "That's my dad. He's probably wondering where I am. Guess I better get going." She thumbed a message into her phone.

"Please tell me you can come back tomorrow," Justine pleaded. "That's the first sign of interest Diva has shown in days. Can you come back and work with her?"

Robyn's face brightened. "I'd like to," she answered eagerly. "I'm sure Dad won't mind. He's been after me to get involved with something ever since I got back from…ever since I got back."

I stealthily pulled my fist in toward my side. My hissed, "Yessss," signaled victory.

"All right. Good." Justine beamed. "Bring your paperwork and come back tomorrow as soon as school is out. I'll see you then."

With a wave, Justine turned and walked off, Mr. K by her side.

Robyn and I walked toward our cars. "That was so cool!" I looked at Robyn. "How did you know that whistle?"

Robyn shrugged. "It just seemed like something to try. No biggie."

"No biggie? It was huge. You heard Justine. Diva hasn't been interested in anything since she got here. And she totally walked right up to you. Aren't you excited?"

Robyn stopped and glared at me. "Just knock it off would you, Sara?" Her face lost the glow of excitement from the encounter with Diva and resumed its normal glare.

I frowned. My mouth gaped open and I stumbled back a step. "What do you mean? Knock what off?"

"The whole chummy, we're best friends, we love horses, isn't life great, crap. We're NOT friends. Life isn't great and girls like you have no idea what it's like to be somebody like me." Robyn's voice dripped scorn. "I came here like you asked. Now it's time for you to leave me alone like you promised."

Resentment boiled in my chest and spewed out my mouth. "What do you mean? Girls like me? What does that even mean?"

"Saint girls. Good girls. Girls who never have anything go wrong in their lives. That's who." Robyn turned her back on me and continued to her car.

I seethed with anger. "Hey! Come back here. Who do you think you are? You don't know anything about me."

I stormed after her and grabbed her arm to pull her around. "Nothing bad, huh?" I snapped. "A lot you know. Last year when you were taking off somewhere, probably Hawaii or something, I was practically murdering my horse in the ocean while I tried to kill myself. Yeah, that's right. I tried to kill myself. And Star almost died because he saved me. Nothing bad, huh? You know what? This so isn't worth it. I've tried to apologize; I've tried to be nice. I actually thought you and I could be friends eventually. But you're so full of your own drama you can't see beyond it to anybody else. Well, I'm done. I. Am. Over. It." I turned my back on Robyn. "And don't call me Saint Girl," I shouted as I walked away. "I told you I don't like it."

I got in the Subaru, slammed the door and raised a cloud of dust when I drove away. I fumed all the way home. I pulled up in front of the barn and got out of the car. Temper caused me to slam the door again. When I heard the sound of a car pulling up behind me, I turned. Robyn. I turned away and stormed toward the barn.

Robyn reached my side and darted in front of me. I tried to duck around her, but she blocked my way and we faced off in front of the barn.

"What?" I demanded, arms folded across my chest, one foot slanted sideways and my other hip cocked out.

We faced each other. Gazes locked onto each other.

"What do you mean, you tried to commit suicide?"

"Duh. What part of tried to kill myself do you not understand?"

Robyn's eyes flashed at the sarcasm. "I know that." She spoke impatiently. "I know what it means. I want to know why. Only miserable people try to commit suicide. How could you have possibly been miserable?"

The emphasis on "you", notched my anger up to rage. "Well, let's see," my sarcastic tone sharpened. "Maybe partly because somebody humiliated me in front of a houseful of kids at a party then spread rumors about me. Let's see, who was that now?" I cradled my chin in my hand and tapped my cheek with a finger. My eyebrows scrunched in mock thought. Then I raised my hand off my chin and pointed a finger skyward. "Oh, I remember now. That would have been…you." My pointed finger landed in the middle of Robyn's chest and gave a little push.

Robyn looked embarrassed. Her eyes studied the ground and her hands jammed into the back pockets of her jeans. "I'm sorry about that," she mumbled.

I leaned in closer to her. "What did you say?"

Robyn sighed and looked up. "I'm sorry about that, okay? It was a rotten thing to do and I'm sorry about how it blew up at school." She folded her arms across her chest and looked around the barnyard then back at me. "It was Travis's idea," she admitted quietly. "But I shouldn't have gone along with it."

Remembered humiliation still had me in its grip. "But you did. And you made my life even more miserable than it was. You with your perfect hair and skinny jeans. You've never had a moment's trouble making friends. I was wretched last year. I felt sick all the time, had to take medication and stop riding Star. And you and Travis just piled it on." My eyes glittered with tears. Irritated, I dashed them away with the back of my hand.

Robyn's anger returned with my renewed attack. "Then what in hel…blazes are you doing with me now?" Her voice increased to a yell.

"I want to be your friend," I yelled back.

We both turned when the barn door slid open a little and Ben's head peeked out. "Uh, Sara?"

"What? What now?" I demanded, my voice still at full volume.

"Uh, nothing, I guess," Ben stammered. "Nothing at all. I'll be going now." Ben's head disappeared and the barn door slid shut.

My gaze whipped back to Robyn. Her lip quivered. I looked down at the ground to cover my own trembling lips. I stiffened them and looked back up at Robyn. Robyn's mouth grinned. A small snorting laugh escaped her lips. She clamped them shut and covered her mouth with one hand. I began to giggle then tried to look stern. A burping laugh leaked out between my lips and suddenly I was full-on laughing. Robyn joined me and soon we were both howling with laughter. Tears tracked down cheeks formerly red with anger and now pink with amusement.

"Did you…did you see the look on his face?" Robyn gasped.

I nodded my head several times. I put a hand on Robyn's shoulder to steady myself. "I don't think he'll recover, do you?" I glanced at Robyn and began to laugh all over again.

"I don't think so. We may have traumatized him forever. His face went completely white."

Our laughter gradually died away. I was breathless, and Robyn looked as limp as I felt. I caught her gaze. We both sobered up. I held out my hand, offering a handshake. "Friends?"

Robyn's hand gripped mine. "Probably? Maybe give it a shot?" Her voice steadied when she added, "Sara."

"Thanks."

We stood quietly for a moment then self-consciously looked everywhere but at each other, suddenly uncomfortable with the dramatic shift in emotion. I offered my solution for any kind of difficult emotion. "So. Like, do you want to meet Star?"

Robyn smiled. "That would be so crisp. I called my dad on the way over here so I have some time."

We walked toward the barn. Just as I reached to pull it open, the door opened and Ben peered out. "Oh, good. I didn't hear anything so I figured you were both maimed, dead, or," he held up a finger like a professor making a point, "you worked it out. I see by your smiling faces; you worked it out. Well done, ladies. Mature choice. But in case you ever decide to go in for women's wrestling I thought of good names for you." He pointed to me and said, "Skanky Sara." Then Robyn, "Ratchet Robyn." He saluted us and headed for the house.

Robyn watched him go. "He's adorbs."

"He's a brat," I replied. "Plus, he's taken. C'mon. Come meet the star of the show."

Star's head was already over the stall door at the sound of my voice. "Hey, boy. How's your day?" I reached out a hand to stroke the inky black softness of his nose. "Somebody's here to meet you." I motioned Robyn closer.

Robyn reached out a hand and let Star sniff her fingers. Moving slowly, she lifted her hand to his cheeks and softly caressed the gleaming black hide. "He's beautiful, Sara. He's like a male version of Diva. Just so, so striking." She reached over the stall door to continue stroking down Star's shoulder. "Hey!" She stretched up on her tiptoes to peer over the top of the half door. "What happened to his chest? That looks like a brutal wound."

I opened the door so Star could step out into more light. I reached under his neck and carefully patted the flesh around the wound to feel for heat or puffiness.

"He got out of the barn a few days ago, spooked and ran off. Mr. K thinks he must have tried to jump a wire fence and cut himself. We're all surprised he wasn't hurt worse. One of the worst days of my life. I had no idea where he was or what happened for a full day."

"You must've been going crazy. I know if Willow, that's the horse I used to ride, was lost I would've been out of my mind and she didn't even belong to me."

I finger-combed Star's mane. "I think it was Travis."

Robyn's hand froze mid-stroke down Star's nose. "Oh. Really?"

I explained my theory. Robyn stroked down Star's neck until she reached his withers then scratched in a circular motion at the base of his mane. His upper lip twitched in ecstasy. We both smiled.

"Well." Robyn took a deep breath. "I told you Travis gets even.

Sounds to me like something he would do."

I looked at Robyn over Star's neck. "Thank you. Thank you, very much. You're the only one who believes me. But I can't do anything about it since there's no proof."

"Yeah. That sucks like a mosquito. He's predictable, but careful."

"Truth," I agreed dismally. Then an idea lit up my brain. "Hey, since you'll be working at Big Sky do you want to help Kevin and me with a group we're going to start for some of the younger clients?" I quickly explained about the Do I Matter? discussion group. "I think it would be great if you were part of the group. It'll be fun. What do you think?"

Robyn's hand slowed against Star's shoulder while I talked. When I asked my question, she dusted off her hands then wiped them down her jeans. "It sounds like a great idea, and I'm glad you're going to do it. There's only one problem with including me."

"What's that?"

"I *don't* matter. See ya." Robyn walked out, and I heard her car start and head down the driveway.

I stared at the barn door. Star's nudging nose startled me out of my thoughts. I led him back into his stall, checked his feed and water then leaned against his side, right arm over his back. "Wow. She's a lot like me, isn't she, Star? Hopefully I'll get a chance to tell her what Kevin told me. The broken places are where God's love gets in."

I gave Star a final pat then headed for the house.

# Chapter 13

*How does a broken heart continue to love when it's in pieces?*
Sara's Diary

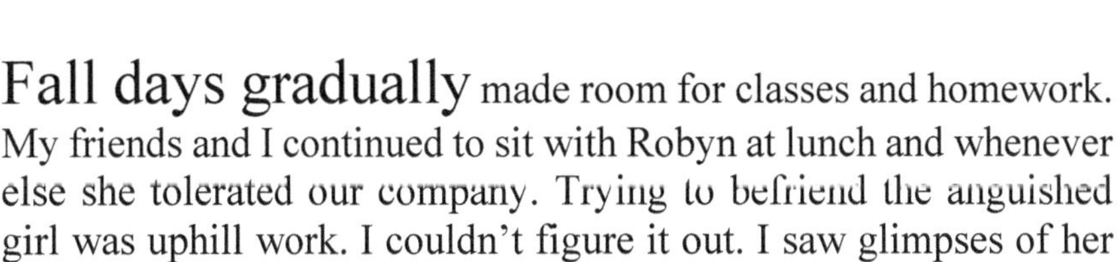

**Fall days gradually** made room for classes and homework. My friends and I continued to sit with Robyn at lunch and whenever else she tolerated our company. Trying to befriend the anguished girl was uphill work. I couldn't figure it out. I saw glimpses of her at Big Sky, but mindful that Robyn, like the bird, could be easily spooked into flight, I tried not to push friendship.

"I don't get it, Justine," I complained. "I just want to be her friend. Why does she keep pushing me away?"

Justine pushed open her office door and motioned me in. "I don't know. I do know she's getting along great with Diva and it's fun to see that horse come to life. Robyn's got a gift. I'm going to talk to her about signing up for the same PATH program you're going to do. I can sure use the extra qualified help around here." "That would be great. Maybe we could do the program together. I'll go ask her…"

"Sara." Justine's tone stopped me cold. "You have to give her room. I'm not sure what her story is, but I've been around enough wounded people to know one when I see one. Do you know how in the Bible it says, "deep calls to deep?"

I nodded. "I didn't know what it meant so I asked Kevin. It's about wanting to dig beneath the surface with God or people, right?"

"That's one way to put it," Justine confirmed. "But I think it's also true that pain calls to pain. I see it time after time in the work I do. People in pain understand others in pain. I think that's happening with Diva and Robyn. It's what will make Diva a great therapy horse. She sensed the ache in Robyn and responded to it. Let them be with each other and don't push Robyn. Her time with Diva is slowly bringing some life back to her eyes."

"Okay. I get what you're saying. It's just that we have stuff in common and I'd like to get to know her better. Plus, I feel bad for her. Travis is making her life hell at school and I know what that's like."

"She'll come around to wanting human friends at some point. God created us for relationships and she'll crave that again. Right now, leave her to Diva. There will be no pain involved with her relationship with the horse."

At lunch the next day, Robyn's sleeve slid up when she reached for her smoothie. I noticed a new red scar line on her inner arm. I remembered Justine's warning and knew better than to ask questions. Finding Robyn sobbing in the girl's restroom during the next period was a whole different story.

Excused from class, I rushed into the restroom expecting an empty space and a chance to clean my irritating contact lens. I stopped short when I noticed Robyn hunched over a sink. Every line and curve in her body spelled misery. Her quiet sobs echoed in the tile-lined room.

"Robyn? Hey. Are you all right? What happened?" I approached her as if she was a spooked horse. I carefully reached a hand to her shoulder and touched her gently.

Robyn rubbed at her eyes and cheeks and twisted away from my touch. "I'm fine. Just, please. Please leave me alone."

"I can't leave you like this," I protested. "Something's obviously wrong. Maybe I can help if you'll let me."

"Nobody can help. Please just go away."

I returned a cautious hand to Robyn's shoulder. "Please? I know how I felt when I was all alone last year. Please talk to me. You just seem so…it's like…I mean, there's like pain oozing out of your pores. If you won't talk to me, will you talk to the school counselor?

Or Justine?"

Robyn's sobs trailed off. She drew in a shuddering breath. But she didn't twitch away from my touch so I moved my arm around her back and offered a tentative hug. Unexpectedly, Robyn turned and clutched at me as if starved for a friendly touch. I returned the strength of her grasp and planted my feet apart for balance when Robyn's weight fell on to me. Her tears felt wet through the material of my shirt. I waited quietly. I strained to hear Robyn's whisper. "I had a baby."

I froze. And waited, hardly daring to breathe.

The soft tone continued. "I had a baby three months ago. I left school last year because I was starting to show. I went to stay with my mom until the baby was born. She came early. And then," Robyn drew in a trembling breath, "I placed her for adoption." Her grip tightened around me. "Three months ago today."

My hug strengthened around her. "I'm so sorry, Robyn. I can't even imagine how hard that would be."

Robyn's fierce hug loosened and she took a step back from me. She used the sleeve of her hoodie to wipe her eyes and cheeks, then leaned back against the sink. I did the same, close enough that our shoulders were touching. Robyn spoke to the floor in a monotone.

"I named her Linnet. The adopting family liked it so they said they'd keep it. They were nice people. At least I did that for my little girl."

I couldn't take my eyes off Robyn's ravaged face. "I've never had to do anything that hard." I whispered. After a pause, I added, "Linnet is such a pretty name."

"My mom's name is Lark. My grandma is Starling. It's a family thing. I guess somebody in our family tree had a thing for birds." She shrugged. "It was the only thing I could give her." A deep shudder shook her body and tears dripped again to the floor. "She was so beautiful. They let me keep her two days, then the case worker took her to the family I chose. I just…I just…my arms feel so empty. Sara, I don't know if I can do this. It just hurts…it hurts so bad. I know it was the right thing-- the best thing to do, but it's agony." She folded over herself, arms hugging her waist. A guttural groan rasped from her throat.

I placed a comforting hand on Robyn's back. She turned toward me and I automatically hugged her to me in a soothing clasp. I held her quietly while her slender body shuddered with deep sobs. When Robyn's sobs slowed, I said quietly, "You're wrong. Linnet's name isn't all you gave her. You gave her life. You didn't have to do that. You could've taken the other way out. You and I both know there are girls in this school who have done that. The gift of life is pretty big, Robyn. That was so brave of you."

I had to strain to hear the muffled response spoken into my shirt. "The baby's father wanted me to have an abortion. My parents said it was my decision and they would support me whatever I decided. They've been great."

She gradually pulled away from me. This time her tear-filled gaze caught mine. "Thanks," she said simply. "I guess I needed somebody after all."

I nodded. "Anybody would."

I reached for the paper towel holder over Robyn's shoulder and grabbed a few. I moistened them at the faucet, twisted out the excess water and handed the moistened towels to Robyn. "Here you go. If there's one thing I found out last year it's that the cold water in these faucets is actually good for something. Press them against your cheeks and eyes. You'll feel better."

Robyn held the chilled towels against her eyes and forehead. She breathed in a deep trembling breath. "I had to come back to town because Dad has custody. Mom's job has her travelling so much we all agreed I would live with Dad. I so didn't want to come back here." Her voice sounded fierce. She lowered the towels away from her face and looked at me. "You know?"

"Yeah. I know. After last year and my suicide attempt, which nobody but my close friends know about, I didn't want to come back to school either. Then I figured out it wasn't the place that made me miserable. I just carried misery around inside me. I felt broken inside. A Bible verse I read during the summer helped me. It basically said God would give me beauty for ashes which I think of as brokenness, joy instead of mourning and a feeling of celebration instead of despair. The verse is in the book of Isaiah. Anyway, I decided to watch for God to make beauty out of broken stuff in my life and he totally has." I met Robyn's gaze directly. "Maybe you'll find that, too. Eventually, I hope. And if I can help, I'd really like to."

"Well, glue could learn something from you about sticking

close, I'll give you that." A little bit of a sparkle shone in Robyn's eyes. "What can I say? You've completely worn me down and I'm exhausted trying to keep you out." We smiled at each other. It felt good.

"Thanks, Sara. I really mean it. Today has just been the worst among some truly terrible days. I'm glad you were here."

A small sound caught our attention. We waited, both of us laser focused on the stall where the sound originated. Finally, I called sharply, "Is someone there?"

The latch on the farthest stall turned slowly and the door opened. Alyssa stepped out. She clutched her phone in one hand and a pile of books awkwardly in the other. One book had almost slipped from her grasp. That must have been the alerting sound.

"Hi girls. Gotta fly. Catch you later." Before either Robyn or I could react, the other girl hurried from the restroom without a backward glance.

Robyn and I stared at each other. Mirror images of pale shocked faces. The unison gulps escaped from our bloodless lips.

"Outed," stammered Robyn.

"Both at once," I agreed.

"It's going to be sharknado halls for us."

"Yep." I thought for a second. "Since it's going to be all over school at light speed, do you mind if I tell Tawny? And Kevin and Ryan? They can help."

Robyn snorted. "Get real, Sara. Nothing's going to help this."

"It'll help if we stick together. Horses do it instinctively. We'll form our own herd," I argued stubbornly.

"I've never really been part of a group," Robyn commented. "I wouldn't know. My family's always moved around too much. I have no clue how to be part of a herd, like, at all."

"Well, it's about time you find out what it's like. Trust me. You cannot even imagine the force of having Tawny for a friend. She's like the exclamation point of every relationship she's part of. The Red Bull of girlfriends. If you have her on your side, you have one powerful bestie. Or homie. I'm not sure what the word is now. But Tawny will." A smile split my face at the thought of my faithful friend.

"I can't believe you're smiling."

"I'm remembering Tawny facing down Travis."

"Oh, yeah, that. That was pretty dope," Robyn admitted. She shrugged. "Guess I don't have anything to lose. They're all going to find out anyway. No way Alyssa will keep this to herself. She was probably lighting up her phone even while we were talking. Sure. Tell your friends. It's still going to be a nightmare."

"Yeah, but having friends will help us survive. You just have to trust me on this." I glanced at my watch. "The bell's going to ring pretty soon so we better get going. Meet us after school in the parking lot. We'll watch for you."

After the last bell, I hurried to meet Tawny at her locker, then we rushed to find the guys. I talked quickly as we went. At one point, Tawny stopped dead in her tracks and stared at me. "Whoa. That is one harsh sit-rep."

I tugged my friend along. "C'mon. We gotta find Ryan and Kevin so we can wait for Robyn. I told her we'd help her out."

"Help her? How?"

"Handle what's going to happen when everybody finds out. She said it will be like sharknado halls."

"Word." Tawny agreed solemnly.

We found Kevin and Ryan by Kevin's old Jeep. Tawny quickly explained Robyn's situation to the guys while I watched for Robyn. I heard Ryan grunt once, and wondered which part of the story had forced the sound out of him. I spied Robyn's pale blonde hair and waved. Robyn returned my wave and headed toward us. Her step slowed uncertainly when she neared the Jeep.

"Hey, Rob. Wassup?" Ryan's casual question and steady gaze helped straighten Robyn's spine and lift her shoulders.

"Oh, no big. You?" Robyn's smiled wobbled, but she seemed determined to hold it.

"Just hanging." He shrugged.

Robyn closed the distance between us. "Sara told you guys what I did?"

Kevin answered for all of us. "We know what happened," he corrected gently. He is such a great guy.

Tawny chimed in. "Sara told us about Alyssa, too. She talks more smack than any pro wrestler I've ever heard. I hope you're ready. And," she nodded over Robyn's shoulder, "here it comes. The big man himself."

Robyn turned and we saw Travis, half the football team and

most of the cheerleaders headed our direction like a mindless school of fish. The lead fish stopped in front of Robyn who involuntarily took a couple steps back until she backed into me. I held my ground and propped her up.

"So." Travis eyed Robyn, his gaze travelling like a predator up and down her body. "The little bird was busy last year. Did you sleep with the whole team or only part of them?" He smirked over his shoulder at the group behind him. Several of the guys laughed and nudged each other. "I always knew you were a tramp you little b…"

Kevin and Ryan stepped forward. Kevin's hands were jammed in his pockets, but Ryan's were crossed like a vengeful Thor, god of thunder.

Travis' words cut off and his gaze narrowed. "So," he drawled. "The princess has a couple knights in shining armor. What? Are you in her pants, too?"

Ryan's arms dropped. His hands tightened into fists and he stepped menacingly toward Travis. Travis backed up quickly with his hands out. "Hey, hey, Ry. My bad. Just gaming you. Robyn knows I'm just messing with her. Right, babe?" He peered around Ryan at Robyn.

Robyn stared him down and didn't answer.

Travis's gaze narrowed. "Good choice. Keep that garbage disposal shut tight and we'll be fine."

"So far you're the only one talking trash," Robyn hissed. "I haven't said a word."

"And let's keep it that way." Travis's icy gaze found me. He lifted his chin in greeting. "Sara." He paused, then took a step forward.

I braced myself like I wasn't at all intimidated by him.

"Heard you tried to off yourself. Isn't that a sin?"

His velociraptor smile left no doubt of his killer instinct. I gasped at the vicious tone and brutal message.

Kevin stepped forward. "That's enough, Trav. Go spread your slime somewhere else."

Travis laughed. "Killer Kev. Standing up for your loser girlfriend. That's sweet."

Kevin stared until the bully's gaze dropped. Travis turned toward his pack, then paused and turned back. His gaze froze onto Robyn. "Just don't you try to pin this on me little bird. You had it off with half the guys in school. No way am I taking the fall for this."

Finally goaded beyond good sense, Robyn snapped back, "Oh, yeah, Trav? Whose daddy demanded a DNA test, huh? Who was that? Oh, yeah, right. Now I remember. It was yours." She took a step forward and thrust her pointed finger in his enraged face. "Convinced his little boy could do no wrong. Guess he found out what you're made of, huh? Lied to him, didn't you? How's that working for you? You couldn't wait to sign off your parental rights with your dad standing right there."

Robyn's brief burst of bravado dissolved when Travis stepped toward her, shoulders hunched and face mottled red. His fingers stretched out forming claws and he reached toward Robyn's neck. She stumbled back in panic, ran into both Tawny and I, while Ryan and Kevin quickly stepped in front of us. Travis's face underwent a lightening change of calculation when he realized the solidarity in front of him. He looked over his shoulder at his so-called squad. Anybody could read the shock on their faces. Shock and disbelief. Their idol had been caught in a lie. He was totally the father of Robyn's baby. Her words carried the clear conviction of truth. Seeing his support vanish into thin air, Travis turned, rushed toward his Mustang and peeled out of the parking lot.

Robyn buried her face in her hands. "What have I done?" she moaned. "What have I done?"

# Chapter 14

*Robyn needs the reliable love of God. Not the artificial kind Travis offers.*
Sara's Diary

**Robyn's shoulders trembled** so I put an arm around her and pulled her against me. "It'll be okay. He knows you have people supporting you this year. It won't be like last year when you were alone."

Robyn stared at me. "You of all people should know this is not going to be okay. Have you learned nothing about Travis? Remember Star's cut chest? And what you did to Travis is nothing like this. I just outed him in front of his whole posse. Made him look bad. You think he'll just let that go? You're dreaming for real. And what I know for sure is that this is a nightmare."

Tawny stepped forward. "Listen. We can't do anything about meta gross Travis right now. I suggest we girls go chill with a latte and figure out some strategy. How about we head to the Crushed Bean? Sara, can you drive?" I nodded and we piled into my car and headed to our local favorite coffee shop.

Robyn played with the straw in her iced mocha. She seemed about to say something a couple times, then drew back. Finally, staring at her drink she said, "It's not true, you know. What Travis said about me and all the other guys. But I wish I hadn't stood up for myself. He's not going to forget I outed him."

Tawny leaned back against the booth. "Why am I not shocked Travis lied? And why was that whole jerk squad surprised? They hang with him all the time."

I laughed. "It would actually be newsworthy if he told the truth for a change."

Continuing to stare into her drink, Robyn said, "Travis was the only one. I…I mean I never did…that…with anybody else. Just him and just once. He kind of talked me into it. Talked about love and how it would complete our relationship. 'Ship, he said." She glanced up at Tawny.

"S'right," Tawny agreed. A slight smile played around the corners of her mouth.

"Anyway, we were at his house by ourselves and he, I don't know, he was just really persuasive. Kept saying he never felt about anybody like he did about me." She sighed. "It was pretty bad. I know he makes it sound like I'm, you know, that kind of girl, but I'm not. It hurt. Really bad. And I wanted him to stop. I tried to get him to stop, but he wouldn't." Robyn's hand shook when she reached up to push her hair behind an ear. "I…" her voice cracked. She paused, took a deep breath and continued. "I didn't know what to do." Her chin quivered. Her gaze returned to her drink. "And I'm so ashamed," she gasped in a quick breath, "but I can't stop thinking about it. It's just…it's just unbearable. And then he dropped me like a hot sparkler." She choked back a sob. "And then the police…" Her voice trailed off.

She looked at me and the misery in her expression reminded me of the pit of despair I was in last year. And the immediate memory of a night last year when Travis roughed me up left me with a punched-in-my-stomach kind of feeling. If Kevin hadn't shown up to help me, would I be in Robyn's place right now?

"That's really awful, Robyn. I'm so sorry that happened to you."

"Jerk. Meta sleazeball creeper," Tawny added for good measure.

"I didn't care that he dropped me. I definitely didn't want to be alone with him again. And the text photos? That started the whole mess."

Robyn's cheeks were pink. Embarrassment? Shame? Probably

both. She continued, "I was so dumb. I still can't believe how dumb I was. Then I figured out I was pregnant. Travis went ballistic and wanted me to get an abortion without telling either of our parents. He was at me and at me and at me. Calls, texts, ambushing me at school." Robyn rubbed her eyes. "But I knew I didn't want to do that. The baby was already alive. It was already like a real person to me. Plus, I knew lots of people want babies who can't have their own." She shrugged. "So, I told Dad. And he called Travis's dad, and it got ugly really fast. But Travis signed off on the adoption and that's all that matters."

She took a sip of her drink and glanced at Tawny and me. "That's it. That's my sad story. And, according to Travis, it's all my fault."

Tawny put a hand on Robyn's arm. "That is straight up the hardest story I've ever heard. But you did the right thing. Hard, but right. And it is not all your fault. Travis made this mess."

Robyn smiled her thanks. "So." Her gaze took in both Tawny and me. "You guys still want to be my friends?"

"Absitively possolutely." Tawny stated firmly. She leaned in close to Robyn. "My grandma says that."

"Of course," I added. "Some kind of friends we'd be if we ditched you now."

"Actually," Tawny added. "Now you're starting to sound like this one." She nodded her head toward me.

Robyn cocked her head in question.

"Last year Sara believed we weren't her friends anymore because she had major problems going on. She totally blew us off because she was going through stuff and thought we didn't care. Moi." Tawny's fingers splayed across her chest. "Like I would not be her friend because she had drama going on."

"No way. You guys are like the best friends I've ever seen."

"Way. She treated us like week-old donuts."

I waved my hand at the other girls. "Hello. Sitting right here."

Tawny turned toward me. "I'm catching our girl up on last year's deets."

"Yeah." Robyn looked at me with mischief in her gaze. "I need caught up on last year's deets."

"Feels weird you guys talking about me while I'm right here," I grumbled. "Let's move on, shall we?"

Robyn regarded Tawny again. "So, are you all about church and God, too? Like Sara and Kevin?"

"Escusez-moi," Tawny's fingers touched her chest again. "I'm not like anybody else. I'm me. God knows all about me and I know what I need to know about Him."

"What about Ryan?"

"Ry guy? He's more of a, hmmmm. Not sure how to explain Ryan. I guess he's a DUO kind of guy."

"I have no clue what that is."

"Me either," I chimed in.

"Duh. Do unto others," Tawny explained. "It says that in the Bible. Do unto others like you want them to do unto you. Isn't that a thing?" Tawny asked me.

"That is definitely a thing," I confirmed. "And I think it explains Ryan pretty well. Though as far as I know, he doesn't go to church anywhere. And I'm pretty sure we would know that." I checked with Tawny.

"Naw. He's not into the buildings and such. He does read the Bible though. And other religious books. He and Kev talk about this all the time. Didn't you know?"

"Nope. Usually when I see Ryan, he's with you. I just know his superpower is niceness."

"How long have you and Ryan been together?" Robyn relaxed now that she was done with her story.

"Uh, let's see. Since seventh grade. I think. Is that right, SJ?"

"SJ?"

"Tawny, don't you dare. Do not go there," I threatened.

"Oh, I'm like, so scared." Tawny clasped her hands and hugged them to her chest in mock terror. "Sara Jane," she said to Robyn.

"Natania Marie Gaynor. You did it. I can't believe you did it. You promised me." I sucked furiously on my straw until it slurped at the bottom of the cup.

"Oh, get over yourself. It's your grandma's name and you love your grandma."

"I do love my grandma, but her name is old-fashioned. My name sounds like some little blonde-haired, blue-eyed girl with ringlets. So not me." I tried to sound stern with Tawny, but we both ended up laughing.

"So, you and Ryan have been together quite a while."

"What can I say? I know a keeper when I see one." Tawny looked like Abby after she's had a taste of cream.

"That is a skill I need to develop," Robyn mourned. "And you've been together all this time. Never broke up?"

A shadow passed across Tawny's face so quickly I wondered if I imagined it. What was that all about? I made a mental note to ask about it later.

"Yeah. We just, I don't know, we just like fit."

"I guess when something fits you hang onto it." Robyn lifted her straw to her lips. Her sleeve pulled back from her wrist. I wanted to ask about the pink scars on Robyn's arm, but something held me back. Instead, I asked a question guaranteed to change the subject. "How do you like working at Big Sky?"

Robyn's face lit up like the fairgrounds on the fourth of July. "I love it there. Justine really thinks I'm helping with Diva. And the best thing is, I'll never see Travis there. He hates horses."

"Do tell," I murmured.

Robyn checked out her watch. "In fact, I'm supposed to be out there right now. I really appreciate how you all helped me this afternoon. Nobody has ever done something like that for me before." Her tone became hesitant. "Can I…would it be okay if I…I'd really like to hang with you if it's okay." She looked from me to Tawny and back again.

"Well, duh. Of course you can. Right, Tawn?

Tawny's fingers were busy with her phone. "Tru dat," she confirmed without looking up. "I'm letting Ryan know to come and get me. You guys take off and do your horse thing. SJ, I'll catch up with you later." She took one hand off her phone to touch Robyn's arm. "Listen, parjarita, you have had a sadventure for real. The saddest ever. Thank you for your story. You hang with us whenever you want to. M'kay?"

Tears shone in Robyn's eyes. "Thanks, Tawny. I'd like that. What did you call me?"

Busy with her phone again, Tawny didn't look up. "Hmmm? Oh. Parjarita. It's Spanish for little bird. S'okay?"

"S'okay. I like it."

I stood up and stretched. "Ready, Robyn? Do you need to go by your house?"

"No, I brought a change of clothes. But can you take me by the school to get my car?"

"Can do. Let's go."

We reached the Subaru and got in. Robyn grabbed the seat belt and fastened it at her hip. "You know, I really hate when Travis calls me his little bird, but it sounds nice in Spanish. Where is Tawny from?"

I checked both ways before pulling out into traffic. "She's from here, but her grandparents are from Cuba. Her mother grew up speaking Spanish because that's all her parents spoke. Tawny speaks both English and Spanish. Oh. And slang. Tawny speaks slang."

"I like her. She says what she thinks."

"Ohhhh yeah." I laughed. "Sometimes more than you want, but I couldn't ask for a better friend. I'm going to drop you at your car, then meet with Mr. K to go over how we're going to train Star and work on his fear of water at the same time."

"You're doing trail?"

"Yeah. Training is slow because we have to get the cut healed and Star over his fear. Which he has courtesy of me. You know, you were maybe dumb for trusting Travis, but how dumb do you have to be to try to drown yourself and use your horse to do it?" I glanced at Robyn. "Maybe you and I can share the dummy of the year award? Sometimes I feel like I'll never get my act together and move forward."

"I honestly don't know how to move forward," Robyn admitted. "I have a little girl. A little girl, Sara. And I gave her away." A sob caught in Robyn's throat. "I know Star is like super important, but he's not a little girl. You know?" Robyn's glistening gaze fastened on me.

I nodded. "You're right. He's a horse and it's not the same as Linnet." I used the baby's name intentionally. "But did you ever think that maybe what you did was the best thing? I mean, I know it's hard, I can't even imagine how hard, but you chose a super good life for Linnet. I know you would've loved her and taken care of her, but you're a teenager. You don't have a job. You haven't finished school. What kind of life could you give her? You found her a family, a home, people who really want a baby and can take care of her. You liked them, right?"

"Yeah." Robyn wiped her eyes with the back of her hand. "I did. They have one little girl already, but can't have anymore and they really wanted another baby. And you know what? They have horses."

"You're kidding."

"Nope. It was one of the reasons I chose them. The mom has a horse named Red Wing. Like the blackbird, you know? I thought that was a sign. Plus, they seem like a really nice family."

"Kevin would call that a God thing. The horse part, I mean."

"Do you really believe God watches out for you? Fixes broken things?" Robyn's voice sounded skeptical. "What about all that stuff that happened to you last year?"

I shrugged. "Bad stuff happens to everybody. Except for the lupus, my bad stuff happened because of dumb decisions I made."

"But isn't God supposed to like take care of you and give you what you want and sh…stuff?"

I laughed. "He's not like a cosmic Amazon where you just order what you want and it's delivered the next day. Listen, why don't you come to church with Kevin and me? See what you think."

Robyn leaned away from me on the car seat. "No way," she protested. "I know you mean well but I don't think church is the place for me. I have too much sh…garbage in my life. Sorry, I'm trying to watch how I talk. But maybe I'll go when I'm a better person. Feeling pretty worthless these days."

"Stop worrying about how you talk. It's not like I don't hear it at the horse shows and around school. And you've got it all wrong. You don't have to get good before you can talk to God. The whole point is He loves you like you are." I dug around in my wallet and found a five-dollar bill. Pretty creased and dirty after passing through many hands. "Look at this five. It's pretty beat up, but how much is it worth?"

Her eyebrows squished together in a frown. "Five bucks. Duh."

"Even though it's disgusting?"

"Yeah."

"This is what I'm trying to tell you. To God, your worth doesn't change if you're good or bad, dirty or clean. You're worth tons to Him just like you are. He loves you no matter what. Hey, do you like music?"

"Some kinds."

"Okay, then how about this. One of my favorite groups is called TobyMac. And I also really like Lauren Daigle's music. In fact, she has a song called *Rescue*. It makes me think about you. Would you listen to it? And maybe some of her other songs? Then tell me what you think."

Robyn cleared her throat and let out a deep sigh. "I don't know." She fidgeted and looked out the window. "Are they both religious?"

"Not in the way you mean. They both sing about relationships and about some of the hard things that can happen in life. Toby's son died of an accidental overdose of drugs. His son was twenty-one. Toby sings about what that was like and how God helped him through that hard time."

"Man. I can't even imagine. So is this guy mad at God? I would be."

"No. He was, and probably still is, super sad. But not mad at God. I think you'd like his music. And Lauren's. She's had some hard things happen to her, too. Maybe just check them out and see what you think. Uh-oh." I nodded forward when I turned into the parking lot. "We've got trouble."

Travis's car was parked in front of Robyn's, blocking her way. Travis leaned against the driver door and watched us slow to stop. His eyes, dark and dangerous, tracked our movement. Like a snake's.

# Chapter 15

*Anger feels better but might get me in more trouble than fear.*
Sara's Diary

Robyn and I sat frozen in tense silence. I turned toward my new friend and met her deer in the headlight gaze. Out of the blue, rage simmered in my mind and boiled over. My hands gripped the steering wheel; my nostrils flared as I sucked in a deep breath. My mind hit replay on all Travis's taunts, leers, lies and threats. A bully. That's all he was. A bully who had finally gotten on my last good nerve. Eyes narrowed, I grabbed my phone, pushed the car door open and slammed it behind me. Chin lifted I stalked up to Travis.

He pushed off his car and opened his mouth to speak. Before he could utter a syllable, I confronted him with a finger jabbed toward his face.

"Don't. Even." I met his gaze with fierce concentration. A faint voice in the back of my mind asked if it was wise to poke the bear. I ignored it.

"I'm sick and tired of your bullying. From now on, any time you're around me, especially if Robyn is with me, I'm going to have my phone on video and you'll end up a viral sensation. Nobody likes a bully. Just leave us alone."

The air felt vibrant with unseen tension. If looks could kill, I knew I'd be dead on the spot. But, riding the high of my anger, I jabbed at my phone and held it up facing Travis. Before he could speak, I continued. "We'll leave you alone, you leave us alone and we'll all be happy."

Eyeing the phone, Travis uncurled his fists and relaxed against his car. "Chill, saint girl. Don't get your undies in a knot. I'm harmless. You know that. Later."

He turned, yanked on the car door and put one foot into his car. Pausing, he half-turned, cocked a finger at me, gun-like, winked and drawled, "Totally harmless. Remember?" His car did his signature rubber burning exit from the parking lot.

I knew on video, his gesture would look like a cocky salute. Only I knew exactly what it was; the same gun-firing motion he'd made toward Star. My anger smothered under an icy blanket of dread. What had I done? Why, oh why had I challenged him? Exactly what Kevin warned me not to do.

Robyn got out of the car and jogged toward me. "What? What happened? I couldn't hear you because you had your back toward me. I mean, how did you even get him to leave? Whatever it was, it was awesome. You were like some avenging Wonder Woman or something."

I groaned. "Did you see the gesture he made before he left?"

"Sort of. It wasn't the right finger for flipping you off so I'm not sure what he was doing."

"It was the exact gun-firing motion he made toward Star before Star got out of the barn and injured himself."

Robyn's face paled. "Ohhhh. So instead of laying low you…"

"…poked the bear." Blood pounded in my ears and my heart raced. "I've gotta get home. I have to make sure Star stays safe."

Robyn put a gentle hand on my sleeve. "Wait a sec. He's not going to race over to your house right now. It's broad daylight. Travis may not be the brightest bulb in the bunch, but he's sly like a snake. If he does anything, it will be something sneaky."

I hesitated. "What do you think I should do? Oh, I'm such an idiot." I pounded my forehead with the heel of my hand.

"Let's go ahead and go about our business at Big Sky. We need to calm down. You let the others know what happened. And your parents. I'll also tell Dad because he knows a lot about legal stuff. Maybe he'll have an idea. We'll keep Star safe, Sara. Honest."

"I couldn't keep him safe before." A quiver wobbled my voice.

"Oh man, my day just keeps getting better and better. First, I'm outed about my suicide attempt and now I've stirred up the worst hornet's nest in school. Killer wasps, even." I groaned. "Stupid, stupid, stupid." A forehead slap punctuated each word. "And I know you mean well, but you're the one who told me the one thing we can count is that Travis gets even. You didn't hear what I said but I totally challenged him. The worst thing I could possibly do."

Robyn swallowed hard. "Well, yeah, that maybe wasn't the smartest move. But we know what he's capable of and now we'll be ready. What about an alarm system? Does your barn have one?"

I stared. "An alarm system? At the barn? That's a great idea! Why didn't I think of that before?" I grabbed Robyn and pulled her into a quick bear hug. "Oh, bless you. You're a genius. That's the best idea ever. I'm pretty sure my parents will agree to it, too. Dad's been saying we need more than Spot to protect the chickens since the coyotes are getting so brave. Actually, both Justine and Mr. K have barn alarm systems so I can talk to them about what works best. You're right. Let's head out there so you can work with Diva and I'll find out what I need to know. Oh, bless you, Robyn. I'm so glad we're friends now." I pulled Robyn in for another hug until I realized she was stiff in my grasp. I released her and stepped back.

"What? What is it? Did I hurt you? Are you okay?"

Robyn smiled at me with a silly smile. "Are you kidding me? No, you didn't hurt me, you goof. Do you realize nobody has ever called me their friend? Let alone been glad we're friends? Or blessed me? Nobody. Not ever. I might have given you a good idea, but you've given me something I never had before. A friend."

"Is that all? No kidding. Well, you've definitely got one now. This is something Kevin would call a God thing, by the way. Didn't seem likely we would end up friends, huh?"

Robyn snort laughed. "No kidding."

"See? That's the kind of stuff God causes to happen. You just wait. You'll see. But right now, we've gotta get going or we're both going to be super late. See you at Big Sky?"

"See you at Big Sky," Robyn affirmed.

# Chapter 16

*Is it really less painful to be alone by choice than left there?*
Sara's Diary

**Robyn and I** pulled into the parking lot at Big Sky within minutes of each other.

"Want to come check out Diva?" Robyn invited.

"Sure. I have a few minutes before I have to meet Mr. K. I'm curious how we're going to get Star over his fear of water. I guess every Trail Competition has some kind of water feature, so we really have to calm Star's fear. Did you know horses can have PTSD? Mr. K gave me some books to read about it."

"Never thought about it, but it makes sense. We share a lot of the same emotions with horses. Like Diva. She definitely has a grief and loss thing going on. Justine says all animals can mourn close relationships within their own species, but domesticated animals also grieve the loss of their human connections. Justine warned me not to expect Diva to forget about her other owner, but to work instead on developing my own close relationship with her."

We walked through the barn to the small corral where Diva stood, head down, ears listlessly back. Robyn whistled her high-low sequence. Sluggishly, Diva's head raised and one ear swiveled forward.

I stopped mid-step. "Wow. I can feel how depressed she is by looking at her. She looks sick."

"Yeah. And this is an improvement if you can believe that. But, at least it's improvement. Justine had the vet check her out and she's healthy. Just really missing her last owner."

"Man. That is some kind of loyalty. But that's one of the things I love best about horses. Once you bond, they are absolutely loyal. They love you no matter what."

"This may sound weird, but I think they see us how we wish we could be. Like I always thought Willow, that's the horse I rode down south, looked at me and saw the me I wished I could be. You know?"

"Exactly. Whenever I feel down about myself, I remember Star loves me so I must not be such a terrible person after all. He has great instincts about people. After all, he despises Travis."

Robyn laughed. "Smart Star. Willow loved me and always watched for me to come to the riding stable. But I never connected how she felt about me to how I could feel about myself. I just…I feel like such a rotten person…and I don't fit in…not really good at anything in particular. Except horses. Maybe I should try to believe I'm okay since horses like me."

Robyn gazed drifted to the distance, not seeing me or the barn anymore. Was she even aware I'm right here? Seems like she's gone to a place I can't follow. I kept quiet.

After a few minutes, Robyn startled as if out of a dream and looked around. "Oh. Guess I drifted off." An embarrassed laugh hiccoughed from her throat. "Right. Diva. Better get going."

Robyn walked toward the corral. "She does look better after being groomed though; don't you think?" She tossed over her shoulder back to me." She tossed over her shoulder back to me.

"I'll say. She was already pretty spectacular, but now she's immaculate. I like how you braided her mane. You're the Tawny of the horse world."

Robyn laughed. "I wish. Mostly I just groom and talk to her. Justine said later this week I can try her in the round pen and see if she'll show us her paces. Plus, she needs the exercise. It's so hard to wait to try riding her."

"I bet. That's how I felt when I couldn't ride Star after he got pneumonia. Still, I was thankful he was getting better and I like just spending time with him no matter what we're doing."

"Same," Robyn agreed.

We reached the corral and leaned over the fence. Robyn coaxed the flashy pinto in a low tone and a with horse cake held out in her hand. Diva considered the invitation then ambled over to the fence. She lipped the treat of Robyn's hand and crunched slowly.

I shook my head and laughed. "That is so not like Star. He inhales any kind of food offered to him."

"I have a feeling Diva's a lady even when she's not depressed. I sure hope I can help her get interested in life again."

"One of the books I read about horse PTSD said something about helping a horse recover from trauma is like helping them learn to be brave again. Maybe with Diva what you're doing is helping her learn it's okay to love again?"

"That makes sense." Robyn tilted her head. "Like, she'll probably never forget about her other owner, but that doesn't mean she can't learn to like me, too. I like that idea. Room for more than one person to love." She pushed back from the fence and regarded me with a thoughtful look on her face. "I hope she can get over separation from her owner, but you know, I kinda get how she feels."

My eyebrows lifted in question. "Oh, yeah? How so?"

Robyn kept her gaze firmly on her hands stroking Diva's neck. "It's like Diva got left alone through no choice of her own and she's in shock because of that. I get it. I always make sure I'm alone by choice, not left there."

"But…well…how do you know when to leave?"

"I don't take any chances. Most of the time I don't let anybody get close enough that it will matter if they leave. But if they seem like it? I make sure I'm the one who ends it." The finality in Robyn's tone made me shiver.

"But that means nobody gets a fair chance to get to really know you," I protested.

Robyn shook her head, a lemon-sucking sour look on her face. "Doesn't matter. I got left by my grandma when she died and my mom when she divorced my dad. Not to mention a couple of guys when they didn't get what they wanted. I truly thought they cared about me. That's not happening again. I get to choose if I'm alone or not. No one else." Robyn's hands gripped the top rail of the fence tightly.

I opened my mouth to argue but was cut off by Robyn's

unexpected question and change of tone.

"Have you met Jeremy?"

The abrupt change in subject left me momentarily in conversation dust. Puzzled, I turned to face Robyn. "Justine's brother? The one who helps with the veterans?"

"Yeah. He does more than that, but that's who I mean. He's been helping me with Diva. He doesn't talk much, but what's weird is I talk a blue streak when he's here. It's kind of like talking to Diva. Anyway, he says he think horses are like people and have their favorites. They even have, like, a soulmate."

"I agree with that. How old is Jeremy? He has all the junior high girls in a twitter. They call him cosmic. He seems kind of unapproachable to me, though. You know?"

Robyn absently smoothed Diva's forelock. "Yeah. He's ruggedly cute. That maple-syrup brown hair and green eyes? Yum. I don't know about unapproachable. He's more just really quiet and kind of shy. He's twenty-one."

"How can he only be twenty-one? He's a veteran, been to war and everything, right?"

"He joined when he was eighteen. Then got an honorable discharge when he was twenty. He was awarded a purple heart."

"Wow. Do you know what happened?"

"Yeah, but I don't think he'd like me to talk about it. He's pretty private. Maybe someday he'll tell you about it himself. I can tell you he said horses saved his life after his discharge." Robyn's gaze shifted from Diva to me. "We both know how that feels, don't we?"

"We definitely do." My mind drifted to how Star had literally saved my life until the memory of my appointment with Mr. K intruded.

"Shoot." I checked my watch. "I was supposed to meet Mr. K five minutes ago. I gotta go. Talk later?"

"Later." Robyn lifted her chin in a good-bye salute then opened the corral gate.

I checked in with Mr. K and he walked me through his training plans for the afternoon. I raced home to get Star and rode him back to the training facility. After a half hour of coaxing him to approach the water obstacle, a foot-deep pit lined with a tarp and filled with water, Star's neck and haunches dripped with sweat. He's normally so eager to master new things. Is my horse broken? I guess part of his spirit is. I hope Mr. K is as good a horse counselor as the human counselor I had.

"That's enough for today, Sara. Take him through a couple of the other obstacles so he ends the day on a positive note. It's going to take patience, but we'll get there. When you feel impatient just remember what it felt like in that surf. Then think how much worse it was for him. He had no reasoning ability or even knowledge of what was happening like you did. He just knew he was caught and exhausted."

"I know, Mr. K. I won't forget I'm the one who put him in that position either. I'll be patient. Is it all right if I put him on the hot walker to cool him down? I need to check with Justine about something before I go home."

"Sure."

We finished our training then I rode Star out to a small fenced in ring that had a contraption in the middle of it that looked like a circular clothesline on steroids. I removed the saddle and bridle, gave him a small sip of water, then attached his halter to one of the long metal arms of the hot walker. I flipped the switch and the machine sprang to life slowly rotating. Star obeyed the tug on the lead rope and followed the metal arm at a slow walk.

I crossed the road to Big Sky and entered the large main barn to take a short-cut through to the training ring in back where I knew Justine had a class. I walked down an aisle and was just about to turn the corner when I heard voices. I stopped, edged closer then peeked around the corner. Jeremy and Robyn faced each other in quiet conversation. Robyn shifted from foot to foot while her right hand hugged her left arm to her side, repeatedly rubbing up and down. She stared at the ground and hid her face behind a waterfall of hair.

Jeremy reached out and took Robyn's hands in his own. He said something I couldn't hear then pushed the sleeves of Robyn's shirt up to her elbows. He traced a finger down the inside of each arm then used a fingertip to catch a tear on Robyn's cheek. He lifted her chin. Holding her gaze with his own, he steadily rolled up the sleeves of his shirt. It was Robyn's turn to trace red puckered scars on the insides of Jeremy's arms.

I leaned partway around the corner, straining to hear. Jeremy's voice, soft as a sigh, reached my ears.

"You can't cut out grief, Robbie. Believe me. I tried."

Robyn choked on a sob. "I feel so empty and like I'm the worst person alive. Cutting makes me forget how empty I am when I feel the pain. What do I do with emptiness?"

"You fill the empty places with purpose. You decide not to live at the intersection of depression and regret anymore. You find a new address that includes loving and accepting yourself. And you trust me to help you carry the pain of loss. Sharing loss is a way of loving someone. And you need to let someone love you. If you can't remember how, let me remind you."

"I don't deserve love," Robyn protested fiercely. "I deserve to be punished. What I did was terrible. I'm such an awful person. I deserve to be punished." Robyn's voice was fierce and determined as she defended her choice to cut.

"Robbie. You don't deserve to be punished." His voice, quiet and kind, caused tears to load in my eyes. "You loved your little girl so much you made sure she had a good life. You did the very best you could even though it was hard. You're trying to fix the wrong things."

Only then did Robyn weep. Not sobs. Not an ugly cry. Slow fat tears overflowed and dripped to the ground. Hopefully healing. Hopefully cleansing. A groan oozed from deep inside Robyn. I recognized that sound. I groaned like that when I was caught in the riptide and couldn't breathe from the pain.

My fingers covered my lips so no sound would escape. Then, suddenly aware of the intense privacy of the scene, I backed slowly for a few steps and then turned and bolted toward the barn door. Blinded by tears, I collided with Kevin. He caught me in a hug and opened his mouth to speak. I quickly silenced him with my hand over his mouth. I tugged him further down the aisle and into an empty stall. I burrowed into his arms and tucked my head under his chin, heart racing.

"What happened? Are you okay?" Kevin kept one arm around me but used his other hand to smooth my hair back so he could look at my face.

"Yeah. I'm fine. Could you just hold onto me for a sec?"

He grinned. "My pleasure."

We stood quietly locked together until my heartbeat slowed. I stepped back and described what I saw and heard between Robyn and Jeremy. I admitted how embarrassed I was eavesdropping on such a private moment.

"Looks like Robyn has found someone who can help her with one of her problems. I know you were hoping she'd talk to you about cutting, but if Jeremy has personal experience with that, he's probably the one to help her out."

"Yeah," I agreed. "But I still hope she'll talk to me about it sometime." I laid my cheek against Kevin's chest, arms clasped around his waist. "But you're probably right. Jeremy is the best medicine for her right now."

"Yep." Kevin gently grasped my chin and tipped my head up so my gaze met his. "And you," he softly touched my lips with his, "are the best medicine for me."

I reached up and slipped my arms around his neck. Our kiss intensified. Kevin pulled me closer. I stood on tiptoe and tightened my clasp around his neck. The motion pulled my shirt up from the grip of my jeans. Kevin's hand froze against the bare skin of my waist. His hands slid slowly up my back, then stopped. He broke off our kiss and placed his forehead against mine. His hands retreated. He pulled my shirt back into place.

My hands unclasped from his neck and slid down to rest on his chest. I drew in a deep breath, blew it out and smiled. "Doesn't get any easier, does it?"

Kevin snort laughed. "Nope. Definitely not easier." He smoothed my hair back and finger combed through the ginger waves.

I drew his face toward me and kissed him.

Kevin's gaze held mine. "I love you, you know."

My lips parted and I felt like I needed to sit down. My tongue moistened my suddenly dry lips. "Yeah?"

Kevin touched the tip of his nose to mine. "Yeah." He grinned.

Not sure I could speak over the pounding of my heart, I reached up, lightly kissed Kevin's lips and whispered in his ear, "I love you, too." I pulled back to search his face for response. Ah. Now I know what people mean when they say someone's face beams.

"Yeah?"

"Yeah. At least, I haven't felt like this about anybody before. I just know I more than like you. Is that love?"

"I haven't felt this way before either. And I more than like you, too. Way more." His eyes sparkled and an impish grin curved his mouth. Just as quickly, his gaze sobered. "Wait. What about Travis?"

My shoulders stiffened then drooped. My lips tightened into a grimace and I shook my head emphatically from side to side. "Nope. Not even close. I'm not sure what that was with Travis, but it definitely wasn't this. It was more like desperation. And I never felt safe. I constantly planned and obsessed about if he liked me. I lied to my parents, dissed my friends and ignored my own good sense. I thought he could make me feel worthwhile. But all that happened was I felt more worthless. And ashamed. Does that sound like love to you? Not to me." I analyzed what I was trying to say then continued. "I feel relaxed around you. And good about myself. Sometimes, when I see you walking across the drive toward the barn, I get this feeling in my chest like…like…I don't know…it's like my heart just swells and I have to take a deep breath and I get this grin on my face. Gosh, how romantic does that sound?" I laughed. "Can you tell I don't have a ton of experience with this?"

"You and me both. But I'm glad to hear this doesn't resemble how you felt about Travis. It sounds uncomfortable. I'm just glad we're rid of him."

"I hope we're rid of him, but I have a feeling he's going to keep turning up. There's this new drama between us that seems like, I don't know, like we're a deeper version of enemies. Like somehow, I've become his reason or excuse for bad behavior."

Quickly I described the scene from the school parking lot when Travis waited for us to turn up. "I did exactly what you warned me not to do and I'm guessing he'll make me pay."

Kevin shrugged. "If he tries, we'll deal with it. I think the alarm is a good idea. Mom has one at her workshop. I'll ask her about it. And we'll stay sharp—all of us. Last year you were on your own. You and Robyn both. This year is a different story." He draped an arm over my shoulder, and we left the barn to find Justine.

"Things might be different for Robyn and me. But Travis is the same. He'll always be a snail leaving a slimy trail wherever he goes."

# Chapter 17

*Connection. It seems Robyn both longs for and fears it.*
Sara's Diary

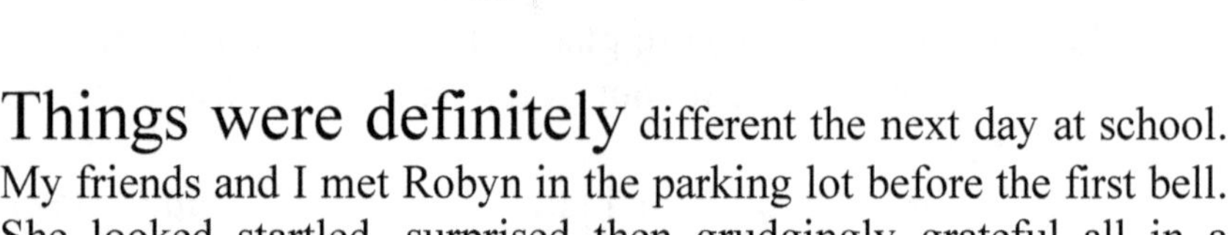

**Things were definitely** different the next day at school. My friends and I met Robyn in the parking lot before the first bell. She looked startled, surprised then grudgingly grateful all in a nanosecond.

"Are you going to do this every day?"

I couldn't tell for sure if there was hope or resignation in her tone.

"Yep," I answered cheerfully. "It's what friends do. They hang out. You'll get used to it. You might even find out you like it."

"Yeah, right."

Now that absolutely sounded irritated, but the relief written all over her face told another story.

Tawny sidled up next to Robyn and shoulder-bumped her. "We are becoming your squad. Get used to it."

Robyn shoulder-bumped Tawny back. Of course. Nobody can resist Tawny's good-natured interfering.

We walked into the building and went our separate ways, but not before Tawny reminded Robyn to find us at lunch.

"Are you sure? I mean after what everyone knows…" Robyn double-checked.

"Positive. I want to find out what blue shade you use for highlights. Sara doesn't speak hair." Tawny winked at me and I mimed a yawn with a hand covering my mouth.

"Okay. I'll find you guys." She gave a tentative wave as if friend was a new language she was trying out. Tawny blew her a kiss, which made our new friend laugh.

Satisfaction warmed my chest as I made my way to English. We will definitely kill her with kindness. Such a change from last year.

Robyn was not the only one experiencing a different dynamic that day. At lunch we gathered at a table in the corner, Tawny and Robyn examining Robyn's blue highlights. Wait. Lowlights? Not totally sure, but they were talking hair. I sort of listened to Kevin and Ryan discussing the current football team but was mostly thinking about my next training session with Star. He still had trouble with the water feature, but Mr. K kept patiently trying new ideas to help Star overcome his fear. The cut on his chest had healed cleanly with only a rough line interrupting his smooth coat.

The sudden hush in the noisy room caught my attention. I looked up to see Travis walk into the lunch room with Alyssa glued to his side. Would my stomach always clench at the sight of him?

Body language can be subtle, but not today. For absolute sure. Everyone's gaze locked on to Travis as he traversed the room to reach the cool table. His posture was his usual, "I'm all that" attitude, and he kept an arm loosely around Alyssa's shoulders. One by one, every person at the table, male and female, deliberately turned their backs on him.

No. Way. I checked out Kevin and Ryan's reactions and met slightly raised eyebrows on each of them. Tawny and Robyn slowed their conversation when they realized everybody was silent and glanced around the room. Robyn's body gave a slight recoil when she saw Travis. She froze in place as if trying to disappear, but she didn't need to worry. Travis stiffened, shock apparently immobilizing him.

As hard as it was to believe, even the GOAT could be ghosted. He tugged at Courtney's hair, but she brushed his hand away. Only Alyssa seemed willing to overlook how he had treated Robyn when she was pregnant. Who knew that crew had a conscience? But the evidence was clear; they were throwing shade Travis's way without saying a word. His face and neck flushed and he straightened to his full height. The arm around Alyssa tightened so hard I'm sure she got bruises. But he put arrogance on like a coat, barked a laugh and turned away from the table. Unfortunately, that put us right in his line of sight.

He couldn't completely hide the rage in his stiff gait, but he kept his pace slow as he headed toward our table. Robyn's hand groped for mine and she latched on with a death grip. When he reached our group, he encountered five pair of paralyzed gazes. It was like being hypnotized by the stare of a cobra ready to strike.

He leaned toward Robyn and me, his voice low and menacing. "This is your fault. You're so thirsty you had to wreck my gig. Won't work. None of you will ever be anything but cringe. And I'll fix you. Especially you two." He looked intense and determined in a really scary way.

Unease churned my stomach when his predator gaze swept Robyn and me. It wasn't a threat exactly. More like a promise.

"You and your tired, lame friends. Just watch it. That's all. Just watch it." He turned in unison with Alyssa and strutted away. An unsuccessful attempt to recapture his swagger.

I gently loosened my hand from Robyn's grasp so I could restore circulation, then turned to Tawny.

"What did he say?"

She rolled her eyes. "Sara. You really are cringe. Which means like extra awkward or embarrassing. Thirsty is more like trying to get attention. Which is the opposite of what both of you try to do. So not true. He's just salty because his peeps have turned on him. Angry," she translated automatically at my blank look. "Interesting that his throwing Robyn under the bus made his crew turn on him, though. I would not have expected that. Neither did he." Tawny snickered. Easy for her to laugh. She wasn't included in that killer stare.

Strangely enough, it seemed Tawny was right. The rest of the day revealed a lack of resentment toward both Robyn and me. The couple times I passed her in the halls, Robyn was treated to slight smiles or chin nods by other students. Or completely ignored. She reported that was fine with her.

I got different treatment. I got averted, uncomfortable looks. Like they didn't really know what to do with me or how to react to someone who had tried to kill herself. Fine with me as long as they left me alone. All in all, things were looking up. Except for Travis.

After school, Ryan and Tawny left to work on a joint project for Civics. Kevin, Robyn and I reviewed our day in the parking lot.

"It's like one of those horror shows where you just know there's a guy with a chain saw hiding in the hall between you and the door." Robyn shuddered and hugged her backpack.

"Agree. I don't know what, but he'll definitely get even. I know that from what he already did to Star."

"You can't be sure that was him," Kevin protested.

Robyn and I turned a disbelieving, "you've got to be kidding," look on him.

"Okay, okay. I agree it's possible, but you have no proof. And I don't think it's a good idea for either of you to react out of fear. What can he do?" He tried to reason with us.

"What can't he do is a better question," Robyn answered. "You just don't know him, Kev. He's not kidding when he says he'll get even. I hope he remembers my dad threatened him with a restraining order when Travis got upset with me when I told him I was pregnant. At least his dad took that seriously. Maybe that will help me out somehow." She sounded hopeful and doubtful at the same time.

"I got nothing," I reported with regret. "I guess I'm open season for him."

"You don't know that." Kevin put an arm around my shoulders. I had a sudden impulse to burrow into the comfort he offered. I know how strong and secure I feel in his arms. Maybe it really will be all right. I'm not isolated like I was last year. I tried to feel hopeful instead of doomed.

"Are you headed out to work with Diva?" I asked.

Robyn welcomed the change of subject. "Yeah. She's doing better. Want to come and check out her progress? You're headed out there, too, right?"

I nodded. "Yeah, but I'm going for training with Star. He's still afraid of the water, but Mr. K says we just have to be patient. I think I'm going to get out Ben's old kiddie pool and put it in our corral at home. Maybe when Star's on his own to investigate the water with no pressure from a human he'll do better." I shrugged. "Can't hurt."

"Might make a difference," Kevin agreed. "I'm on for helping Mom this afternoon. See you later?"

I nodded and leaned in for a goodbye kiss.

Robyn stared after him when he walked toward his Jeep. She stared so long I finally broke her attention by asking, "What?"

She startled and turned toward me. "Oh. Nothing. He's just so nice. He and Ryan both. I don't think I'll ever trust a guy like you can trust Kevin. Travis was the last in a long line of guys who lied. Guess I have no guydar."

"Guydar?"

"Guy radar. Like, reliable instincts about guys."

"Oh, I don't know. Maybe you just need to look for different things than you settled for before. My counselor used to say if I can't find the answers I'm looking for, maybe I need to change my questions. Maybe you should change the things you think you want from a guy."

"I'd have to be a different person to do that. Problem is, I'll always be a loser. See ya." Robyn gave a small wave and walked away. She left me frustrated and at a loss for words though I knew there had to be a way to change her self- definition.

"Help me, God. Give me the right words to change her heart."

# Chapter 18

*Star fears water because he thinks water was the enemy. The enemy was really my despair.*
Sara's Diary

I rode Star over for his trail class training, but first Kevin and I held the beginning session of our Do I Matter? group. We had ten kids and decided right away that would be our limit from then on because ten was plenty. The session went well once we got the kids talking about bullying, self-confidence and how to handle negative emotions.

After we reported to Justine, I crossed the road to Madrona Acres and found Mr. K in the training ring. Our session that afternoon did little to dispel Star's water phobia. We've already mastered the rest of the obstacles. I knew Star would. The next step would be a matter of tackling them against the clock. But the water? That turned out to be a real problem. In his mind, even a foot of water was equal to the ocean. It didn't make sense. To me. Fortunately, Mr. King seemed able to get into Star's mind and understand his fear with no trouble.

The first thing Mr. K had me do, I accomplished at home. He instructed me to use a hose like I used to when I washed Star before a show. He wanted to find out if Star was afraid of all water, or just water on the ground. The hose didn't bother Star at all, so we knew we had to tackle his fear of ground water.

We got him through small-to-medium size puddles in the potholes all over Madrona Acres, then tackled the water feature in the ring. My thighs burned from tightening every time I encouraged Star toward the water only to have him swerve abruptly to the side as we approached. We were inching closer so Mr. King felt confident it was only a matter of time. I wasn't so sure.

As I rode home, Star's fear of water consumed me. Surely there had to be a faster way to get him over the trauma. After grooming, feeding and cleaning his stall, I closed the barn door, set the newly installed alarm system and contemplated the corral. Inspiration hit when my gaze fell on Star's beloved soccer ball. He was as attached to that thing as much as Spot was to the stupid squeaky toy he slept with and carried around the house. Excited to try out my idea the next day, I rushed to the house for dinner and a study session with Tawny.

Dinner over and my friend and I grilling each other over physics formulas, I remembered Tawny's slight hesitation when Robyn, Tawny and I were discussing sex at the coffee shop. My brain fried on formulas, I put my set of flash cards aside.

"Tawn, remember when Robyn told us her story at the coffee shop?"

"Yep. Anybody who would ghost a bae because he got what he wanted is a real tool. New level of underground for Travis to sink."

"Agree, but I remember when we were talking about when Travis and Robyn, well, you know, when they…"

"Just say it. Smash is what you're looking for."

"I am? Is that the same as, well, as sex?"

"Duh."

"Well, when Robyn talked about that, you sort of hesitated and changed the subject a little bit. What was up with that?"

Maybe for the first time ever, Tawny's golden gaze avoided mine. She stared at the cards in her lap, bit her lip then glanced around my room like it was a brand-new place she needed to check out.

"Tawn?"

"Yeah." She sighed, paused, then looked straight into my eyes. "There is nobody I am as tight with as I am with you. But this is really hard to talk about, so I never have. But I see you and Kev getting about as tight in a ship as Ry and me, so I'll spill the tea."

I had absolutely no idea what she was talking about. But I wasn't about to interrupt the mood and ask for translation. Hopefully all would soon be clear.

"You know Ryan and I have been together since junior high, right?"

I nodded. I set down the cards I held and grabbed a pillow to hug. All my attention focused on my friend.

"Once when we were in eighth grade, we were watching a movie at his house. In his room. His mom left to go pick up his dad because their car had died. Long tale short, we ended up having sex. It just sort of happened. You know Ryan, he didn't talk me into anything, and he wasn't pushy. It really did kind of just…happen. We just…there wasn't really any reason to stop, so we just kind of kept going."

Tawny's focus turned inward and it was like I wasn't even there. She was remembering something I wasn't part of. I sat quietly and waited for her to continue. I could tell she wasn't at the end of her story. A deep sigh signaled her return to my bedroom.

"He took me home. We didn't really talk. But things got weird. Do you remember when we broke up for a while?"

"Yes. You seemed really sad, but you weren't mad or anything. Told me you both decided to take a break."

Tawny nodded. "Yeah. I went all emo on him."

This time she noticed my blank look and translated. "Emotional. We were both kind of freaked out, I think, so we decided to split. But we still really liked each other. Finally, Ry texted and asked me to meet him after school. We sat on the bleachers and talked about what happened. We kind of both had the same reaction. It was like, we didn't feel guilty or like we did this bad thing; it just felt wrong for us. Except, if it wasn't wrong, why did we both feel like we needed to make it right? I don't know. It was just super confusing. But Ry said he wanted me to be his girlfriend. And I really hated not hanging with him so we agreed we would keep seeing each other, but not participate in sex. Not unless we both agreed with no pressure from the other. We've stuck to that."

"So you hooked up, but now you're unhooked?"

"Yeah, that's not a thing. But points for trying." Tawny

laughed. "And don't ever say that to anybody. Unhooked." She shook her head. "You can be so dense."

She leaned forward and gave me a big hug. "Don't ever change. You're basic in the best way possible."

Was that an insult? Likely, yes, but I returned her hug anyway then grabbed her by the shoulders and pulled back so she could see my face.

"Thank you for telling me your story. I understand it would have been awkward to talk about it before, but I appreciate you explaining it to me now. Kevin and I have talked about this, too, and pretty much made the same decision as you and Ryan. Sometimes it's hard, but so far, we haven't changed our minds."

"All I can say is sex changed Ryan and me and not in a good way. We had to work hard to get back to our ordinary selves. Those girls at school who are regulars at this? They act like it's no big deal, but I know they're lying to themselves. For one, it hurt, and for lots of other reasons, it changed Ryan and it changed me. I feel bad for Robyn. At least Ryan actually cares about me. Travis def did not care about Robyn."

"One hundred percent agree. And I can't imagine how hard it was for her to give up the baby. I think Robyn's really depressed." The memory of the scars on Robyn's arms flashed into my mind, but I decided that information was not mine to share. "I hope she doesn't get to the same dark place I got last year."

"We'll just have to make sure we stick by her. I kinda like her. She's feisty."

I nodded. "She is, but in a good way now that she's starting to trust us. Last year the worst thing I did was pushing away my friends when I needed them most. Robyn seems willing to give us a try as friends. I hope that continues because I would hate for her to go down the same road of despair I took last year. Letting all those negative messages to myself just sit and fester in my mind was such mistake. I definitely learned my lesson about talking to someone about depression before it turns to despair."

Tawny flopped back on the bed. "I'm glad you're not going down that road again. I'll never understand how you could think I wasn't your friend, but I guess that just shows how unpredictable emotions are."

"You know how sorry I am, right?"

"'Course. We're good." She sat up, gathered her set of physics cards and leaned forward to give me the signature Tawny hug which included a short back rub. Best. Hug. Ever. "My brain is fried. I'm glad tomorrow is Friday." She leaned back but kept her hands on my shoulders. Her gaze locked mine. "Never, ever forget. AGYB. Yes?"

I nodded. "Yes. Me, too. Always got your back. Always."

Tawny smiled. Then smothered a huge yawn. "I gotta go. See you tomorrow?"

"Absolutely."

My friend left and I tried to study, but my brain wouldn't concentrate on formulas. My idea to help Star get over his water phobia kept interrupting my concentration. Finally, I gave up, slipped into some crocs and shrugged into a jacket to go put my plan in motion. I knew I wouldn't sleep until I took some action.

An hour later, in the last few minutes of daylight, I surveyed my project in the corral with deep satisfaction. This had to work. Or at least help.

Confidence put a bounce in my step when I returned to my bedroom to finish homework and go to bed. Tomorrow couldn't come quickly enough.

# Chapter 19

*I think Robyn's discovering that having friends can make anything bearable.*
Sara's Diary

I got up extra early so I'd have time to put my plan into motion. It was going to have to be casual Friday because I was definitely not going to have time to change. Big whoop.

After a quick breakfast, I headed to the barn. I turned off the alarm, grabbed a spare hay net and stuffed it with hay. Then I got Star out of his stall, swung the net over my shoulder and led him to the corral. Star kept nibbling at protruding pieces of hay until I heaved the net over the fence and fastened it in place. Concentrating on his food, he didn't notice the new addition to the corral while I opened the gate and led him through.

Last night before bed, I unearthed Ben's old plastic kiddie pool out of the storage shed, washed it out, placed it in the center of the corral and filled it with water. It was probably five feet in diameter and I filled it as full as possible. Floating gently on the surface of the water was Star's beloved soccer ball. I hoped that, left to himself during the day, he'd get bored enough and want the ball bad enough that he'd at least get near the water. I had no idea if it would work, but Mom said she'd keep an eye on him while I was gone.

I closed the gate and walked over to where I hung the feed net. He pulled mouthfuls out of the net and crunched away until his first pangs of hunger were satisfied, then he grabbed a mouthful of hay and looked around the corral while he chewed. His jaws stopped when he saw the pool and his head raised up, ears perked towards it. The ball was bright yellow and blue, so I knew he could see it. He took a few paces toward the toy, then stopped, head still held high, nostrils flaring. He shook his neck, blew out a breath and returned to the hay.

The thing is, Star and I are a lot alike. He has a stubborn streak and so do I. I don't like to be rushed into things and would rather have time to think and consider my decisions. He's like that, too, in his own horse way. I wondered if he might just need privacy to consider and experiment with the whole water thing without human interference.

The school bell wouldn't wait, so I reluctantly turned from the corral to grab my backpack to get to school. I knew the day would drag until I could get back home to see if there were results from my experiment. But I had a surprise for Robyn that helped me tear myself away from Star's little drama playing out in the corral.

When I reached school, Kevin waved to me from his Jeep so I parked nearby. I explained what I was trying with Star, and, like the stellar boyfriend he is, he was totally impressed with my idea.

"I've seen him with that soccer ball. I bet this is going to work. Maybe not to get him actually down on the beach, but I bet he'll be okay with the water feature for your competition."

"I hope so. Mr. K keeps giving us variations of challenges with the obstacles and it's actually kind of fun. If we can only get past the water feature, I think we have a good chance of competing in the trail classes. The rest of the course is going well."

"See you at lunch?" He leaned in and kissed me.

"Yes. Have you noticed Robyn doesn't hesitate to join us anymore? I think we're making progress with making her feel accepted."

He nodded. "Yeah, and the kids who dissed her are mostly ignoring her, so I think her drama is dying down. What reactions are you getting now?"

I shrugged. "Nobody has mentioned my suicide attempt this week. Last week Alyssa said something about offing myself, but I kept going and didn't really hear. I can't seem to escape the Sara the Saint label though. So irritating. That whole crowd keeps bugging me with that one."

"Teflon, remember? Make like Teflon and let it slide."

"I try."

"No try, there is. Only do, there is," he intoned in a perfect imitation of Yoda.

I slugged his arm. "Very funny."

We kissed goodbye and headed our separate ways.

At lunch, Ryan, Tawny and Robyn beat us to a corner table. Once we settled down to eat, Ryan spoke up.

"Hey. Check it out. I went by the car dealership yesterday afternoon and saw Travis out on the lot talking to a customer. Think he quit school? I figure he's working at his dad's dealership."

"Can he do that?" I wondered.

Kevin joined in. "Sure. He's eighteen. If his friends let him down, I can see where he'd quit."

I quickly checked Robyn to see how she took the news. She swallowed a bite of energy bar. "I suppose you all think that means we don't need to worry about him?" Her gaze took in all of us.

"Well. Yeah," I answered for everybody.

Tawny nodded. "If his fam friends are ghosting him, I can see where he'd pop off to car land."

Robyn shook her head. "You guys just don't get it. Travis doesn't get lost. He gets even. He doesn't have to be at school to mess with us. Though I think only Sara and I are in his sights. You three," her gaze singled out Ryan, Tawny and Kevin, "aren't really on his radar."

"So you and I need to stay sharp?" I asked.

"Def. You got a security system for the barn, right?"

"Yep."

"And my dad talked to Travis's dad so I think he'll think twice about messing with me, but you never know. One thing's for sure about Travis, you don't know what he'll do next because of the drugs. He did some pretty crazy things last year once he started bad seed."

"Bad seed?" Ryan asked.

"Marijuana mixed with H," Tawny answered.

Robyn nodded. "He gets bizarro."

Ryan pointed at Robyn, Tawny and I in succession. "Don't any of you go anywhere alone. Promise?"

I'd never seen Ryan look so serious. Kevin mirrored Ry's expression.

Tawny looked from one to the other. "So. We continue to stay away from Travis the tool."

The look on Kevin's face made me laugh. One more thing we have in common-we are both totally slang illiterate. Tawny caught his look of incomprehension.

"Tool equals rude and obnoxious. Also seriously delulu if he's taking bad seed."

This time Robyn put us out of our misery and translated, "Delusional."

"Why can't people just say what they mean? What's wrong with plain old English?" Kevin complained.

"Get over yourself," Tawny advised. "You talk science with your greenie friends, I've heard you. You're part of that squad. Sara talks horse. Same thing. And I bet your grandma used to say 'far out' just like mine back in the day." She shrugged. "We all have our own vocab."

Ryan stood up, stretched and grabbed his trash. "You all need to chill. As long as we've got translators, who cares what we say and how we say it? Nothing Travis does surprises me and the fact that he's blaming two girls for all his trouble is nothing new. He's never taken responsibility for any of his crap, I don't know why you expect him to start now."

Tawny's eyes glistened with admiration. "That's what I'm talking about. Isn't he the best?"

She stood and reached her arms around Ryan's waist. "Thanks, babe. I'll make sure these two," she nodded toward Robyn and me, "watch their backs. We'll be careful."

Ryan leaned down and kissed the top of her head. "Anybody messes with any of you will deal with me," he promised.

The rest of us gathered up our garbage and walked toward the door. I pulled on Robyn's sleeve to slow her down and handed her an envelope.

"I got you something."

"Should I open it now?"

I shook my head. "No. Just when you get a chance. See you

after school?"

She nodded while she slipped the envelope into the pages of a book. "Yeah. Later."

After school, Kevin had to help his mom and Ryan and Tawny stayed in the library to work on their project. I checked my phone while I waited for Robyn. I glanced up to see her walking slowly, reading the card I gave her as she went. She paused when she replaced the card into the envelope but held onto the bookmark I had given her. When she got close, her trembling smile seemed opposite to the glisten of pain in her eyes. Her mouth signaled hope, but her eyes looked like black despair. For once I didn't rush to fill a silence. I leaned against the car and waited for her to get emotional balance.

She piled her school stuff on the Subaru, held the envelope in one hand, the bookmark in the other and gestured with both.

"How did you know?"

"About Linnet's four-month birthday?"

"Yeah. How could you possibly know?"

Still not sure if I'd made a mistake or not, I crossed my arms and kicked at the gravel of the parking lot. "When you told Tawny and I your story at the coffee shop, I kind of tracked the timing clues from when the whole sexting thing broke at school, to when you left town last spring, to when you got back in town. I figured this month had to be Linnet's four-month birthday though I don't know the actual day of course." I paused to get my thoughts in order. I didn't want to mess this up. Not something this important. "The thing is, after my suicide attempt, people kept telling me to put it in the past and move forward. Like I should just forget about the misery that was so overpowering I wanted to die and almost killed my horse doing so. How can I forget that? And I don't want to forget it because I don't ever want to go down that path again." I took a deep breath and looked out over the quickly emptying lot before bringing my gaze to meet Robyn's.

"Are people telling you the same thing? Forget and move on?"

Robyn nodded. "My parents."

I drew in another deep breath for courage. "I don't think you should. I don't think you can, actually. What you did was brave and full of love. Your little girl has life because you did the hard thing. I wanted to remember that with you and celebrate her life."

Robyn swallowed hard then set her jaw in determination. She

looked at the bookmark in her hand. It had a cute photo of a linnet bird sitting on a tree branch. The bird was obviously in full song and the bookmark advised "Sing happy notes." Cheesy, right? But the bird was really adorable.

Robyn hurled her whole body weight toward me in a giant hug. I leaned against the car to keep my balance, but hugged her back as hard as I could. Finally, she let go.

"I can't believe you figured it out. I can't believe you took the time to figure it out. Why did you?" Her head tilted; honest puzzlement furrowed her eyebrows.

"Because I'm your friend. Well. I mean, I want to be your friend. And I care about you. I know I was a jerk last year..."

"So was I," she interrupted.

"Yeah, well, maybe. Neither of us were the best versions of ourselves last year, but there were reasons for that. And who we were with didn't help. And you know what I'm talking about."

"Travis and the poison-tongued girl squad of his?"

"Exactly."

We were both quiet for a few minutes then I asked. "Do you think we can be real friends? We actually have a lot in common if you think about it."

She stared at the bookmark again, then pulled the card out of the envelope and opened it up. "Do you really believe this? That God cares about how sad I am?"

"Yes," I replied firmly. "And so do I."

She held a hand toward me. I gripped it solemnly and we gave each other a decisive shake.

"Are you and Kevin getting together tonight?"

"No, he helps his mom most Friday nights because she makes a lot of sales on Saturdays. Why?"

"Could I come over later? Maybe talk a little? Get to know Star? Get to know you?"

"That would be great. What time?"

"Seven?"

I nodded and she leaned forward again to hug me, then turned and walked off. I watched her for a minute then remembered my big experiment and scrambled into the Subaru to hurry home.

I drove up and stopped a few feet from the corral. Star lifted his head to check out the commotion then lowered it again. My heart felt like it might burst when I saw what he was doing. He pushed the soccer ball around the perimeter of the pool with his nose, following it like a bloodhound on the scent. Then he planted a forefoot right by the ball inside the pool causing a huge splash and making the ball bounce wildly. He lifted his head and did a few bucking jumps away from the pool, then returned to do the process all over again. My plan worked.

Robyn and Star. I was definitely on a roll!

# Chapter 20

*Time does not heal all wounds. Sometimes it just allows them to scab over.*
Sara's Diary

Robyn drove up at 7:00. There was barely enough light left for us to prop our arms on the top rail of the corral to watch Star for a few minutes before I returned him to the barn. He had enough of his soccer game, apparently, but did take a drink of water out of the kiddie pool while we watched.

Robyn looked at me. "This is a mega step, Sara. You really do know your horse. I think he's well on his way to conquering his fear of water. Way to go." She lifted a hand to high five me.

"I sure hope so. We'll see what happens tomorrow during training. I might bring the soccer ball with me just in case. The water feature in the ring looks a bit different than the kiddie pool, so we might be starting all over. Hope not."

I walked over to the gate and called to Star. Knowing food was in his future, he stepped quickly to meet me. I haltered him, then led him to his stall, Robyn on his other side, a hand resting on his shoulder.

Robyn helped me get clean water and feed. Clearly, she was comfortable with the barn routine, then we sat on a bale of hay while Star steadily munched his oats and hay.

Robyn filled me in on Diva's progress.

"She's finally responding to me in active ways. Yesterday she actually gave a little nicker of welcome when I got to her pen. Justine's going to let me try riding her tomorrow. Want to come?"

No way was I going to smother that sparkle in her eye. I nodded. "Absolutely. What time will you be there?"

"We're shooting for 11:00, but it always depends on Justine's classes. She goes over a lot."

"I would say the timing of Justine's classes is sort of notional rather than an actual schedule. She really loves working with her clients."

"Totes. Her enthusiasm is catching, too. She's getting me signed up for the PATH program just like you. I'm not sure what that's going to look like. Dad really wants me to go to college. He doesn't see how I can make a living working with horses. I might have him talk to Justine so he'll understand better."

"You can do both. Justine told me about a college in Oregon offering a Master's program in Equine Mental Health Therapy. I guess the bachelor's degree would be psychology or something related, then the master's program would concentrate on using horses as therapy animals. I've been thinking about it and I'm going for it. The PATH program fits right in."

"That is so lit! I'll ask Justine about it and ask if she'll talk to Dad. He's not unreasonable. For a parent. He just worries about me."

"Same. My big problem is leaving Star and Kevin behind. Kevin's going to the community college in Santa Rosa. Partly because of cost, but also so he can keep helping his mom. If you go to Oregon, at least I'll have someone I know."

"Oregon's not that far. Dad said he's getting me a car for graduation this year so if I go, we'll have wheels."

My heart did some happy somersaults at how matter-of-fact Robyn was about our sticking together. Maybe I'm not as lame at friendship as I thought?

"That would be awesome. Or lit? Is that a better word?"

"Awesome is old school, but always allowable," she teased.

"Noted."

Except for Star's steady munching sounds and an occasional bird call, the barn was quiet. Peaceful. Hay and horse are my favorite aromatherapy. If Kevin's mom could bottle it, I'd buy her out.

We'd both been sitting quietly for a few minutes when I noticed Robyn's fidgeting fingers tapping a drum beat on her knees. I reached over and placed a hand over hers to still them.

"What's up?"

She stared at her hands. Then at Star. Then turned to me. "I still can't believe you wrote me a card and found the linnet bookmark. Like, how did you change so much from last year?"

I got up, went into the tack room and came back with a Bible in my hands. I sat back down and thumbed through until I found what I was looking for.

"Read that."

Robyn took the book and squinted at the page. "If it possible, as far as it depends on you, live at peace with everyone." Her gaze returned to mine. "So?"

"Last year I was awful to you. But you weren't the only one I was terrible to last year. I totally dissed Tawny, my best friend ever, and even Kevin when he did nothing but try to support and love me. All because I wanted Travis to like me, and I wanted to fit in. I just kind of lost my mind for a while, and my emotions completely took over. After Star saved me from the riptide, I talked to my parents about God. I was raised in the church, but never really understood who God was and, in particular, who He was to me. Dad made me think back and I realized God was with me the whole time I was slowly going out of my mind. Dad challenged me to just ask God to make my faith real. He said one of the ways to do that was to read the Bible. When Star was still really sick, I sat out here, opened up my Bible and this verse is the first thing I saw. I knew right away I needed to talk to my friends, tell them what was going on and apologize for lying to them. For not trusting them. For being a terrible friend. I even tried with Courtney and Alyssa."

"Shut up." Robyn looked shocked.

"I did. Courtney and I used to be good friends until high school. Once I talked to her, well, texted, she's backed off being such a brat. Not friends, but not enemies either. Alyssa? No way. She still has it in for me. Anyway, I knew after I read about being at peace with people also included you. That's why Kevin and I came to your house that day."

"Huh. Weird." She closed the Bible but held onto it. Like she needed an anchor or something. Keeping her gaze on the floor, she murmured, "I was so miserable that day. You interrupted one of my worst days ever."

Her hands gradually tightened around the book until her knuckles whitened. She stared at Star, but it seemed to me she wasn't seeing him at all. Then her gaze turned to me and it was like looking at black despair. Whatever she relived in that moment had to be the deepest pit of grief possible. I gently pried her hands off the Bible and gripped them with mine. Hers were ice cold. I waited.

Robyn's throat worked while she tried to swallow anguish. She looked down at our hands. Finally, her voice hoarse with emotion, she said, "When you came that day I was getting ready to cut. I know you've seen my scars." A smile briefly lifted her mouth. "How you kept from saying anything I'll never know."

"You have no idea," I agreed solemnly.

She nodded. "Thought so. Anyway. I started cutting not long after Travis shared my photos with the whole football team. How could I have been so dumb? It was so humiliating. And I've been so ashamed. Cutting…I don't know…somehow it relieves the pain inside. Then when Linnet was born and I placed her with a family." She shook her head. Her fingers tightened around mine. "It just hurt so much I thought I might die from the pain."

"Did you consider suicide?"

"No. At first, I wanted relief from the pain inside and cutting provided that. But then I just wanted to punish myself. Not die. Punish. Actually, in a weird way, I'm trying to stay alive. Cutting is the only way to do that. Anyway, Jer…a new friend of mine is trying to help me stop. He says everybody has things they're ashamed about and everybody has things they feel guilty about. He says I'm using cutting to solve the problems of shame and guilt, but you can't physically cut those out of your life. He wants me to go to a counselor. He does, and it's helping him. I went to a counselor while I stayed with Mom until Linnet was born. I haven't gone since I moved back home with Dad though. My parents don't know about my cutting. I just feel so ashamed. And so empty. I don't know what to do."

Robyn's last statement was more wailed than spoken. She choked up and looked at me with eyes flooded with tears. Mine felt like they were drowning, too.

"I went to a counselor after my suicide attempt and she helped a lot. I still visit her occasionally to check in. I could give you her phone number."

Robyn nodded. She freed a hand to wipe tears off her cheeks. "That's probably a good idea. Dad's been after me to find someone because he knows I'm depressed. I just…everything seems so hard and I can't…I can't." She choked on a sob. I leaned forward and hugged her.

"Listen. I don't know about cutting. But I know about feeling ashamed and guilty. I went from hating my life so much I wanted to be the opposite of myself to not wanting to be alive at all. And at least you're only hurting yourself. I almost killed Star. I still struggle with guilt about that. His life is changed forever because of the damage I caused. My counselor said guilt is believing I did something bad, but shame is even worse. Shame is believing I'm bad myself, and I really struggle with both. Sounds like you do, too."

Robyn nodded. "It's like I can never say enough sorrys so nothing will ever change. It'll be like this forever."

"Seems to me neither one of us can have a healthy future until we heal from our past. I don't know how you can heal if you keep cutting. That is an actual continual wound that you don't ever let heal."

"That's what Jer…" Robyn's lips closed on the name. "Okay, if I tell you this you can't tell anybody because it's not my story. But he's become a part of my story and it's awkward to talk around him. Jeremy cuts, too. He started when he came home from Afghanistan."

"I know. I've seen your scars accidentally a couple of times."

"Man. You know everything." Her wide-open gaze gave me too much credit. "Your nickname should actually be Sara the omniscient."

"No. That would be God. You guys," I started talking with my hands like I do when I'm nervous, "you're cutting actual skin that leaves scars. You think people don't notice?"

Robyn's face and neck got pink. "I think we both thought we were hiding our scars."

"Yeah, no. No can do when working with horses. Your sleeves pull back too often."

"Does everybody know?" There was a note of desperation in her tone.

"Tawny has noticed, but we haven't talked about it. The boys are clueless. I don't know about anybody else. My guess is Justine has seen your scars. You've worked with her too much with Diva.

But Justine is one of the kindest people I know."

"What about at school?"

I shook my head. "Nuh-uh. You've kept pretty much to yourself or lately with us since you moved back. I don't think anybody else has noticed."

Relief eased her tense shoulders. "Thank God for that."

"Actually, now that you mention it, there's a lot to thank God for."

"Oh boy. Here it comes." Robyn rolled her eyes.

"I'm not going to preach. But I know for sure God cares about you and will help if you let Him. Remember that song I told you about? *Rescue*? Have you listened to it?

Shaking her head and looking at the time, Robyn said, "I told Dad I'd be home by nine o'clock. I really should get going." She started up off our hay bale. "I'm really glad we talked, but I don't know about any God stuff."

I had already thumbed through my playlist to Lauren Daigle's song and started it playing. "Just listen."

The opening chords of the song cut off her protest. She gave in and sat back down.

The closing chords faded away. I glanced at Robyn. Slow tears coursed down her cheeks. She seemed in a faraway place. Then she startled back to reality. She turned a bleak gaze my way. "That's nice, Sara. And I like her voice. There's just one problem. Rescue? Me?" She shook her head. "No way. A princess gets rescued, Sara. And trust me, I'm no princess. See ya."

She was out the door before I could object.

# Chapter 21

*Robyn believes hope is terrifying. What she doesn't understand is
no hope leads to despair.*
Sara's Diary

The next morning, since it was Saturday, I was up, ready to ride over to Big Sky for Robyn's training session with Diva before the rest of my family was even awake. I had Star's soccer ball in a sack tied to my saddle just in case we needed it for incentive during our training later that morning. Today was definitely going to be an interesting day.

I took a deep breath of crisp fall air and nudged Star into a ground-eating canter. I could tell he itched to stretch his legs and run, so I leaned forward and let him go. Speed and cold air brought tears to my eyes. The black silk of his flying mane whipped around my face and head.

"Woo-hoo!" My delighted yell caused Star to stretch out and go for it. Maybe I only had one horsepower under me, but it felt like riding a speeding train. So much power. When I sighted the buildings of Madrona Acres and Big Sky in the distance, I gradually pulled Star down to a walk so he could cool down a little.

Justine spied us riding up to her facility and waved us over. Star headed right for her and nudged her jacket pocket for a treat.

"Okay, okay. Let me get it you big goof." She pushed his nose away from her pocket and pulled out a molasses cake. While Star slobbered over his treat, Justine stroked his neck and looked up at me.

"Here for our next step with Diva?"

"Uh-huh. Wouldn't miss it. Are you happy with how Robyn's working with her?"

"Absolutely. We're finally getting a glimpse of what kind of personality the horse has. I believe she's going to be a great therapy horse. One thing concerns me, though. So far, she only responds well to Robyn. If she turns out to be a one-person horse, which can happen, I'm not sure what we'll do. But we'll cross that bridge if we get to it. One step at a time. You can put Star in that pen over there. Then come and find us in the back training ring."

After taking off the saddle and bridle, I turned Star loose and followed Justine to the back ring. Diva was already bridled and had a bareback pad cinched up tight. Robyn stood at the horse's head whispering to her and smoothing her forelock. Mr. King was at the fence, his arms crossed on the top rail and one booted foot perched on the bottom rail. His first lesson was mine at nine o'clock. He was curious about Diva and Robyn, too. I joined him.

Thirty minutes later four happy humans and one flashy mare with a new spring in her step gathered in the center of the pen. Robyn perched on Diva's back and regarded Justine with a query in her expression. Robyn's face radiated such joy she seemed like a whole different person. One I'd never met.

Justine patted Diva's shoulder then rested a hand on Robyn's knee.

"That was great Robyn. She's coming right along. You've accomplished so much with her. I'd like you to do a similar training session every day next week in the corral, then we'll try her outside. Maybe with Sara and Star? We'll figure that out later. Groom her and move her up to the pen next to the main herd. We'll see if she feels more sociable with her own kind now that she's accepted you."

After Justine and Mr. K walked away, I held out my hand toward Diva before stroking the white blaze down her face.

"How did it feel?" I asked Robyn.

"She's a dream. It was like I've already ridden her a hundred times it was so easy to connect. I think Justine wants Jeremy to start working with her to see how she responds to a man. I'm a little jealous," she glanced at me with a question in her gaze. I nodded.

"I feel the same way with Star. He lets Ben ride when I can't, but he's kind of a one-person horse. Have to admit I like it." My neck felt suddenly warm from embarrassment. Was it kind of juvenile to admit I was jealous of my horse's attention? But Robyn bobbed her head in agreement.

"I know, right? I like being the only one she likes right now. Hey, what are you doing later?"

"After training I'm meeting Ben and his girlfriend, Zoe, at our house. I guess Zoe wants to talk to me about Star. Or maybe horses in general? Not sure. Anyway, I'm meeting them and then checking in with Tawny at the coffee shop. Want to meet us? Probably around three o'clock?"

Robyn uncinched the bareback pad and lifted it off Diva's back before she answered.

"You sure?"

"I'm sure. It'll be fun. See you then?"

She nodded and turned her attention to Diva. I retrieved Star, tacked him up and headed across the road to my own training session. Mr. King listened closely while I explained the successful experiment I dreamed up for Star with the soccer ball. He gripped my shoulder in approval.

"That's great, Sara. Really using your head. This is why it's so important to really know your own horse. I would not have thought of that. Let's see what happens when you approach the water in the training ring. Do a couple of the other obstacles first, there're two new ones, then we'll try the water."

We spent some time on the new challenges, reviewed the familiar ones then Mr. K motioned me toward the water. I took a deep breath and turned Star toward the water pit. His ears told me he knew what was coming. They flicked forward and back, but he didn't slow his step until we got right up to the edge of the pit. I sat still and let him look. He sniffed the water and blew out a breath causing ripples to fan out. I held my breath when he lifted a foot and tentatively moved it forward. He placed it firmly into the water and stretched down to smell the surface again. His other front foot followed. He lifted his feet high at each step and rushed the last yard when we neared the other side, but he did it. I leaned forward, hugged his neck and made a huge fuss of stroking and praising him.

Mr. King's mouth turned up in a huge grin.

"Take him through the pool noodle curtain and over the bridge then come back around to the water," he directed.

I did as he instructed. When we came back to the water, Star hesitated momentarily then walked forward with his head held low so he could see the surface more clearly. He rushed the other side again, but I knew we could train that away.

Mr. King had us go through the entire course as if we were in a show then signaled an end to our session. I couldn't wait to tell Robyn we were two for two with our horses today. I was definitely celebrating with a grande caramel macchiato later on!

Star and I headed home where I gave him a quick grooming and turned him loose in the corral. I grabbed a quick lunch, finishing just as I heard Ben drive up. I went out to meet the famous Zoe whose name meant life.

Ben and Zoe stood by the corral fence when I came up behind them. Star held his head over the top rail, greeting Ben and his friend, but Zoe stayed safely back. I liked that she didn't assume anything about my horse. Smart girl.

Ben's girlfriend regarded me with a steady hazel gaze when Ben introduced us. Her thick brown hair waved softly around her face, blunt cut at her jawline. She had a side part and used a braid along her forehead to hold her hair off her face.

"How did Star do today?" Zoe's voice was soft, but not fragile.

"Really well. I think he's over the worst of his fear of water. Did Ben tell you about it?"

She nodded. "I've always liked horses, but this is the first time we've lived in a place where having a horse is common. I hope it's okay I came over today."

I laughed. "Totally fine. Star loves company. Especially if they come with food. Here," I handed her a piece of carrot from my pocket. "Hold it like this and offer it to him." I demonstrated with the piece of carrot held out on my flat palm.

She copied my movement and held the treat toward Star. He whisked it off her palm without even touching her.

Zoe's eyes widened. She glanced at Ben then turned a sparkling gaze on me. "Can I feed him again?"

"Sure. Here." I handed over another piece of carrot.

Eyes shining, she carefully held her hand flat and repeated her offering. Star neatly lifted the orange fragment and crunched away. When he reached his nose forward to snuff her empty hand, she giggled.

"That means he likes you," I assured her.

"He does?" She looked at Ben again and a silent message passed between them. He nodded and nudged her shoulder.

Zoe turned to me, fingers clasped in a knot at her waist. "Could I pet him? I mean, like, right next to him? Would he care?"

"Nope," I answered cheerfully. "Come on over to the gate."

She turned a beaming smile on Ben before she followed me. No wonder he likes her. She looks at him like he's an unopened present.

The three of us slid through the gap I opened in the gate. Star ambled over to meet us. Zoe grabbed Ben's arm and half moved behind him.

"Gosh. He's really big." She swallowed hard as she took in the raven-black gleaming hide broken only by snowy white patches with black spots on his rump. "Is it…are you sure it's safe? He's safe?"

She glanced at me, but her gaze returned to Ben. Fine by me to let my little brother shine. She seemed like a nice girl and he'd never had a girlfriend before.

Ben stroked Star's neck. "He's as safe as can be as long as you treat him right. Here," he took Zoe's hand and tugged her in front of Star.

"Hold your hand by his nose and let him smell you. That way he'll know you when you come over again."

Ben demonstrated and Zoe faithfully copied his move, even moving her hand up toward Star's forelock and softly stroking his face.

When Star reached out his muzzle and sniffed Zoe's neck, the girl froze. But when he carefully nuzzled the hair along her cheek and neck, Ben's gaze sought mine in astonishment. No one was more shocked than I. My horse regularly caressed my hair, head, neck and shoulders, but I'd never seen him react to anyone else that way. I had a momentary selfish impulse to push her away. I know, I know, juvenile, right? Instead, I stayed quiet to see what would happen next.

Zoe stroked Star's cheek while staring steadily into his, as I well knew, mesmerizing eye. Then, as if drawn like a magnet to iron, she moved forward under his neck, stood on tiptoe and stretched her arms on either side of his neck as far as she could reach, then hugged for all she was worth. Star stood like a protective statue. My hand came up to cover my slack-jawed open mouth stare. What in the world was going on? Star never acted like that with anybody but me. Curiosity outweighed jealousy when I saw a tear escape between Zoe's closed eyelids. What was it with this girl? Evidently, Star knew something neither Ben nor I had a clue about.

# Chapter 22

*I can't believe I ever thought Travis was hot. He's attractive like a*
*velociraptor and just as dangerous.*
Sara's Diary

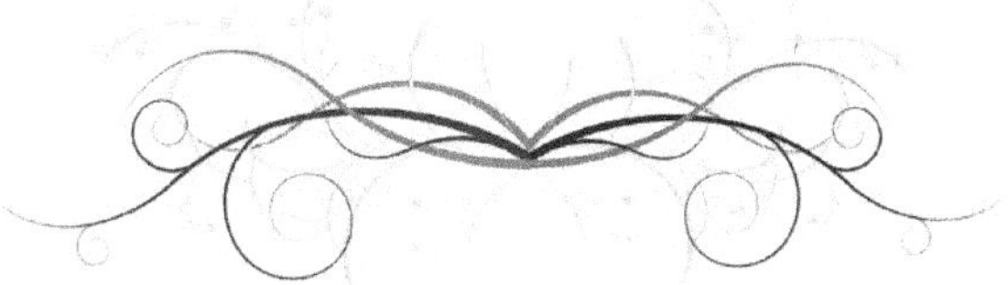

"So Star likes Ben's pookie?" Tawny lifted her straw to lick off whipped cream.

"Pookie?" I mouthed at Robyn.

She gave me a subtle thumbs up. Pookie must be something good, I guess. What do I know?

"Apparently. I've never seen Star act like that with anybody but me. I don't get it; but I'm completely okay with it. I mean, Star's great and Zoe seems like a nice girl, so no biggie." I took a drink of my macchiato and pretended indifference.

"Bzzzzzz!" Tawny made a sound like an off-key buzzer. "I call cap on that."

"Ditto," Robyn seconded. "You know you want Star to like you best."

"Okay, okay." I held both hands in front of me, palms up and leaned back in the booth. "I admit it feels weird and it shook me a little. But, guys, she held onto him like he was a rock in a flood. What do you suppose is up with that? She told me she's never even been around horses."

"Well, Star is definitely something big and strong to hold onto.

Maybe she's afraid of something?" Robyn shrugged when she guessed.

"I don't know. And, yeah, I do wonder why Star is acting this way, but it didn't stop me from agreeing to teach her to ride. Those big eyes pleading when she asked. What could I do?"

"You could have said no," Tawny acknowledged, "and I'm kinda surprised you didn't. Is she going to ride Star or will you teach her at Mr. K's?"

"She asked specifically if I would teach her to ride Star. She said he looks safe." I snort laughed. "Safe. He towers over her. But she feels safe with him." I gave a bewildered shake of my head. "I don't know. Seems wrong. Even my saying yes feels unbelievable. But also like the right thing to do. Guess I'll trust God has a plan here even if I don't have a clue."

"I've seen her with Ben and I'm sure she's not sus. I say you go ahead and see what happens. If nothing else, you'll have Ben's undying affection. He, at least, is in a serious situationship," Tawny advised.

I rolled my eyes. "Once again in English, please," I begged.

"I see them together a lot and I don't think you need to worry she's a suspicious character. She and Ben are in that place where they're more than friends, but not a full-on couple yet." She rolled her eyes back at me. "You're such a boomer, Sara."

I'm pretty sure that's an insult, but I've got to keep some dignity so I changed the subject.

"Robyn, what's that magazine you're looking at?"

"Tawny's going to give me a new do and I'm deciding what I want." She turned the pages slowly and I could finally see different styles of hair featured.

"Listen, parajita, meet me at Mom's salon tomorrow afternoon, okay? The shop is closed on Sunday so we'll have the place to ourselves. Pardon moi, but you just don't look like yourself. Or I guess your outside doesn't match what I think your inside looks like." Tawny tipped her head while she considered our new friend.

"Sounds like you plan on introducing Robyn to herself," I joked.

"I wish somebody would." Robyn's voice sounded wistful. "Mostly I think I'm the worst person in the world, but you guys keep telling me that's not so. I wish I could see what you're seeing."

"You have self-blindness," Tawny proclaimed. "I just made that up. It's when you can't see who you really are and believe you're someone else. I could so be a life coach," she mused, chewing on her straw. "Anyway, tomorrow, yes?"

Robyn nodded. "I'll meet you around two o'clock."

I checked my watch and groaned. "Listen, I've gotta get home. I have to help Mom then change to meet Kevin. Are you guys ready to leave?"

They nodded and we gathered up our phones. On our way to the parking lot, we were all head down checking for messages when a rough, "Hey," caught us by surprise. We stopped and looked up to be confronted by an angry-looking Travis.

A tsunami of emotion swept over me. Fear, anger, apprehension, anxiety–all took turns somersaulting through my mind. My neck and cheeks grew hot when anger won. I crossed my arms over my chest.

"What?" I snapped.

He moved forward to block our way. His eyes looked dark and wild. He had a couple days growth of beard, which might be the fashion right now, but it just made him appear threatening. His hands tightened into fists at his sides didn't help.

"What do you want, Travis?" I prompted.

"You two have wrecked my game." His gaze darted between Robyn and me. "I can't go to school; my friends are blanking me. You've totally snatched my life right out from under me. I'm gonna get you. Get you both. You can't do this to me." He took a step toward me, but Tawny distracted him.

"Watch it, Travis." Tawny had her phone held out in front of her, aimed at the enraged man. He grabbed at it, but she pulled back. "There's an emergency app for women that notifies the police of street harassment. Keep it up and I'll hit send. Or be smart and make like a tree and leave."

Travis's dagger stare caused chills down my spine. I swallowed and my stomach clenched like I'd swallowed a knife.

Finally, he hissed curses at us through clenched teeth, turned and stomped to his car. He'd traded the Mustang for something long, low and sleek, and it peeled out of the parking lot leaving the smell of burning rubber heavy in the air. Signature Travis.

The three of us stood frozen until Robyn took a deep shuddering breath and looked at Tawny. She tried for a smile that was more of a wonky grin.

"Make like a tree and leave? Really? Pretty sure my uncle says that."

Tawny shoved her phone in her back pocket. "Hey," she protested. "I was under a lot of pressure." She ran her fingers through her hair to fluff up the curls. "And my uncle totally says that." She laughed, shaky, but a laugh. Robyn and I joined her.

I sobered up first. "What are we going to do? He's getting worse. His eyes looked creepy. Is that drugs?"

Robyn nodded. "He was pretty blown up. Losing it big time." She glanced at me. "You have the security alarm turned on all the time, right?"

"Right," I confirmed.

"Dad got me some pepper spray," she admitted. "But mostly I forget it."

"Bring it with you tomorrow," Tawny advised. "Who knows if he's following you or what."

"You can give me a ride to my car at Justine's?" Robyn asked, her eyebrows raised in question to me.

"Yep. Let's go. See you, Tawn." I gave her a quick hug then followed Robyn to my car.

The drive to Big Sky went quickly while Robyn and I talked about how off Travis was. When we drove into the Big Sky drive, I spotted Robyn's car and pulled up beside it. She grabbed the door handle then hesitated. She looked down at her lap and mumbled something about a song.

"What? I can't hear you when you're talking to your lap."

She glanced over at me then stared out the windshield. "I listened to that song again."

I thought quickly. "You mean *Rescue*?"

She nodded. "Yeah. Listened a few times actually. You really believe God feels like that about me."

"Yes, and about me. In fact, He's already done all that for me so I'm positive it's true." I waited while she thought.

"I liked Lauren's voice so I found some of her other songs. Sometimes I wondered if she was living my life. You know her song, *You Say*?"

"Yes. That's another of my favorites."

"I don't believe everything that song says, but when I listen to it, I feel such an empty space inside of me just waiting to be filled. And I wonder if I believe what that song says, and *Rescue*, would that empty place be filled?"

"I believe so. Why don't you try and see what happens?"

She was quiet for so long I wasn't sure she heard me, but then she spoke again. "I tried to pray. Well. I did what you said and just talked. And I asked for something. So I'll see if I get an answer and then I'll know if God is real."

I shook my head. "It doesn't work that way. God's not like a big cosmic vending machine that you put in a request and blam, there's your answer. What if what you're asking wouldn't be a good thing? God's not going to give you something that wouldn't be the best for you to have. That's what the promise is. That He will work things out for your good. And since He's God, He knows what is best for you and will be best in the future."

"But you said He answered your prayer," she protested.

"He did. And He helped me when I didn't even ask, too. But His answer could have been no whenever I asked for something. No is an answer, too. It's about trusting Him to know what is the best thing for you."

"So I can keep asking?"

"Sure. Tell me what you're praying for and I'll pray for it, too."

She considered that. "Nope. If it's real, you can pray without me telling you what it is. If it happens, I'll know God is real. Bye, Sara. See you Monday."

She hurried out of the car before I could object.

Now what do I do? Pray, advised a little voice in my mind.

# Chapter 23

*Everything broken leaves a scar. That's how we know there's a story.*
Sara's Diary

**Sunday after church**, Kevin sat on a hay bale in the barn while I laid on my back with my head resting on his thigh.

"Is Ben going to be around while you're teaching Zoe?" Kevin asked. His fingers stroked through my hair and almost had me asleep.

"Nope. She told him this was for her and she would see him after we're done. She's little, but mighty that one." I laughed. "Ben didn't even try to argue."

"Smart. Everybody needs space to do their own thing."

"Are you saying you need some space from me?" I teased.

In answer, he hauled me up by shoulders and sat me in his lap. I leaned against him and looped one arm loosely around neck.

"Nope. In fact," he pulled me in close for a kiss, "I could do with less space."

I laid my head against his chest and relaxed with the steady beating of his heart echoing in my ear. Steady. That described Kevin perfectly. I looked up at my kindhearted boyfriend and felt a warm glow of appreciation. What would it be like to leave him behind if I went to Oregon for school?

"Are you still planning on classes at the community college next year?"

He nodded. "Mom will still need my help until her products are featured in more stores. She has a pretty steady income, but hiring someone isn't in the budget right now. Neither is paying for me to go to a four-year school. It's okay. I can wait."

"I'm thinking of how it will be for us to try a long-distance relationship."

He grasped my shoulders and propped me up beside him on the hay bale. "Worried?"

I picked at pieces of hay sticking out of the bale. "Not exactly. Just not sure how it will work."

"We'll keep in touch. Facetime, texting, visits. It's about an eight-hour drive. I could do that for a long weekend, easy."

"If you have time," I agreed. "But I know you'll want to keep your grades up and with helping your mom, I don't think it will be easy for you to get away."

"Not easy." He grasped my hand and brought it to his lips. "But worth it."

Oh. Man. How did he do that? Make my insides go all warm and mushy? My heart raced, and I had to moisten suddenly dry lips. I gulped.

"Yeah?"

"Yeah." He smiled, raised a hand to cup the back of my head and pulled me close for a kiss.

"A-hem," Ben's loud interruption startled us. I confronted my brother indignantly. "What is up with you? Think you're a ninja or something, sneaking up on people?"

"Hey," he shot back. "If you're looking for privacy, in the barn with the door wide open is not the place. Get over yourself. When is Zoe coming?"

I checked my watch. "Any time now. Why? She doesn't want you around," I reminded him.

"Yeah, I know." He ran a nervous hand through his hair. "But I kinda have to be. I mean, what if she needs me?"

I hid a grin behind my hand.

"Why would she possibly need you? She'll be perfectly safe with Star and me."

I took pity on him. I liked being around Kevin all the time, too.

"I'll try to figure out a way to include you while we're doing our first lesson. That's all I can do. But no promises," I insisted sternly.

Clearly uncomfortable, he ducked his head in embarrassment. "Thanks," he mumbled. He lifted his head and his gaze met mine. "It's just…I need to…that is…"

"I get it," I assured him gently. And I did. I felt the same way about Kevin. The Mitchell siblings had it bad.

The sound of tires crunching on gravel outside the barn door interrupted our conversation and caused panic on my brother's face. He looked wildly back and forth. I reached forward and touched his arm.

"Go out the back door. I'll lock it behind you."

"Yeah. Yeah," he brightened. "Thanks. Bye." He scurried past me to back corner of the barn.

I said goodbye to Kevin and walked out to meet my pupil. Zoe's mom waved through the windshield before she turned her head to maneuver out of the driveway. Zoe stood frozen; uncertainty mixed with anticipation playing tag across her expressions. Her shiny new cowboy boots lifted a smile to my lips. They'd be scuffed and dirty soon enough.

"Ready?"

Zoe nodded.

"Okay," I motioned her forward, "come on then. We're going to start at the beginning.

We walked into the barn where I opened the tack room door.

"Here's where all Star's tack is stored. If you decide to stick with horses as a lifestyle, or hobby, you'll clean yards and yards of leather to keep it soft and water-resistant. Grain is kept in bins that can be securely fastened. Partly to keep out the mice, but also to keep Star out. Horses will overeat and can even kill themselves by eating too much grain, so this is really important."

"Like me with sour gummy bears," she commented, mischief in her tone.

"Exactly." I smiled. This was going to be fun.

We went through all the different kinds of tack, examined both my English saddle and the western one I used the most. I grabbed a couple brushes and a curry comb and nodded toward a rope halter with a lead rope attached.

"Grab that and let's go get Star."

I opened his stall. He already had his head over the door wanting to know what was going on, so I urged him back. When I motioned Zoe through the open door, she swallowed hard and hesitated. Then determination lifted her chin and she walked toward me with the halter held in a death grip.

"Hold out your hand like you did yesterday."

She obeyed; her fingers unable to resist stroking his soft muzzle. I handed her a horse cake. She offered it correctly from the flat of her hand.

"The best way to get to know each other is by grooming. Trust me, Star loves this part. You'll see," I promised.

I pulled the halter over his nose and fastened it behind his ears. I nodded toward the posts in the center of the barn. Large metal rings were attached to each post. "Lead him out to the posts and we'll tie him for grooming. Use one hand to hold the rope and the other to hold the halter under his chin."

She drew in a deep breath through her nose and took the end of the rope. She moved closer to Star and reached up to clasp the halter. Her head barely reached his mouth. He dwarfed her. I knew from experience this could feel intimidating. I already had a relationship with Star by the time I actually got to ride him so it wasn't a big deal for me. Why was she challenging herself with something obviously personally alarming?

And what was up with my horse? My. Horse. Who was presently lipping the hair at the back of Zoe's neck like she was a popsicle. He never touched other people like that. Me, yes. Anybody else? No. Why was he so drawn to her? I shrugged and followed behind him to the hitching posts.

I showed Zoe how to tie the rope in a quick release knot. She fumbled a bit but got it on the third try. I fetched the stool I used to groom him when I first brought Star home. We walked around him while I showed her the different patterns of hair growth and explained the importance of brushing and combing in the direction the hair grew. She nodded seriously and I could tell she was cataloging mental notes. When we progressed to picking up and examining each coal-black hoof she stood back and stared at me.

"It'll be fine," I assured her. "He's not picky about his feet like some horses. Just grab around his pastern like this," I demonstrated, "lean against his shoulder and tug. Voila'. You can see if he has any rocks caught in his shoe or if there are any other foot problems."

She stared at me. Then at Star. Gulped. Set her shoulders in resolve and stepped in front of me. I took her by the shoulders to move her in place. She ducked down and backed away like a spooked crab on the beach. My mouth fell open and my head jerked back in surprise.

She faced me, hands wringing in front of her, face white as a sheet, and stammered, "I'm sorry. I didn't mean…I mean, it's okay…I just…" She took in a deep breath blew it out. Then she wiped the palms of her hands against the sides of her legs.

"I, ah, I guess I don't like to be touched. Surprised by being touched I mean. But, it's okay, it'll be fine. I was just caught off guard," she stammered. Her face instantly went from pale white to flaming red.

"That's okay, Zoe. Really. I just didn't know." I talked to her like I would a spooked horse. "How about if I warn you if I need to touch you? Would that work?"

Silently, she nodded and looked at me with relief clear in her gaze. What was going on with this girl? Curiouser and curiouser.

She mastered her fear of picking up Star's feet and was confidently patting and walking around him by the time we finished a thorough grooming. I gave myself a congratulatory mental pat on the back for how well Star was trained.

Zoe and I stood back and admired my horse's handsome, gleaming appearance. I thrust out my hand toward her. She took it. I gave her a decisive shake. "Well done, young jedi," I intoned in my best Obi-Wan impression. She giggled. "We have a few minutes left before your mom comes to pick you up. Want to try a short ride? It'll be a quick bareback walk around the corral, but at least you can see what it feels like."

She nodded eagerly. I directed her to lead him out to the corral and through the gate. Once in the corral, I took the lead rope from her.

"I'll boost you up. For this first time, I'm just going to lead you around the corral, okay? Hold onto his mane. You can't hurt him, so don't worry about that. Got it?"

Eyes sparkling and mouth in a wide grin, she nodded.

"I have to touch you, okay? Just to help you get on and settled."

"It's okay. I'm ready."

I cupped my hands and directed her to put her foot in the hand cradle. Once she stepped into my hands, I boosted her up and onto Star's back. I put my hand on her hip to steady and center her. Her mouth formed an O of astonishment. Her eyes widened and she gripped Star's mane for all she was worth. I kept my hand on her hip.

"You okay?"

She nodded enthusiastically. One hand stroked Star's shoulder. She looked down at me.

"This is awesome!"

I could tell. Her eyes sparkled and she leaned forward to hug Star's neck with a laugh of pure joy. He turned his head to nip at the toes of her boots. Again, not usual behavior for him with anybody but me.

I tugged on the lead rope. We walked the perimeter of the corral. I checked on Zoe a couple of times. Her rapt face told a story all its own. Another horse girl was born. I smiled.

We circled back to the gate just in time for Zoe's mom to drive up. I instructed the girl how to swing her right leg behind her so she could slide down Star's side on her tummy. She stumbled. I reached out a hand to steady her and she slid out from under my hand before it connected. Man. That was some serious touch aversion. Reading her body language told a story I hoped wasn't true. Time would tell. Or maybe she would tell me herself? I hoped so.

# Chapter 24

*Talking about what happened makes it real. Is that why we stay quiet?*
Sara's Diary

**Walking into school** the next morning, I heard Tawny call my name. I searched the halls for my friend. Her waving hand caught my attention and I headed in her direction. Then squinted. Who was that next to her? When I got close enough to distinguish features, I recognized Robyn. Sort of. Just not the Robyn I knew.

Tawny completely transformed her. Robyn's long, blue-streaked, blonde hair was somewhere in a trash bin at the salon. In its place, Tawny created a short, blue, layered bob that stuck out at odd angles. She looked like a super cute frozen porcupine. The bright blue tint caused her eyes to appear like twin tropical lakes. I'm positive Tawny called the new look adorbs.

"Hey! You guys were busy yesterday. I like it."

Robyn touched her blue-spiked cuteness. "Really? It's not too much?"

"Not for you. I'd look like an idiot. You look like a supermodel."

I turned to include Tawny. "Way to go, Tawn. You've outdone yourself."

"Well, I am extremely skilled, I have to admit." She laughed off her bragging tone. "To be honest, it was easy. Robyn's hair is lusciously muy bien." She kissed her fingertips in homage to Robyn's hair. One hundred percent hair stylist to her last cell.

"When I see myself in a mirror, I do a doubletake and wonder who the girl with the pixie cut is. I've never worn my hair short before." She felt the back of her neck like it was unfamiliar territory.

A bell rang and the three of us turned toward our first classes as we waved to each other.

At lunch, we met up with the boys. Ryan's response to Robyn's new hair was a chin lift salute and a, "Nice, do." Kevin just smiled and gave a thumb's up.

Once we settled down to lunch, Robyn fidgeted with her sandwich, put it down and cleared her throat.

"I have something I want to say. All of you," her glance included the four of us, "have been really nice to me when I didn't deserve it."

Kevin started to object. She held her hand up to silence him.

"I don't, Kevin. I never made any effort to know any of you last year, let alone be nice or even polite. But you've become friends and I appreciate that. I want to be different." She touched her hair. "I want to change my insides as much as Tawny changed my outside. So," she took in a deep breath, "I'm going to start by being honest. I've been cutting myself for over a year now. More since I moved back home with my dad. I can try to explain reasons, but I know it doesn't make sense in any version of sanity. I want to stop. I want to be more like you." Once again, her glance swept the four of us. She paused so long Kevin asked quietly, "What are you looking for?"

"Each of you, I don't know, it's like…" she lifted her shoulders in a frustrated shrug. "Like you know who you are. Or maybe it's that you know how to be who you are. Like take Sara, for instance. I know her best because I spend more time with her because of the horses. And because, well, we had to work out some junk from last year."

"What about Sara?" Kevin prompted.

"Yeah, what about me?" I leaned toward her. "Mostly I'm a mess." I indicated my messy bun.

"No. No you're not. Maybe last year," she admitted, "but this year is different. It's like you have kind of a confidence and a sort of, I don't know, like calmness you didn't have before."

"Truth," Tawny agreed. "SJ, you're way different than last year. Last year you were despo in the worst way possible. I'm with Robyn. What happened? And close your mouth. It's not attractive." She smiled and bit into her apple.

I snapped my gaping mouth shut. Me? Confident? Me? Calm? Were we even talking about the same person? I didn't recognize the person Robyn described at all. Then I stopped and thought. I am different than I was last year. And suddenly I knew what that difference was. And why.

"Last year I wanted desperately to feel like I belonged. So, I changed and tried to be like everybody else. I could sort of fit in as long as I acted like the rest of the group. But I didn't really belong. The sad thing is, I would've settled for fitting in even though it meant I couldn't be myself. This year I'd rather belong. Even if it's only with a few people. I guess I'm at peace with who I am and even like myself. Most of the time," I amended. "But the real change was when I got to know Kevin better." I reached over and took his hand. He squeezed gently. "Kevin taught me more about God. Who He is and how I could trust Him with my life. I never really got that before even though I went to church all the time. The inside changes you're talking about came from letting God have some say in my life."

Kevin added, "It's pretty simple, Robyn. Change comes when you let go of control of your own life, and let God take over."

Robyn studied the sandwich in her hands. Then she looked up. "I've never really had friends I could talk to. And even after you guys were nice to me and became my friends, I didn't want to talk about what I was doing because that made it real. Like as long as I hid what I did, I could pretend it away. I want to be a real person. I want people to know the real me. Maybe you won't like me so much, but at least I'm being honest. And I think maybe that will help me stop cutting, too. And I want to. Stop. And I'm going to call that counselor you told me about, Sara. I know somebody else with my problem and he sees a counselor. I guess I can finally admit I need help."

By this time, she had completely picked her sandwich into little pieces so she swept them into a pile and onto a napkin.

"Not throwing shade or anything, but a lot of how you were last year had to do with Travis," Tawny commented. "Both of you. Kind of like he infected you with sus vibes. We know how mad sketchy he is."

"Word." Robyn replied.

I piped up. "I'm not sure exactly what you said, but I know your opinion of Travis, so guessing it's not good. And being around Travis wasn't good for me last year, I agree. But it was my idea to use him to become popular. Definitely not my brightest move considering how insane he is, but it's not all his fault."

"Fair," Tawny agreed. "But he's still like an infection of some kind. It was like you two were under some kind of evil spell or something."

"Maybe. But we both have to take some responsibility for what happened to each of us. Don't you think, Robyn?" I glanced at her.

Robyn nodded. "I agree he's not a good person, but I didn't have to get pulled into his vibe."

Ryan gathered all his trash and loudly squashed it together to jam into a brown bag. "That's enough review of past junk. Robyn, you are straight up fair for talking about hard stuff and we appreciate it. But let's move on, shall we? You're making changes, Sara's already swapped out last year's cringe feels, we should all focus on what's ahead."

"That's what I'm talking about," Tawny leaned over and checked Ryan's watch. "I've gotta stop at my locker before my next class so I'll see you all later."

Ryan left with Tawny. The rest of us gathered up our backpacks, dropped off our trash and headed for our next classes.

Head down checking to make sure I had the paper due next period; I almost ran into Alyssa. Mostly kids parted around me without acknowledgment, like I was contagious or something, but Alyssa planted herself in front of me, challenge in her stance. When I looked up, the expression in her eyes caused chills down my spine.

"You think you're so smart," she hissed through clenched teeth. "Just wait. Travis is going to fix you good. You're nothing. Got it? You're nothing." She twitched away and rushed past me.

I stared after her. What was that all about? Faint unease caused my stomach to tighten.

When I reported Alyssa's behavior to Kevin after school, he reminded me how dramatic she'd been in the past. "Consider the source," he advised. "Besides, you're being careful and you've taken precautions with Star. What else can you do?"

His practical calm eased my fear. "You're right. She didn't tell me anything I don't already know. Travis hates me."

Kevin changed the subject. "Want to get together later? Or are you meeting with Zoe?"

We walked toward the parking lot hand in hand. I nodded. "She's meeting me at the house right after school. But I'm free after dinner. Want to study together?"

He nodded. "I'll see you later." He stopped by his Jeep and I continued to my car. After tossing my backpack into the back, I slipped into the driver's seat. I fastened my seat belt, started the car and eased forward to the exit. Movement in the side mirror caught my attention and I looked closely. A long, low shape pulled slowly out after me from a couple rows away. My gaze returned front so I could pull out of the parking lot onto the street. I checked the rearview mirror. The dark shape of a large vehicle kept a steady distance. By the time I reached our driveway, my hands clutched the steering wheel in a death grip and my skin felt clammy. I couldn't see through the tinted glass of the ominous car, but it couldn't be anybody but Travis. He pulled out from behind me and roared away when I signaled at our driveway.

I think I know how a mouse feels when Abby has it in her sights. Hunted.

# Chapter 25

*Sometimes there's not enough light available to completely dispel the darkest dark.*
Sara's Diary

"Quiz time." I handed Zoe a grooming brush. "See if you can remember what to do to prepare him for our lesson today."

We figured out pretty quickly Zoe couldn't groom Star without a step stool to reach his head and back. Once we got her high enough, she thoroughly brushed every inch of his hide. Following the whirls and curls of his hair growth, he was show ready by the time she finished. She even polished his hooves with a soft cloth, tip of her tongue showing at the side of her mouth as she concentrated. Watching her helped the growing panic of my drive home recede. It was hard to feel scared in the sanctuary of the barn.

Zoe smoothed down an imaginary scuff of Star's mane and looked at me with anxious anticipation. I wish I could get her to relax. She's so tightly wound I'm afraid she'll shatter. Except with Star. She's completely unafraid of him. Sticks as close to him as a chick by a mama hen. And him? It's like he's adopted her. He noses her cheek then lips at her hair whenever she's within reach.

"He looks great, Zoe," I congratulated her. "Let's get the bareback pad and get to work. Ready to actually ride?"

Her eyes glistened with excitement. She nodded.

"Okay, lead him out."

I walked beside her as we walked out to the corral. I placed a hand on her shoulder to praise how quickly she learned grooming techniques. She froze, her back as rigid as if she was backed up to a wall. I forgot. I removed my hand and motioned her to stop.

"I'm sorry. I'll remember from now on. Okay?"

She nodded; eyes tightly shut. Tears shimmered on her closed eyelids. Embarrassment? Probably. I didn't want to make whatever it was worse, so I started to walk and she followed me. By the time we got Star inside the enclosure, she regained her composure.

"Ready for me to boost you up?"

She nodded and put a foot in my clasped hands. Once she settled onto the pad, I explained what we would be doing. I kept pushing Star's head away when he repeatedly turned to nose Zoe's foot. It was like he could tell she was upset. And why not? I reasoned. He could read my emotions like a book. Apparently, there was a whole subtext going on between them that I was not in on. Anybody who works with horses has learned patience and I was no exception. Whatever was going on would come out eventually.

I explained Mr. King's rationale for learning to ride each gait bareback before graduating to a saddle. He believed a rider learned best by learning to balance on the horse's back and feel how the horse moved. It's how he taught me. Once I explained, I looked up at her and drew in a quick breath.

"Zoe, I know you don't like being touched and I will do my best, but there are times I'm going to have to correct your posture, or your knee and foot alignment. Is that all right?"

She nodded, both hands wound tightly in Star's mane.

I stroked Star's neck a few times, then glanced at her again. "And if it would ever help to talk, I'd be glad to listen. Okay?"

She nodded again, a delicate pink flushing her neck and cheeks. I caught a quick glimpse of her gold-flecked hazel eyes when she gave me a tiny smile. A hundred questions played tag in my mind, but they'd have to wait. This girl was as timid as a hummingbird and I knew if I questioned her, she'd be gone in a flash.

We worked for a half hour before I motioned her over to the fence where I perched on the top rail. "Once more around. Walk halfway then trot the last half. You're doing really well."

She followed my instructions, hands clasping the reins low on

Star's neck, heels down, knees drawn in for balance, back straight and eyes forward. She rode like there was Velcro between her and Star. She's a natural and my thoughts were busy with a plan. When she reached where I sat on the fence, she brought her right leg over Star's back and shimmied down his side. I jumped down from the fence, held my hand out for a congratulatory shake which she accepted after hesitating, then took the reins from her hand to lead Star toward the gate.

"I'm going to leave him out here for a while so let's get his bridle and the pad off him. You uncinch the pad."

She tugged at the buckle while I loosened the bridle and slipped it over Star's ears. Zoe pulled the bareback pad off at the same time. Star shook himself all over and ambled over to the water trough. I motioned Zoe toward the barn with a nod of my head. After we stowed the tack away, I sat on a handy bale. I motioned her to the same.

"Listen. I have an idea for you to think about. You're about as natural a rider as I've seen. And Star likes you. And he doesn't take to just anybody. In fact, hardly anyone. Even Ben he mostly just tolerates. Next year I'm going to college in Oregon. What would you think if we continue lessons until you're comfortable riding Star then we'll audition you with Mr. King and see if he's willing to train you in my place with Star? It's up to him if he wants to work with you or not. How would you feel about showing in a horse show? Would your parents let you?"

"I think so. When we knew we were going to move here I asked Dad if I could finally get a horse and he said we'd see once we were here. We can't afford one right now, but he's glad I'm learning to ride Star. You would have to talk to my mom and dad, but I think they'd be okay. Ben told them all about how you show and win championships and stuff."

"I can't take Star with me, and I'd never sell him, but he can't just stay here and do nothing. He'd go crazy with boredom. If you can take over his training it would help a lot. I have to admit I'm surprised you wanted to learn to ride him. You weren't afraid?"

"Yeah, at first. But I'm trying to not let fear stop me from doing things. The first time I came here to visit Ben, you were riding Star and I thought he was so beautiful. I kept wondering what it would feel like to ride him. And I need." She paused. "I'm trying to do things even though I feel afraid."

It seemed like there was something more. I waited.

In a tone so low I had to strain to hear, she added, "I have to learn to be brave." Desperation tinged her voice.

"Why?" I kept my voice as neutral as possible hoping she'd continue to talk. She did but changed the subject.

"I hope it's okay, but Ben told me about what happened to you last year. Were you afraid?"

"When? Like all year?"

She nodded.

"No. I was afraid in the riptide because I didn't think I'd be able to get out and I really didn't want to die once I came so close. But most of the year I was depressed. And angry. What messed me up is I acted how I felt. I had all these feelings of depression, anger and, I don't know, feeling like I was an outsider or misfit. Like I didn't belong or matter to anyone. The problem was that was how I felt, but it wasn't the truth. I know better now."

Her gaze was on the scene outside the barn door, but I had a feeling that's not what she was seeing. I'm not even sure she remembered I was beside her. And I'm not sure she was talking to me when she spoke again.

"I'm kind of trapped in a riptide, but there's no escape. I'm afraid I'll be caught forever. And I can't, I can't live this way. I have to get brave."

I tried to hear what she wasn't saying. "What do you mean, Zoe? I'll be glad to help if you let me know how." I spoke softly, but she startled out of her reverie and glanced at me wide-eyed.

"Uh, it's okay. I'm fine. Really, everything is okay. I just get afraid sometimes. Oh! There's Mom, I gotta go. Thanks for the lesson. Bye." She was out the door before I could protest. Weird.

I went to the house to help Mom with dinner and get ready for a study session with Kevin later on. After dinner, I got Star settled for the night, set the alarm and spread my physics homework out on the dining room table. Kevin joined me and we worked on formulas and problems. With Kevin's help, we finished quickly. He speaks fluent science. I get more out of studying with him than I ever do in class. Bonus boyfriend points for him. It was still early so we agreed on a movie and settled in to watch. I curled up against Kevin with his arm holding me close.

Partway through, my parents went up to bed with a reminder of school tomorrow and warning not to stay up too late. Hooked into the drama taking place on an alien warship somewhere in the galaxy, I barely nodded and waved goodnight.

Suddenly, Kevin paused the intense onscreen battle.

"What?" I started up, but he pulled me back against him.

"Not sure. Hold on a sec."

We listened intently.

"I thought I heard Spot barking. But there's nothing now."

"He could have seen a raccoon."

Kevin nodded and we returned to a galaxy far away. But after a few minutes, Kevin paused the movie again and got up.

"Maybe I'll just go check. Stay or come with?"

"Come with."

He held out his hand to pull me up off the couch. We made our way through the dining room and kitchen to the back door. Kevin opened the door. Next thing I knew, he slammed through the opening at a dead run toward the barn. "There's smoke. Call 9-1-1."

Once he cleared the doorway, I could see what panicked him. Smoke curling up from the far back corner of the barn. I pulled my phone from my pocket and punched out 9-1-1 while following Kevin. I quickly explained the emergency to the operator then hurried around the side of the barn to see Kevin kicking at piles of burning rubbish piled around the back door. "Grab a hose," he yelled over the sound of crackling flames.

I rushed to the front of the barn to grab a hose, but could hear Star neighing in terror inside the building. Indecision cost me valuable seconds, but I turned the faucet on full and raced back to Kevin with the streaming hose.

"I have to get Star," I screamed.

"Don't. Sara, don't go in the barn," Kevin's voice sounded a desperate warning even while he aimed the rushing water at the flames.

"I have to get him," I shouted and sprinted back to the front. I pulled the barn door open and the alarm blared. It barely registered as I pulled the door wide and dashed to the tack room. The main space filled with eye-watering smoke though there were no flames. Yet.

I grabbed the closest halter and started talking to Star before I even got to his stall. Shrill with panic, his neighing cancelled my voice. I opened the top half of his stall door and he rammed into the secure bottom half.

"Whoa, boy, whoa." With one hand I grabbed his nose, the other feverishly stroked his neck until my voice finally registered in his instinct-driven panic. In the few seconds he was distracted by my presence, I drew the halter up and over his ears, clasped it and took a tight hold. With my free hand I slipped open the door clasp and pushed it open. As soon as he felt the door move, he lunged forward with me trying to control a thousand pounds of terrified horse. I kept talking and used both hands to keep hold of the halter while he bolted for the door. Once clear, his white-eyed gaze searched frantically for safety. The familiarity of the corral drew him and he headed that way with me barely keeping up. I grabbed the gate latch and flung the gate wide open. Star bolted through. I let him go, quickly shutting the gate behind him.

My parents erupted from the back door, their voices as frantic to locate me as I had been to find Star.

"Here, I'm right here." I raced to intercept them just as we heard sirens screaming toward our property.

They clutched me in a tight hug, then Dad grabbed my arms and held me in front of him.

"What happened? Where's Kevin?"

"He's at the back of the barn trying to put the fire out. We thought we heard Spot, so came out to check. Kevin saw the smoke."

Dad handed me off to Mom and ran toward the smoke. "Disable the alarm," he called back. Mom and I hurried to the system where she punched in the code. My hands shook uncontrollably now that I had Star safe. Oh, the indescribable relief of the cessation of the alarm ringing. Ben joined us just as the noise of the alarm stopped.

The sirens from the fire truck soon filled the barnyard with more blaring noise. The firemen erupted into an organized ballet of movement as they each raced for their assigned positions. It wasn't long before the chief came around the corner of the barn with Dad and Kevin beside him. They all reeked of smoke and their eyes watered from the irritants of the fire.

"It's pretty well under control, folks. You wait here and I'll return with a preliminary report shortly. By the way, I'm Fire Chief Powell." The fire chief turned and headed toward the back of the barn again.

"I'm going to check Star."

"Sara," Mom protested.

Dad put a hand on her arm. "Let her go. Kevin, go with her?"

"Yes, sir."

We reached the gate and slipped inside the corral. I searched through the dark until I saw the glow of Star's eyes shine through the gloom. Kevin and I walked slowly forward while I talked to my horse in a soothing voice. I put a hand on Kevin's arm to stop him when we got close and walked forward to Star on my own. He thrust his head into my chest and leaned into me. I clasped my hands along the ridge of his neck behind his ears and held on. Every so often a violent tremble shook his body. I stayed close, stroking and talking quietly until he seemed calm. I motioned Kevin forward.

Once we made sure Star wasn't injured and he seemed quiet, Kevin and I returned to the house. We found my family huddled on the back porch, waiting for the fire chief's report.

Kevin and I repeated our story for Ben. When we concluded with the fire truck pulling up to the barn, Ben looked around. "Where is Spot? He's the hero of the hour." He began calling, but no hefty and wiggly black body showed up. Ben went into the kitchen and came back with a flashlight. "I'm going to look for him. Maybe the sirens scared him off."

"Don't go near the barn," Dad warned.

"I'll stay back," Ben promised.

He walked away calling and whistling for the old black lab. His friend since childhood. We could see the rays of the flashlight as Ben searched. Saw the light still about halfway down the driveway, then vanish.

Mom started up, but Dad pulled her back to her perch on the steps.

"I'll go." He disappeared into the darkness down the driveway. A few minutes later he and Ben emerged from the dark into a circle of light from the house. Ben carried Spot's still body in his arms like a baby.

Mom's fingers reached up to touch her lips when she murmured, "Oh, Benny."

# Chapter 26

*You can't drown sorrow. It bobs back to the surface when you least expect it.*
Sara's Diary

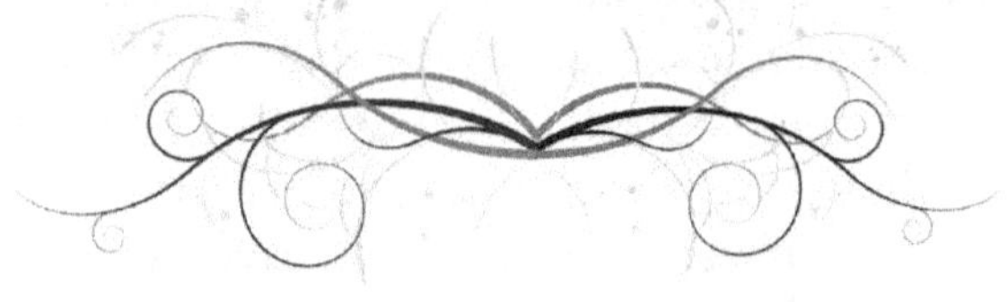

The next morning, I woke early to go check on Star. I left him in the corral for the night because the barn reeked of smoke. While I brought out hay for him, a fire department SUV drove up. I recognized Chief Powell from last night. Another official-looking man was with him. They got out of the SUV and came over to the fence.

"Good morning. Sara, isn't it?" Chief Powell asked.

I joined them at the fence and nodded. I recognized the police officer as the one who responded when Star escaped the barn and was lost.

"This is Officer Talbot. Steve, this is Sara Mitchell. She and her boyfriend discovered the fire last night."

"We've met," the police officer acknowledged. "I'm sorry for this incident. I'm glad you and your family are safe."

Mostly safe, I amended to myself. But a police officer likely wouldn't consider the family dog a serious casualty.

Chief Powell continued. "We have a report for you and your family. May we come in?"

Lights were on in the kitchen so I nodded and led them toward the house. The two officers waited on the porch while I checked to see who was up.

Mom and Dad sat at the table nursing cups of coffee. Dressed in similar versions of sweats and flannel, they decided they were presentable enough for the officers and asked me to invite them in. No sign of Ben. Probably just as well.

Mom offered both men coffee, which they accepted, and we all took seats at the kitchen table. The fire chief started.

"Last night we were able to determine the fire was arson. The perpetrator used dry twigs, old hay and paper to start the fire at the far back corner of the barn." He looked at me. "If you and young Mr. Richards had not acted so quickly, the fire would likely have caught the hay on the corresponding inside wall on fire and the structure could easily have been lost. What made you go check? The arsonist deliberately avoided the alarm."

"We thought we heard our dog bark. Kevin decided we should check."

The chief nodded. "It's well you did. Once we extinguished the fire, we used flood lights to look for evidence. We found the makings of the fire and this." He removed a plastic bag from his pocket and handed it to me. "Recognize it?"

The bag held a silver cigarette lighter. I examined it curiously; positive I'd never seen it before. I was about to hand it back to the chief when the design on one side of the lighter caught my eye. My eyes widened and I shivered as if from cold. Just as quickly a hot flash of rage filled my chest. I pointed to the ornate design etched into the metal.

"That design. I've seen that before. It's a snake and Travis Baker has a tattoo just like it on his arm." I brought the lighter closer so I could see better. "And see, the initials TB are entwined into the design. It's his, I know it is." I shifted my gaze to the police officer. "I told you. I told you it was him when you came here last time. He let Star out and spooked him and last night he tried again."

"Miss. Sara…"

Officer Talbot tried for a reasonable tone, but it didn't work. I was halfway out of my chair shaking the plastic bag in his face.

"It was him last night, wasn't it? The first time didn't work, so he came back. If only you had listened…"

"Sara." Dad's voice held quiet authority. I sat down. Fuming, but down.

Just then, Ben shuffled into the kitchen. "What's going on? What's all the noise?" Ben's hoarse voice and red eyes suggested a sleepless night. Grief etched lines in his forehead. I could feel his pain like it was my own. I loved Spot almost as much as Star.

Mom got up and walked over to Ben, sliding an arm around his waist. "Chief Powell and Officer Talbot are giving us their report from last night. You don't have to stay."

Ben's grief-stricken gaze regarded the officials. He hesitated. Then scuffled to an empty chair and slouched down. "No, I want to hear."

Officer Talbot cleared his throat. "If I may?" He indicated the lighter in the bag. I handed it to him.

"We found this at the scene. One of our firefighters remembered the design as a copy of the tattoo on the arm of a car dealership salesman. Our firefighter was there last week checking out the new models. We followed up this morning and met with Travis Baker and his father. The younger Mr. Baker had deep scars on his right hand and wrist. They looked like dog bite wounds. That's likely why he dropped the lighter. The dog grabbed his hand."

Ben's eyes sought mine. His teared up. Mine welled, too. Spot saved Star. And the barn. First by barking the alarm, then by actually going after Travis.

"Do you own a dog?" Officer Talbot's question broke my silent communication with my brother.

"We did." Ben's raspy voice choked on a sob. "He died last night. We think probably from a heart attack. He was pretty old. I found him halfway down the driveway."

The officer nodded. "Likely chasing the arsonist. Once we confronted Mr. Baker with the lighter, he confessed. He appeared to be impaired so we administered a breathalyzer which was negative."

"He takes drugs," I murmured.

Officer Talbot nodded. "That would not register on the device."

"What will happen to Travis?" Mom asked.

Who cares? I thought. But Mom worries about everybody.

"I'm not sure," Chief Powell admitted. "He's eighteen so could either be tried as an adult or as a juvenile. Arson is a serious crime. The lawyers will decide on how he's charged. In the meantime, there's no structural damage to the barn so it's safe for you to go in.

I'll leave a copy of our report for your insurance company. If there are no more questions, we'll be on our way. We just wanted to let you know the results of our investigation."

Dad got up to shake both officer's hands. "Thank you. We appreciate your coming by. Thank you for your help."

"Just doing our jobs, Mr. Mitchell," the Chief replied. There was a smile in his tone. "You folks have a nice day."

The officers left. The four of us sat at the table until Mom stood up and placed her hands flat on the surface. "How about my special cinnamon roll French toast for breakfast? With bacon? Any takers?"

She glanced at each of us in turn. Dad matched her energetic tone and replied, "That sounds great. Sara? Ben? What do you think?"

Instead of answering, Ben asked, "Dad, could we bury Spot this afternoon? Maybe in that sunny spot by the barn he liked so much?"

"Sure, son. We can do that. How do you feel about school today? Want to stay home?"

Ben nodded. "Yeah. I'm pretty wiped out." He looked at Mom. "I'm not very hungry. Maybe we could have breakfast for dinner tonight?"

"Sure, honey. It will taste just as good later on. Need some more sleep?"

"Yeah. Think I'll go to my room for a while." He stood and walked toward the stairs, but not before I saw a fresh sheen of tears on his cheeks.

Dad turned his attention to me. "How about you, Sara? Need a day?"

"No, Dad. I checked on Star and he's fine. It's going to be a nice day so he'll be fine in the corral. I'm going to open the barn doors to see if we can get rid of some of the smoke smell. And I'll come straight home from school so we can bury Spot together. I bet Zoe will want to be here, too."

"I'll take care of the barn. You go ahead and get ready for school."

"Okay, thanks. Cereal's fine for me, Mom. But I'll look forward to dinner." I kissed her cheek and ran up the stairs.

I knocked softly on Ben's door, but there was no answer. I understood. Spot was Ben's Star. He was even the same inky velvety black. I would miss him, too. I honored my brother's preference for solitude and hurried to get ready for school.

In spite of hurrying, I was late for school so didn't see my friends until lunch. As unemotionally as possible, I told them about last night and this morning's conclusions.

"O-M-G." For once Tawny was speechless. She sat, eyes filled with tears, holding tightly to Ryan's hand. Finally, she turned to me, eyes kind with the understanding of deep friendship. "Spot. He was there when we first became friends. Always with some kind of squeaky toy or tennis ball. Poor Ben. Spot was his all in all. Goofy dog." A tear escaped down her cheek. Whether for Spot or Ben, who knew? Probably both.

Tawny visibly gathered herself and shook off melancholy. "Shazam. Travis is totally whacked. He must have been blasted out of his mind." She shook her head. "He's really in for it this time."

Robyn was as silent as falling snow.

"Are you all right?" I nudged her arm.

She nodded, but her face reflected doubt. And guilt? Was that what I saw?

I nudged her again. "C'mon. Not buying it. What's going on?"

She slowly tore open the wrapper of her candy bar then said, "Is this my fault?" Her gaze rested on each one of us in question.

"What? Wait, you mean Travis? And the fire?" Astonishment raised my voice an octave. "No. Way. How could this be your fault?" I protested.

"If I hadn't told everybody he was the birthfather, none of this would've happened. He was okay until then."

"There is no version of any dictionary that would define Travis as okay," Kevin chimed in. "Even before you outed him, which you had every right to do since that was part of your story you were telling people, he's been unstable. Ever since he graduated from alcohol and started taking drugs. And the more hardcore the drugs got, the more hardcore his behavior got. He made all his choices, Robyn."

Kevin is the most likely person she would believe, so I kept quiet. Even so, her expression was skeptical until Kevin added, "Trust me, Robyn. This is not your fault."

The tension in her body relaxed. "Thanks, Kevin. In spite of everything he did to me, I feel sorry for him. This is really bad."

"Especially if they try him as an adult," Ryan piped up.

"How's Ben?" Tawny wanted to know.

"Gutted. He stayed home today. We're going to bury Spot this afternoon. Who knew silly old Spot would be a hero? But, boy, he definitely is. Star…" I choked up at even the thought of what could have happened. "Thank God for Spot."

A soft, "Amen" from Kevin and nods from everyone else were a tribute to the old lab.

"There is some good news though." Everybody perked up and gave me their attention. "You know how I've been rattled about how to figure out if I should go to Oregon for college, stay here or whatever? When I was working with Zoe, I realized she's the answer to my prayers. She is going to be an excellent rider. She's a natural. So I asked if she would be willing, once she's got more experience under her belt, to take over Star's training with Mr. King. I'm pretty sure he'll be okay with that. That way, I can go to college and not worry about Star anymore. And I know this sounds weird, but it kinda feels like she needs Star somehow. There's something going on with her I don't get, but she sticks to him like glue and he's already bonded with her. Which he's never done with anybody but me."

"And you're okay with this?" Robyn's skeptical tone made me laugh.

"I know, I know. I can be pretty jealous of Star's attention. But I figure his being drawn to her is something different than my bond with him. I can't really explain it, but it's different enough that I'm okay."

"Would Ben mind if I come this afternoon when you bury Spot?" Kevin gathered his trash in one hand and hooked the strap of his backpack with the other.

"I think he'd like that. I'm pretty sure Zoe will be there, too. It's not going to fun for any of us. Spot has been in our lives since Ben was five years old."

Robyn pushed up from the table and scrambled off the seat. "Ben can be thankful he has people who will help him grieve. It's tough alone. Just when you think you've pushed the grief down where it can't bother you, up it bobs just like a cork in water."

# Chapter 27

*Hate consumes a person just like fire consumes property. I need the power to walk away from hate.*
Sara's Diary

**After we honored** Spot and placed him in his favorite sunning place, I asked Zoe if she wanted a riding lesson. She opted for a walk on the beach with Ben. I get it. I saddled Star and we rode over to Big Sky. I wasn't scheduled for training, so I decided to check in with Robyn and Diva. Kevin went to help his mom. He was joining us for dinner tonight so I would see him later.

I found Robyn in a big training ring. She put Diva through her paces with Justine in the center of the ring calling out instructions. Diva was a different horse with ears perked forward and a spring in her step.

After about ten minutes, Justine motioned horse and rider to the center of the ring. They conversed quietly for a few minutes then Justine walked toward the gate with a wave to me. I climbed the fence and joined Robyn in the ring. Robyn dismounted and walked toward me, Diva trailing behind her.

"What do you think?" Her eyes glowed with inner excitement.

"I can't believe how changed she is. It's like you waved a magic wand over her or something."

"She's a dream to ride. Justine's wondering if we should show her. So far, Diva hasn't wanted to engage with any of the clients in the classes. Could be she needs more time, could be therapy horse isn't her destiny."

We walked toward the gate, Diva following close behind Robyn. They reminded me of Star and me. While Robyn removed tack and groomed Diva, we chatted about possibilities for showing and what that would be like.

"Not going to try trail are you? I'd hate for you to come in second to Star and me," I teased.

"As if," she shot back. "No, Justine's thinking more like dressage. Let Diva strut her stuff. She really is a diva." She gave the flashy pinto a final swipe with a soft brush and left her to her hay. "Do you have a minute?"

"Sure. We canceled Zoe's lesson today so she could spend time with Ben. What's up?" We grabbed a couple of beat-up folding chairs in front of the barn.

"You didn't say much today at lunch. What's going on?" Robyn asked.

"I talked a lot. I explained the whole fire story and everything." I protested.

"Yeah. But you didn't talk about Travis's part in it. Talk. This is where I get payback. You've been at me and at me and at me to talk honestly with you. Your turn."

Immediately my jaw clenched and my heart pounded. I stood up and paced a few steps with my hands clenched into fists at my sides. Loathing burned in my heart when I thought about Travis. How did Robyn know? This is when having a friend who really knows you backfires. In some ways, Robyn knows me better than Tawny because of our shared experience with Travis. Tawny tries to understand the humiliation and anger, but she's never had a guy treat her that way so she doesn't really get it.

I paced back to my chair and sat down. Elbows on my knees, I braced my head in my hands and stared at the ground. Robyn waited.

Finally, I ground out between gritted teeth, "I hate him. I hate him so much. He's evil. Pure evil. How could he set that fire knowing Star was inside? That's just wicked."

Robyn let me rant for several minutes. A gentle hand on my arm interrupted my tirade.

"Sara. Stop. Take a deep breath and just listen. When I didn't think I could stop hating Travis and get on with my life, you encouraged me to try. I'm going to tell you the same thing. Just try. You helped me understand hate consumed me and did nothing to Travis. It's the same for you. And besides, doesn't your God have something to say about hating people?"

Man. Talk about advice coming back to bite where it hurts. Rage battled self-control. I knew for me anger easily turned into depression and I did not want to go down that road again. Could I practice what I preached? I prayed a silent plea, "Help me, God," and tried to calm my breathing. I inhaled a breath so deep that it hit the very bottom of my lungs and blew it out. Glancing sideways at Robyn, I shook my head. "Quit hating Travis, huh? Just like that? After what he did?"

"No. You didn't say that to me and I'm not saying that to you. I'm also not saying it's easy. But you showed me it's possible to walk away. Just quit. I was the one hanging onto to anger and fear. Travis was happy as could be. You can walk away. It just takes steps."

While Robyn talked the pressure in my chest eased. Muscles unclenched. My heart stopped pounding. A quiet voice in my mind suggested, *Let me help you forgive. You can't do it on your own.* I recognized that voice. And knew I would have the strength I needed to let go of hating Travis. Forgiveness? That would have to come gradually.

"Have you forgiven Travis?" I asked Robyn.

"No. I don't hate him. I just feel nothing."

"God would help you forgive, if you ask Him to."

She shook her head. "You don't know all the bad things I've done, Sara. God isn't interested in helping someone like me. I can't forgive myself. How could God forgive me? No, I'm learning that cutting isn't the answer and I feel more peaceful than I have in a long time, but God doesn't want to mess with someone like me."

I thought for a few minutes then asked. "If Linnet needed something and asked you for help, what would you do?"

"Duh. I'd do or give anything to help her."

"It's the same with God. You're His child and He's always ready to help with whatever you need. Doesn't matter how you act or what you've done. You're His child. All you have to do is ask. Just try talking to Him sometime. Just try."

"You and your just try." She sighed and dropped her head back. "Okay. I'll try."

We sat quietly for a few minutes then I turned to her. "Who would ever have thought that you and I would be sitting here friends?"

Robyn snort laughed. "Not me, for sure. But I'll tell you something. If the reason we're friends is because your God told you to get right with me, or whatever, then maybe what you say about Him is really true. You definitely would not have been friends with me on your own. We hated each other."

"True. That's why I think it's worth your learning to pray and find out about God personally. Our friendship is pretty much in the miracle category, you think?"

She laughed. "Agree. I told you, I'm checking out the whole prayer thing. We'll see what happens."

"You're being so mysterious," I complained. "Oh well. Listen, I've got to go. Kevin's coming over for dinner so I'm going to help Mom. See you at school tomorrow?"

"Yep. Later." She headed back toward Diva.

When I got home, I found Dad in the barn busy clearing away hay bales that reeked of smoke.

"I'll pile them outside under cover and we'll see if the smell goes away. There aren't too many. Just that front row near the fire. What do you think about the smell in here? Okay for Star?"

I walked around inside and found it breathable. Opening the main door and all the windows made a big difference. The back door was a black mess of partially burned boards. Dad had lifted it off the hinges and propped it outside against the barn.

"Someone from the insurance company has to assess everything before we can really clean anything up, but at least it smells better."

"I think it will be okay. After dinner I'll bring Star in and see if he objects. As long as the weather's nice, he can stay in the corral. I'm going in to help Mom."

Zoe joined us for dinner, too. Ben seemed quiet, but okay. While we feasted on Mom's excellent cinnamon roll French toast, bacon and fresh fruit, Zoe and I took turns telling my family about our plan to have Zoe take over training Star for me when I go to college next year. Kevin was quiet and I made a mental note to talk to him later. Once we finished dinner, Kevin said he had to go home to finish homework. He gave Ben a combo handshake and half hug, said how sorry he was about Spot and walked down the path toward home.

Since it was still early, I asked Zoe if she'd like to ride for a while. She eagerly agreed.

"Great," Ben chimed in. "I'll come and watch."

Zoe cheeks immediately bloomed pink. She looked down and suggested, "Maybe later?" She looked up at him through long dark lashes with a puppy pleading look. "I'm not very good yet. I'd be nervous with you watching."

Ben smiled and nodded. "That's okay. I get it. Let me know when you're done and I'll take you home." He leaned forward as if to kiss her cheek, caught sight of me and smoothly changed the movement to a turn to go inside. I grinned.

We groomed Star and I instructed Zoe through a walk, trot and slow canter for about a half hour then we quit. When we returned the tack to the barn and I reached to hang up Star's bridle, I tripped over a water bucket and grabbed for Zoe to avoid a fall. She froze momentarily then pushed me forcefully away from her.

"No!" She flinched then gasped, "Get away, get away" while she frantically scuttled away from me. She cowered against the feed bin.

I rolled from my side where I had fallen to my back then sat with my arms propped behind me. What in the world? Zoe trembled against the feed bin, arms wrapped tightly around her, face set in a grimace of fear. "No, no, no, no," whispered through her clenched teeth.

I got up slowly, talking to her like I would a startled horse. When I reached her side, I asked, "Zoe, may I touch your shoulder?"

She shrank away from me, turned her frightened gaze on me, then finally nodded.

I lightly touched her shoulder. "I won't hurt you, Zoe. I'm your friend. I won't hurt you. I promise. Can you come and sit on the hay?"

She dipped her head and I lead her to the baled hay against the wall. We sat in silence for a few minutes. She shivered occasionally and kept her arms tightly wrapped around herself. Finally I spoke softly.

"Zoe, you have to tell me. Or somebody, but I'm right here. You really have to tell somebody or you'll make yourself sick. What happened to you?"

She shook her head violently from side to side.

"Zoe. Remember when you told me you had to be brave? This is part of being brave. Telling your story takes courage. Would you feel better talking to Mom? You know she likes you."

A panicked gaze sought mine. She clamped her lips shut and shook her head again in a negative motion.

"Then tell me," I urged gently. "Listen. When I had to tell my parents I tried to commit suicide I was so afraid. I thought they'd be angry. That they wouldn't understand. And I was so ashamed. And I thought it was all my fault. It felt like the truth was a monster that would harm everybody I loved, but that was a lie. The monster was keeping everything in. Once I talked about it, the monster had no power. Please tell me what's going on." Then I had an idea. "Hold on. Wait here a sec. I'll be right back."

She looked at me with a face drained of color and dread in her gaze. I was quick to reassure her. "No, no. I'm not going to get Mom or anybody. I'm going to get Star."

Her immediate look of relief told me I was on the right track.

I grabbed a halter and rushed out to the corral. Star came willingly with his usual curiosity. I tied him loosely to the center pole, then, moving calmly and quietly, directed Zoe out to sit on the hay bales near the pole. Star ambled over immediately and snuffed her hair then her cheek. A tremulous smile melted her clenched jaw.

Star continued to nose Zoe's hair, then he nibbled on her shoulder. It didn't take long before she threw her arms around his neck with a sob and clutched tightly. I gave her a few minutes to sob then suggested, "Zoe, sit down and tell Star. Tell Star what's going on."

She nodded against his lowered neck and sat down. He pushed his head carefully against her chest then left it there. She stroked his nose and scratched under his forelock. And out came the story.

"My cousin's friend always comes when he visits. They're best friends. He." She stopped, drew in a shuddering breath. "He touches me. He watches for when no one's around and catches me alone. And I try." Tears flooded her eyes and down her face. "I try to avoid him, but he finds me when no one's around. And I tell him no." Her agonized gaze sight mine. "I tell him no, Sara. But he doesn't listen. Just says we're good friends and it's all right. But it's not. And it's my fault." She laid her head against Star's cheek and cried while her body trembled beside me.

I tried hard to contain my rage. I breathed in deeply and exhaled quickly, trying to control my anger and sadness while Zoe cried out the secrets and tension she'd been holding in for who knew how long? Finally, spent, she stood up, reached her arms as far up Star's neck as she and cried quietly against him. Every so often, her body shuddered with escaping emotion.

I waited a few minutes, stood behind her and asked quietly, "Zoe, may I touch your shoulders?"

She nodded and I put my hands around her shoulders. Without warning, she pivoted and clutched me around the waist like I was a life buoy. I hugged her while Star nuzzled the back of her neck and her hair. When her sobs subsided, I guided her to our hay bale and sat beside her, arm around her shoulders. Exhausted, she leaned against me.

"This is NOT your fault. It's against the law, Zoe. It's called sexual assault and it's against the law," I repeated firmly. She stilled against me. "I think you need to tell somebody besides Star and me. This is where being brave comes in. If you can ride a giant horse and not be afraid, you can tell someone you trust about what this boy is doing. It's very wrong. Nobody should touch you at your age and especially if you said no. Nobody has the right to do that."

She sat quietly against me, her breathing returned to normal.

"I can't. Everybody will be upset. And they'll say it's my fault. I just need to be more careful."

I shook my head. "No, Zoe, that's not the solution. You told Star and me, the next time will be easier. I'll come with you if you want. But you really have to say something. What if he's doing this to somebody else? Somebody younger than you."

Her body stiffened. "He started with me when I was nine." She admitted softly.

"You have to say something. Unless you want me to tell someone? Your parents? The school counselor?"

She shook her head violently. "No, you can't! Promise me, Sara. Promise!"

"Okay, okay, I promise," I soothed. "Then you really have to."

"But they'll be so mad at me. My cousin, my aunt and uncle."

"I don't think they will."

"What if they don't believe me? He said no one would believe me."

"I believe you. And I barely know you. Your parents love you, Zoe. They want you to be safe."

"Can I think about it? And would you really come with me?"

"Absolutely. Whenever you want me. If Star could talk, we'd bring him, too. But I don't think people would understand."

That prompted a small smile. Small, but there.

I hesitated, but decided to check out my hunch. "Does Ben know?"

Her face grew even more red, if possible, but she nodded. "He knew something was wrong. He promised not to say anything. But he told me the same thing you did. That I have to tell. He got really mad." She looked at me through red-tinged eyes. "He punched the wall. But he wasn't mad at me. Just like you aren't."

"Your parents won't be either, Zoe. I think they're the best ones to tell. What do you think?"

She drew in a huge shuddering breath. "Yeah. I think you're right. Would you really come with me?"

"Yes," I reassured her again. "Unless you want Ben?"

She shook her head. "My mom freaks him out a little bit."

"When would you like to tell them?" I wanted to nail this down.

"Can we wait a few days? And you won't tell anybody?"

"A few days is fine. And I won't tell anybody. We'll figure it out," I promised. And we would. It might take a while, but we would find a way to make Zoe safe.

I glanced outside and saw it was almost dark. "I think we better get you home. Want Ben to take you?"

She nodded.

"Okay. Give Star a hug and we'll put him back in the corral. Lesson tomorrow?"

She nodded again, but this time a small smile lit her face.

# Chapter 28

*God's specialty is beauty out of brokenness.*
Sara's Diary

**The next day** after school, Kevin asked if we could get together after Zoe's lesson.

"Sure. I'll text you once we're done."

"Can you come to Mom's workshop? I'm finishing up stocking the shelves and you'll be a nice distraction." His smile warmed me all the way home.

During our lesson, I followed Zoe's lead and didn't refer to our emotion-charged encounter in the barn last night. She seemed more at ease. It's like finally telling someone has lightened the stress she's been carrying by herself. I knew it wasn't going to be easy to tell her parents and whatever followed was bound to be awful at first. But the darkness she'd tolerated out of fear was finally pierced by the light of truth. That part would only get better the more she pressed into honesty.

When we finished our lesson, I texted Kevin and took the well-worn path to his house. Mrs. Richards's workshop smelled like the best potpourri in the world. I inhaled deeply as soon as I got in the door. So many smells.

Kevin stopped transferring small decorative boxes from a shipping container to neat shelves against the wall. We sat on the stools at the sorting bench and faced each other. He reached for my hands.

"I'm glad you've figured out a plan for Star. I know you've been worried about next year would look like. Your idea to have Zoe take over working with him is a great solution. She seems like a nice girl."

"She is. And more importantly, Star accepts her. I feel like a weight has been lifted off my shoulders. I really want to go to school in Oregon and learn about equine therapy, but I just wasn't comfortable leaving Star with nothing to do. Now I just have to figure out how to manage with not seeing you. I'm going to miss you so much." I scooched my stool close and leaned forward until my head rested on his chest. He propped his chin on the top of my head and sighed.

"Yeah. That's what I wanted to talk to you about."

I jerked myself upright and demanded, "What? You sound worried. What are you thinking?"

He put his hands out, palms up. "Relax. I'm not worried. I'm going to miss you, too. I just think we should talk about what it's going to be like. We should talk about dating, or not, and stuff like that."

"I don't want to date anybody else. Do you?" Suddenly uneasy, my brows puckered together and I gripped my knees.

"No. But we should talk about what happens if either of us meets someone. That could happen. I know we have about a year before we're separated, I just think we need to agree to be honest with each other. That's all."

"Okay. If I meet somebody I think I might like more than you, I promise to talk to you about it. I just don't see that happening," I answered honestly.

"Same." He grinned. "I'm going to go nuts waiting for your visits home."

"Same," I echoed. "But we'll figure it out."

He stood, gripped my hands and drew me up off the stool. I put my arms around his waist and leaned into his warmth. It felt like I was home. With one finger he lifted my chin and placed his lips against mine. My hands slipped up his chest and clasped around the back of his neck. His arms held me close. When our kiss ended, his arms tightened.

"I love you, Sara," he murmured.

"I love you, too, Kev." I pulled him close and we stood quictly, heart-to-heart, for a few minutes. Slowly, he loosened his grip and took a step back. His deep cocoa-brown eyes regarded me steadily. He pulled a small box out of his pocket and handed it to me.

"To remind you of me," he explained.

I opened the box and saw a delicate silver ring. I picked it up and examined the design. Two hearts intertwined together so it was hard to tell where one began or ended. I gently drew it out of the box, my mouth dropped open in awe. I'd never seen anything so pretty. So me. Simple, clean lines. I slipped it on my finger. It fit perfectly. I looked up at Kevin. I hope my smile reflected the bright warmth of my heart. I threw my arms around his neck.

"It's beautiful. I love it so much." I placed my lips against his for a different kind of thank you.

He returned my hug. "I'm glad. It reminded me of you. I don't know what will happen to us in the future, but I wanted you to know how much you mean to me. I thought this was a good way to say it."

"It's perfect," I agreed.

We talked a few minutes more, then Kevin glanced at the shipping container with a frown. "I hate to say it, but I really need to get back to finishing up out here. I still have homework. See you tomorrow?"

"Fo sho, as Tawny would say." I laughed, we shared another kiss and I waved goodbye.

Feeling light as helium on the walk home, I kept admiring my ring. My phone beeped a text notification. I thumbed it open. Robyn.

**Headed your way. Home?**

**Almost. I'll be there in a minute.**

**We need to talk.**

That's the problem with texting. That could either be ominous or terrific. I hurried so I'd be there when she arrived.

I made it home before Robyn and headed upstairs to wait in my room. Mostly I sat and admired my new jewelry. Well. My only jewelry. Not bad at all for a first.

A car pulled up in the driveway. Robyn. I went downstairs and we met at the back door. Definitely not ominous news. Her face beamed with a wide smile and her eyes sparkled like snow crystals in the sun.

"Can we go to your room?" She was already hurrying me up the stairs before I answered. We reached my bedroom and she closed the door behind us, turned to me and blurted, "You're never going to believe this."

She practically vibrated with whatever news she had. I motioned her toward the bed and turned toward my desk chair but never made it. She grabbed me in a sideways hug that practically broke my ribs. I eased out of her arms so I could face her. From there I edged us over to the bed and sat us both down.

She grabbed my hands in an unyielding grip. "It worked. Your prayer thing worked." With each word she gripped my hands more tightly until I felt like I was trapped by a boa constrictor.

"What do you mean, it worked? What happened? You mean you got an answer to prayer?"

She nodded.

"Robyn."

"Yeah?"

I nodded down to my hands. My fingers were turning white from her strangle hold.

She laughed. "Oh, sorry." She loosened her grip, but kept hold of my hands.

"Here's the deal. I knew placing Linnet for adoption was the right thing. It was the hardest thing I've ever done, but I knew it was right. But what I wanted more than anything was an open adoption."

"What's that?"

"It's where the birth mother maintains contact with her baby. How much contact depends on the adoptive parents. Linnet's family wasn't sure they could do that, so they initially said no. But I really wanted them for Linnet's family, so I said it was okay but would they think about it." She shook my hands in excitement. "And they did. I just heard from them that they've changed their minds and agree an open adoption will be best for Linnet. They'll send me pictures of her and I can visit every few months. We won't tell Linnet I'm her birthmother until her parents feel she's ready, but I get to be in her life." Robyn burst into tears, leaned forward and gripped me in a fierce hug. "God heard me, Sara," she sob talked. "He rescued me just like you said. You can't believe," she paused to take a breath and pulled back to grip me by my shoulders. "You can't believe how happy I am. I never, ever thought they'd change their minds and it broke my heart. I've been so miserable. It seemed like I would be broken my whole life."

I beamed at her. "Then it's a good thing God's specialty is to make beauty out of brokenness, isn't it?"

Did you read Riptide, book one?

Reading Group Discussion Questions:


1.  Sara says something mean to Robyn even though Sara has experienced girls saying mean things about her and knows how painful it is. Have you ever said something mean to someone then regretted it? What did you do?


2.  Sara distinguished between knowing what Robyn did, but not knowing who Robyn is. Does how a person act describe who they are? Why or why not?


3.  The Biblical standards for sex are that it should take place only between married couples. Do you agree this is a good standard? Why or why not?


4.  Robyn participates in sexting with Travis in an effort to hold his interest in her. Have you ever done something to make someone like you that caused you to feel ashamed?


5.  Robyn says fitting in isn't the same as belonging? Do you agree? Why or why not?

Follow the continuing story of Sara, Shooting Star and the rest of their friends in the upcoming novel, *Tide Pool*.

Susan Thode lives in Enumclaw, a small town at the base of Mt. Rainier in Washington State. She enjoys the rural setting dotted with many horse farms...and the beautiful mountain.

A former high school English teacher, Susan has been a licensed mental health counselor and certified trauma/crisis counselor for twenty years. She helps people answer tough questions about God's plan and purpose for their lives in spite of pain and confusion. She also gives them tools to navigate emotional journeys of discovery through trauma and crisis.

As much as Susan enjoys her writing and counseling responsibilities, her greatest joy is being Grandma to her 14-year-old granddaughter, Moxy, from whom she is learning Tik-Tok dances.

Visit Susan at

Instagram      doyoumatter1

TikTok      suethode

Web page      doimatter.org

Facebook       Susan Thode

www.ingramcontent.com/pod-product-compliance
Lightning Source LLC
Chambersburg PA
CBHW060706010826
48977CB00007B/785